Deadly Secrets

Also by John MacDonald

The Widow Esposito

The Cassiatorre Quartet

The Mario Mystery
Deadly Secrets
The Oligarch Murders
Get Me Moretti!

Deadly Secrets

A Dino Moretti Novel

JOHN MACDONALD

Cassiatorre

First published 2025
by Cassiatorre

Paperback ISBN 978-1-917862-03-5
Ebook ISBN 978-1-917862-11-0

For Carol –
who gave me Italy.

ACKNOWLEDGMENTS

With thanks to everyone who has shaped my writing and given so generously of their time to read my work and share their experience.
Myra Duffy, Richard Louden, Margaret McMillan, Helen Williamson.
My editor, Christine McPherson.
And my wife Carol for believing.

CHAPTER ONE

The Questura phone rang as Commissario Dino Moretti passed the front desk. Alfiero, a portly, red-faced officer in his fifties, replied then held his hand up to stop Moretti.

The desk officer covered the mouthpiece and looked up at the tall detective. 'Can you take this, Commissario?'

Moretti paused, and his compelling dark brown eyes skewered Alfiero.

'I was about to go for breakfast.'

Alfiero's expression changed from puzzled to pleading. 'I can't make it out.'

Moretti frowned, sighed, and took the phone.

'Hello. Commissario Moretti speaking.' He paused, waiting for the usual reply. Instead, he heard a stream of disjointed Italian in a very heavy Chinese accent.

'Police? We need help. Motherlaw robbed. Case stolen. You must help.'

He glanced at Alfiero's worried face, nodded, and raised his hand.

'I will help,' he replied slowly and clearly. 'What is your name, and what has happened?'

A confused mixture of Chinese and Italian made it impossible for him to understand.

'I will help,' Moretti repeated, separating each word. 'Please speak slowly. What is your name?' He mimed writing to the desk officer, and Alfiero picked up a pen.

'Zhao Yu.'

'Zhao Yu,' Moretti repeated for Alfiero. 'Where are you, Signor Zhao?'

'In restaurant.'

'Where is the restaurant?'

'Bar Roma.'

'Ah, I see, Bar Roma,' Moretti repeated for Alfiero's sake. 'Please stay there and I will come to you, alright?'

'You must help. Come now.'

'Yes,' said Moretti, nodding. 'I will help. I am coming now. Two minutes.'

'Hurry.'

Moretti handed the phone back to Alfiero. 'Did you get that? It's the Chinese family that bought Bar Roma.'

Alfiero nodded and turned the pad for Moretti to read. He had no time to question Alfiero's phonetic rendition of the names.

'Good. Log it against my name. That's where I'll be if anyone is looking for me.'

'Yes, Commissario.'

Moretti hurried to the former Bar Roma and knocked on the glass door. Almost immediately it was opened a crack by a wiry Chinese man of about fifty, wearing a short-sleeved white shirt and neatly pressed black trousers.

Moretti held up his ID to the narrow opening.

'Signor Zhao? I'm Moretti.'

'Come in, Moretti. You must help. Motherlaw robbed.'

Moretti entered. The place was in chaos. The original glass-topped wooden counter that once held pastries, snacks, and drinks, had been removed to reveal tiles which looked new compared to the well-worn ones beside them where almost a century's customers had stood to drink their breakfast coffee or evening aperitivo. The fruit machines and the billiards table had gone, as had the glass-fronted fridge from which thousands of customers had chosen a cool drink on a hot summer's day.

'Motherlaw robbed,' Zhao repeated. 'You help now.'

'Where is your mother-in-law?'

'Train station.'

'In Maghicchio?'

'Yes. Go now.'

'Does she speak Italian?'

'No Italian.'

Moretti rubbed the nape of his neck. 'How will she tell me what happened?'

Zhao looked puzzled.

'How will your mother-in-law speak to me?'

Zhao's eyes widened, and he called behind him in Chinese.

A slim woman of perhaps thirty appeared, wiping her hands on a cloth. Her straight, jet-black hair was tied back in a ponytail. She, too, wore a white blouse with dark trousers.

Their exchange was fast, but from their body language and sidelong looks in his direction Moretti understood that the discussion was about him.

The young woman finally nodded and turned to face Moretti.

'My name is Cao An Na.' Her Italian was still heavily accented but fluent. 'My grandmother is at the railway station. A trunk of hers has been stolen. The authorities have her, but they can't communicate. Can you help us, please?'

'Of course, Signorina Cao. What do you need me to do?'

She glanced at Zhao.

'They need me at the railway station to translate for my grandmother,' she explained. 'But we do not have a car. My father is very old-fashioned and does not want me to go with you on my own.'

'He can come, too.'

'No, he is expecting a delivery, and he cannot leave the restaurant. We plan to open in a few days. Is there a woman officer that I could go with?'

'There is one, but she is working on another case. I can call her, but I can't say how long it will take her to get here.'

The young woman turned to her father and explained the situation.

Zhao narrowed his eyes and scanned Moretti from

top to bottom, pausing at his huge walrus moustache, then barked an instruction.

'My father says I can go with you, Moretti, but I must sit in the back of the car.'

Moretti suppressed a grin.

'Of course.' He nodded and directed his answer to the older man. 'That is how we often transport witnesses.'

She kissed her father on the forehead and left with Moretti.

The young woman remained silent, with her head turned to watch the passing scenery, until they arrived at the railway station in Maghicchio. They made their way to the stationmaster's office, where a distraught, tiny, white-haired woman was sitting on a huge piece of luggage. She stood up and threw off her torment like a wet coat when she saw her granddaughter. They hugged and cried, swaying gently, before the old woman spoke. Moretti guessed that her words were part apology, part explanation. He stood beside the stationmaster in silence until they finished, separated, and wiped their faces.

'Moretti, this is my grandmother.'

'Good day, Signora,' he addressed the old woman. 'Can you please tell me what happened?'

The stationmaster sat at his desk, and Moretti leaned against it while the old woman sat back on her luggage and her granddaughter stood beside her.

An Na translated Moretti's question and nodded while her grandmother began a lengthy account of what had happened. The old woman's hands were shaking, so Moretti poured her some water from the cooler. She looked at her granddaughter, who nodded again, before accepting the water and completing her story.

An Na held her grandmother's hand and turned to Moretti.

'My grandmother came from China with two large trunks: this black one, and another – the same size – in navy-blue. She had help at the airport and in Rome to put the trunks on the train. She did not understand the announcements that tell passengers when they are coming to a station.' She paused and took a crumpled piece of paper from the old woman's hand. 'But she had this.' She handed the paper to Moretti. 'On one side is written Maghicchio, and on the other side is the address of the restaurant and our phone number.'

Moretti examined both sides of the paper and handed it back to the old woman.

'She showed the destination to passengers, who shook their heads until it was her stop.' She held the old woman's hand in both of hers. 'When she arrived at Maghicchio, she managed – barely – to get the navy-blue trunk along the corridor, through the swing doors, and down the steep steps to the platform. She left it there and got back on the train to collect the black one. She was struggling along the corridor with it when the guard blew his whistle, and the train began to move off.'

She rubbed the back of her grandmother's hand. 'She screamed, but the train gathered speed. One of the passengers fetched the train guard and explained what had happened. She got off at the next stop and waited for a train to bring her back to Maghicchio. A train guard came with her and helped with her black trunk. But when she got back here, the first trunk had vanished.'

Moretti looked at the old woman. She had the face of someone who had spent her whole life outdoors. She wore baggy black trousers and sandals and held her unzipped black quilted jacket closed at the neck.

'The first thing I want to say is how sorry I am that my countrymen did not offer to help you with your luggage. Their actions have brought shame on all of us, and I apologise.' He paused while An Na translated. The old woman's eyes flicked to him when his name was mentioned. 'I want to assure your grandmother that we will do whatever we can to get the trunk returned safely to her.'

He turned to the stationmaster as An Na translated.

'What happened?'

The stationmaster's face was red, and he was sweating profusely.

'Like the old lady said, she left her trunk on the platform and got back on the train. The platform was busy, so the guard didn't see her. He did the usual check to see if there was a latecomer running for the train, but it was all clear, so he blew the signal to go.'

'Didn't he notice the trunk?'

'No, Commissario. His focus is only on getting passengers on the train and setting off on time.'

'What happened next?'

'We got a call from the train, explaining what had happened. One of my colleagues checked, but the platform was empty. Like the young woman said, I advised the next station along the line. The old lady and her trunk were helped off and taken to the other side of the tracks to wait for the next train back here. She showed me her paper and we called the number for her.'

'Did the train guard get the details of any passenger who saw it happen, or the one who reported it?'

'I don't know, but I can quickly check.'

'That would be helpful. Also, I need to speak to your colleague who checked the platform, and the one who accompanied the old woman.'

The stationmaster picked up the phone. 'I'll organise it immediately, Commissario.'

'And I need to see the CCTV recordings for the platform and the exits.'

'Of course.'

Moretti turned to explain what he had said, but An Na had already translated everything.

'Can you take us back to the restaurant, Moretti?'

The Commissario gauged the size of the trunk.

'It'll be a squeeze,' he said. 'The trunk won't fit in the boot. I'll have to put it on the back seat, so one of you will have to sit up front beside me.'

An Na translated.

'No problem, Moretti, I will sit in the front. Grandmother can watch from behind.'

'I noticed a trolley outside. We can put the trunk on it.'

An Na held the door for her grandmother, while Moretti grabbed the handle of the heavy trunk and wheeled it to the door on its little castors. He held up a hand to wave to the stationmaster, who cupped the mouthpiece of the phone.

'I did what I could.'

'I'll be back shortly. Make sure everything I asked for

is here.'

Outside, they heaved the trunk onto the trolley. The two women walked in front while Moretti followed, pushing the trolley. Even with the rear doors open fully and the passenger seat pushed forward, it was a struggle to get the bulky luggage inside, but they managed. An Na opened the other rear door for her grandmother, who sat inside with her hand resting on the trunk. An Na squeezed into the front seat.

'Now we can go, Moretti.'

Outside the restaurant, An Na opened the car door and helped Moretti extricate the trunk while her father and grandmother hugged.

'Moretti, how long until the trunk is found?'

'Signorina Cao, I must be honest. I'm ashamed to say that I don't know when or if it will ever be found. All I can say is I will try my very best.' He gave her a card. 'Call me on either of those numbers if there is anything else.'

The young woman nodded once, thrust out her hand, and shook his.

'I trust you, Moretti,' she said then turned, picked up one side of the trunk, and shoved it inside, closing the door behind her with her foot.

By the time Moretti returned to the stationmaster's office, the personnel had been assembled. He spoke to each of them and rang the numbers of the passengers. None could add anything further to the story except to emphasise how distraught the old woman had been. The CCTV recordings of the platform showed the trunk disappearing in the midst of a crowd who had disembarked from the same train, but the views from the exits didn't capture the action.

Moretti sat alone in the stationmaster's office, wondering what was in the trunk. He closed his eyes and opened his mind to imagine all the ways in which the luggage could have disappeared. Instead of the answer, a bitter recollection took its chance to return and remind him of the only case in his career that he had been unable to solve. He opened his eyes to banish the memory, but the fact remained – the old woman's luggage was lost.

CHAPTER TWO

Over an hour later than usual, Moretti stood in Bar Italia. He paused, mouth open, warm pastry poised at his lips, and looked at the approaching reflection in the mirror behind the counter.

'Commissario.'

He put down the pastry and his coffee cup on the counter, half turned, and looked up at the tall ispettore.

'Good morning, Cristina. Have you had breakfast?'

Cristina Furlan tightened the edges of her mouth, and the tendons in her neck stood out temporarily. At almost two metres, she was very tall by local standards, and her dark trousers, white short-sleeved shirt, and ankle boots contrasted with the colourful, light summery dresses and sandals that the local women wore.

'Sorry,' she said, removing her sunglasses. 'A call has just come in. Can we talk about it?'

Moretti reached back, brought the cup to his lips, drained it, and wiped the froth from his thick moustache.

'I'll take this to go, Carla,' he said, wrapping the croissant in a fresh serviette from one of the dispensers on the counter. He handed the owner of Bar Italia a ten.

Carla smiled and held out the change she had ready. 'See you tomorrow, Dino.'

'Thanks.' He nodded as he passed the table where three older women sat, pretending not to eavesdrop.

'Ladies.'

'Sorry,' repeated Cristina, putting her sunglasses back on as they stepped out into the bright heat of the morning.

Moretti squinted up at her as he peeled back the thin tissue paper, exposing a third of his pastry.

'What was the call?' He bit into it, sending a little shower of tiny flakes to the ground, while the icing sugar topping transferred itself to his moustache.

'It's from the traffic police in Maghicchio. A car driving all over the road – both sides – with multiple near misses, a minor collision, and other vehicles forced off the road.'

'A car?' Moretti said, chewing. They crossed the road and headed up the slope of the main square in the direction of the Questura. 'Can't the traffic cops deal with it?' He swallowed and took another bite.

'They were dealing with it. Their cars accounted for the minor collision and two of the other vehicles.'

'I still don't see why that involves us.'

'The driver of the car lost control, hit a tree, and was killed. He was an English tourist, so there will have to be an investigation in case it's thought that the traffic cars somehow caused it. The station head in Maghicchio was the one who made the call.'

Moretti popped the last piece of pastry into his mouth and wiped his fingers. Cristina cleared her throat and tapped her top lip. Moretti cleaned the crumbs and icing sugar from his moustache.

'Now I see,' he said, as he finished the last of his breakfast. 'Carlo thought he'd call us and get ahead of the internal investigation. Why didn't you say that in the first place? Let's take your car. It'll be quicker if we don't have to push back the seats in mine.'

They changed direction and headed past the memorial fountain and down to where Cristina's car sat in the shade of a gnarled olive tree.

'How did Carlo sound?' asked Moretti, buckling up.

Cristina reversed out of the parking space, joined the main road, and took the road to Maghicchio.

'Like he needed help,' she replied. 'I think he'd have

preferred it if he'd been able to speak with you in person.'

The morning sun was already high in the sky, so Moretti lowered the visor on his side, took a pair of black-rimmed wraparound sunglasses from the top pocket of his linen jacket, and put them on.

'Carlo's an old friend, but he worries too much. I think that he's still smarting from his men letting our Mafia visitors slip past their roadblocks at the funeral in the spring.'

'Hmm.'

'How far down is it?'

'About eight minutes,' replied Cristina. 'Just at that series of hairpins.'

'That sounds about right,' mused Moretti. 'A tourist unfamiliar with the road could easily have an accident there if they were driving too quickly.'

A few hundred metres from the scene, Cristina slowed because a bashed and dented blue and white traffic car with flashing lights was parked across the road ahead. Traffic officers were stopping and turning back the traffic. She lowered the electric window as she reached them. One of the men looked into the car, recognised the detectives and waved them through.

'Stop here, Cristina,' said Moretti, straining forward against his seatbelt a moment later. 'I want to get out.'

Both detectives got out and walked to the verge. They had an aerial view of the crash scene across the olives, vines, and open fields below them.

Moretti pursed his lips and exhaled slowly.

'That's some mess. Look,' he exclaimed, pointing. 'No tyre marks on the road. It looks like it didn't even slow down before it ploughed straight through the olives then rolled onto its roof.'

Two more police vehicles with flashing lights were parked below them. The nearer car was at the crash site, where its occupants were already taping the area off; the other was further down, turning back traffic. Two civilian cars – one sitting at a crazy angle, the other tucked in at the verge, hazards flashing – completed the scene. In the far distance, the long klaxon note with its two staccato sixths faintly heralded the approach of an ambulance from Maghicchio.

Moretti took off his jacket and rolled up his shirt sleeves. 'Let's drive down there.'

They stopped beside the traffic car which was enclosed in the same incident tape as the overturned car in the olive grove. An officer was sitting with a man a little apart from a woman who was alternately dabbing her head with a wad of tissues and sipping from a frosted bottle of water.

The two detectives put on latex gloves and stepped out. Cristina immediately joined the woman and knelt on one knee beside her.

'How are you feeling?' she asked, placing a hand on the woman's shoulder.

'I'm fine,' the woman replied shakily. 'I bumped my head a little on the dashboard. Our car doesn't have airbags.'

'I'm Ispettore Cristina Furlan. What's your name?'

'Paola. Paola Grilli.'

'Were you driving, Paola?'

She nodded her head to the side and winced. 'No, my husband was.'

'How's your head? Let me see.'

The woman removed the tissues and tilted her head back.

Cristina carefully teased away some stray hairs.

'You'll have a lovely bruise there for a few days.' She smiled. 'There's a good-sized egg there already.'

The woman returned Cristina's smile and put the tissues back.

Cristina patted her arm. 'The ambulance is on its way. They'll check you over and maybe take you for an X-ray.'

Moretti, meanwhile, stood beside the seated officer, leaned forwards, hands on thighs, and addressed the man.

'Commissario Moretti. What's your name?'

'I told your colleague here. Giorgio Proietti. I was driving when that madman appeared.'

Moretti saw that Proietti's hands were shaking.

'I'm sorry if I'm asking you to repeat yourself, but can you tell me briefly what happened?'

Proietti looked up under his brows at Moretti.

'We were driving downhill to Maghicchio. Suddenly this car appeared on our side of the road at a crazy speed. I swerved and slammed on the brakes. He narrowly missed me before he went off the road. The cop car chasing him only managed to stop in time.'

Moretti turned to the traffic officer. 'I wonder if you could help your colleague with the tape.'

The officer rose, gave half a salute, and sauntered towards the crashed car. Moretti waited until he was out of earshot, and when he spoke again, he lowered his voice.

'What speed was the traffic car doing?'

Proietti looked over at his wife.

'About the same speed as the crazy guy. Fast.'

'But they managed to stop.'

Proietti turned back to look at Moretti. 'Yes. And they stayed on their side of the road.'

Moretti studied Proietti's face.

'Signore, how closely was the pursuit car following the speeding car?'

Proietti's eyes narrowed as he replied.

'If you're asking me if I think the cops caused him to crash, the answer is no. I could hear him before I saw him. Loud music playing. You know, that boom, boom, bass beat that youngsters like. And he was either singing or shouting at the top of his voice as he came around the corner. The cops weren't on his tail. I'd say they were two or three car lengths behind him.'

'That's not much at that speed.'

'It was enough, Commissario. Now, if you're finished, I'd like to sit beside my wife.'

Moretti straightened and held out his hand to help Proietti up. The man ignored the offer and joined his wife as the ambulance arrived.

Cristina left her and stood beside Moretti. 'She had a bad fright, but I think she'll be okay,' she said. 'How about her husband?'

'I gave him every opportunity to drop the cops in it, but he's quite clear that they are not to blame.'

'Their commanding officer will be relieved.'

Moretti grinned mischievously. 'That depends on

what I tell him.'

One of the ambulance crew climbed to the overturned car, looked inside, and spoke to the officer while the other stayed with Proietti and his wife. The detectives made sure that the couple were safely in the ambulance with their contact cards before they walked downhill to retrace the path of the crashed vehicle.

'Nothing on the road surface that would cause the car to lose traction,' noted Moretti. 'And from the marks on the verge and into the olive grove, it went straight off.'

Cristina followed his gaze to the overturned vehicle.

'Is that the passenger of the other car up there beside the traffic officer?'

Moretti felt oddly queasy. 'Let's find out,' he replied, striding off.

Another car arrived behind them, and two officers began to photograph and measure the scene.

The detectives ducked under the incident tape and climbed towards the smashed car. They could see that the dead man was still suspended upside down by his seatbelt.

Cristina stopped to photograph the number plate while Moretti examined a tree stump.

'This is what caused him to flip the car,' he said, walking on ahead. The queasiness was now a chill.

'The tyres are new, which would fit if it's a hire car,' she observed. 'It looks like a tourist, not used to driving on the right, took the corner too fast and lost control.'

Moretti ignored her and headed to the opposite side of the car from the officer and the kneeling figure. He bent over and looked through the car, past the blood and vomit on the dead man's face and chest, and gasped.

'You.'

Dr Sergio Vanni turned his attention away from the dead man and looked up. 'Hello, Dino. It's been a while.'

CHAPTER THREE

Each weekday in Cassiatorre, one of the smaller squares hosted fruit and vegetable merchants or fishmongers. These were small-scale local businesses, set up quickly on trestle tables with the contents of a small white van that would sell out before one o'clock.

The weekly Saturday market was altogether different. Harking back to the time before supermarkets, when most food was produced and sold locally, the weekly market in Cassiatorre took up the entire large municipal carpark. The weekly market attracted bigger vehicles whose sides cantilevered up to form protective coverings against sun or rain, and from which a vast selection of goods was on sale. Typically staffed by a couple and one or two of their children, the sellers moved in a smiling choreography, offering, suggesting, explaining, and ultimately selling their produce.

Agente Gennaro Santoro loved visiting the weekly market. It was his chance to meet friends, have a laugh, buy produce from his native Puglia and, importantly, gauge the atmosphere and underlying mood of the townsfolk. Today, with the bright, warm sun bringing out short sleeves and summer dresses and the return of the season's first tourists, the mood among the stallholders and their clients was lively, welcoming, and friendly.

Santoro stopped at one of the vehicles fitted with eye-level glass counters, holding a dizzying selection of cheeses, cold cuts, preserves, and dry goods sourced from every part of the Italian peninsula. The agente allowed himself a day's dispensation from his diet every Saturday, and he eyed the salami – vacuum-packed, whole, and suspended from hooks in the ceiling of the van. His mouth watered.

A small scrum of older women stood in front of him in what seemed like a disorganised gaggle. Each pressed forward to be served, as if the quantity or variety that she had chosen to buy would imminently run out, but each knowing and fiercely – often vocally – defending her exact position in the queue.

To his left, a woman was buying a few salted sardines from huge tins to add to the dried baccala already in her bag. To his right, others chatted, tasting the free samples, and buying cheese cut to the portion of their choice.

A young, dark-skinned woman wearing a white apron looked down past the women nearest the counter while she adjusted the red bandana that held the coils of her black hair off her face.

'What will it be, Agente?' she grinned. 'We have mortadella today.' She cut a wafer-thin slice from the huge salami above him and presented it to him on the tip of her knife. The women moved aside to avoid the blade, and Santoro reached through them to take it.

'The long arm of the law,' muttered a stocky woman wearing a floral shift.

Santoro popped the mortadella into his mouth and shook his head, taking in the meaty panorama before him. Beef, boar, and pork were preserved in every possible way.

'Hurry up, queue jumper,' bristled another woman at his shoulder. 'Some of us are expecting guests for lunch.'

Santoro ignored her.

'Something spicy,' he said to the young woman.

'How about *spianata calabrese* or *'nduja*?'

'I'll take an *etto* of each.'

'Last of the big spenders,' said the stocky woman, to the chuckles of the others.

'Thank you,' said Santoro, exchanging his money for

a small plastic bag. 'And have a good weekend, ladies,' he added as he left.

Couples came to the bustling market together, and while the women queued and shopped at the front of the vehicles, their husbands – dressed in denim dungarees, checked shirts, and hats even in summer – shuffled in little knots at the side of the vans. Not all market stalls were equal. The ones that attracted the menfolk were the few which had *porchetta*, a whole roast pig – from snout to tail, minus its legs – supported on a trencher on the countertop, from which hand-cut slices of the still-warm, aromatic, moist, fatty meat and salty crackling were cut and folded onto dry bread rolls to make a calorie-laden panino the size of a sore hand.

Santoro joined a group of pensioners who resembled emperor penguins waddling tightly together at the side of a porchetta van. Panino in one hand, and a small plastic tumbler of free red *sfuso* wine in the other, the men chewed, chatted, teased, and laughed with friends they'd known for sixty or seventy years. The huddle opened to let him in.

'The cops are here,' joked one.

'Hide the booze,' quipped another.

Santoro shook his head, grinned, and made his way to the side of the truck.

'Day off, Gennaro?'

'No. Just getting a few goodies before I go to the Questura.'

The stallholder saw him and called down, 'The usual?'

Santoro gave him the thumbs up. 'With plenty fat.'

'Coming up. Help yourself to wine.'

Santoro separated a small plastic tumbler from the stack and poured a splash of red wine from an unlabelled bottle into it. The old guys took it in turn to speak.

'Cops are turning back traffic on the road down to Maghicchio.'

Santoro sipped his wine and nodded. 'There's been a bad accident.'

'Someone dead? How'd it happen?'

'You know I can't talk about that.' Santoro's look closed the subject.

'Leave Gennaro alone.'

The stallholder held out a large panino stuffed with warm pork. Santoro handed over a note and waved away the change. He folded back the top of the paper napkin and bit into the roll.

'Heaven!' he exclaimed. 'So, what's new with you guys?'

Between munches of their panini and sips of wine, the men's conversation ranged from coping with the lack of rainfall, where they were going for Sunday lunch, to how their children and grandchildren were doing. Santoro left them when they all headed over to the other end of the market where live poultry, vegetable seedlings for planting out, and heavy-duty gardening equipment and spares were sold.

Stopping every few metres to chat, Santoro eventually arrived at a fruit and vegetable stall, donned a plastic glove, and filled several paper bags with produce. He smiled with amusement at the antics of a Dutch tourist at the neighbouring stall. She had chosen two dresses from the racks and was asking the seller, or rather miming, where she could try them on. She was invited, by mime, to climb up into the van and try them on behind the privacy of a curtain that slid on a plastic-coated spring hooked to the sides of the open door, closing it completely – or nearly so. She gauged the space inside the back of the van against her own height and decided to risk the purchase without trying them on.

On the way to buy fresh mozzarella, Santoro passed two huge, square umbrellas that covered a messy rummage of second-hand clothes, towels, and bedlinen. Eager women winnowed and sometimes fought over the goods, keen to profit from the prices handwritten in red marker pen on pieces of cardboard torn from food cartons. A smiling Angolan youth with short, braided hair struggled to keep the separate bundles tidy, while a surly Sicilian made up the prices on the spot, argued with the customers, and took the cash.

Still full after his panino, Santoro ignored the aromas from the rotisserie van selling whole roast chickens, rabbit, and deep-fried vegetables, which provided a ready-cooked family lunch for women whose morning was lost to shopping.

He was heading for the Questura with his purchases when voices, raised above the general hubbub of the market and of a discordant tone, attracted his attention to two stalls which sold similar bits and pieces. One sold every spare part for every size of Moka, vacuum cleaner bags and filters, and parts for myriad small electrical appliances. The stall next to it also sold small electrical goods, batteries for every device, watches, sunglasses, beads, and everything for making jewellery. Both stalls sold pots and pans.

The argument was about the positioning of the tables and large umbrellas. Despite the different pitches being marked in red paint on the surface of the carpark, there was an occasional territorial dispute if an owner felt that a line had been crossed or if the prevailing wind caused an umbrella to overshadow his stall. Such petty nonsense was usually resolved by the Municipal Police officer who patrolled the market checking for permits, but on this occasion she was busy at another part.

Santoro shook hands with the locals he had been talking to and weaved his way over to sort things out. He arrived, smiling and palms up in a placatory gesture, with his shopping bag in the crook of his elbow.

'Rocco, Signor Chen, good morning,' he began. 'What's all the fuss about?'

Both men answered at the same time, so Santoro put his hands up again to stop them.

'Signor Chen, you go first, please.'

The Chinese man pointed to the ground, where the legs of his neighbour's trestles were outside of the red line allocated to that pitch.

'Look. Illegal,' Chen said in very broken, heavily accented Italian.

Santoro looked at the two red L-shapes separated by a space of about ten centimetres that defined the limits of their spots.

'You're right, Signor Chen,' Santoro agreed, as one or two shoppers stopped to watch. 'Rocco's trestle legs are over the line, but they don't come over your line, do they?'

Chen knelt and pointed at his table legs. Rocco feigned nonchalance and moved some stock about on his table.

'Look. Leg inside line. Legal.' He then pointed to Rocco's. 'Leg outside line. Illegal.'

'I agree, Signor Chen, that Rocco's table leg is outside the red line, but it doesn't interfere with your table, does it?'

Chen folded his arms while Rocco, with contrived casualness, focussed his attention on rearranging items close to the table leg under discussion. Another couple stopped to look.

'Outside line,' Chen insisted. 'Illegal.'

'Well, it's not strictly illegal, Signor Chen,' soothed Santoro. 'Rocco's table leg is in what might be called no-man's-land.'

Chen frowned. 'No-man's-land? Never heard of it.'

'Rocco's table leg is in the empty space between his pitch and your pitch,' Santoro explained. 'The Municipal Police always leave a little distance between the pitches, so that if someone strays over a little, it doesn't actually go into the next space. That space between the red marks doesn't belong to anyone. It's no-man's-land.'

Arms still folded, Chen muttered, 'Looks illegal,' until a passer-by showed interest in some of the beads in his stall. So, he broke off and passed the customer a plastic bowl to collect an assortment.

Santoro now turned to Rocco.

'And how can I help you, this fine sunny day?' he asked with a smile.

'Don't give me all that, Gennaro,' said Rocco. 'Look at his stock. Look at his prices. He's undercutting me.'

Santoro sighed. 'I'm only a cop, Rocco, but forgive me, isn't that how business works?'

Rocco put his hands on his hips.

'I don't mind competition,' he said. 'As long as it's fair.' He stabbed his finger at the neighbouring stall. 'Chen imports all that stuff from China. It's probably not been checked. I don't even know if it's safe, and I don't think he even pays the taxes to the damn government that I do. And did you know some Chinese have bought Bar Roma?'

Before Santoro could respond, Chen shouted over, 'I pay taxes. I pay all taxes.'

He reached into the van behind him, fished out a ring binder, and flicked through the plastic pockets inside it. 'Look,' he exclaimed, holding out one of the pockets. 'Accountant letter. All tax paid.'

Santoro took the paper and read it.

'Thank you, Signor Chen.' He returned the letter and faced Rocco. 'Signor Chen pays all his taxes,' Santoro said firmly. 'If he can buy stock at a better price, then you maybe have to think about what you're selling.'

'My family have been coming to sell goods at this market for over forty years,' Rocco continued. 'Chen's only been here three or four.'

Santoro thought about making a comment on the age of Rocco's stock but thought better of it.

Chen called over. 'Chen leaving soon.'

'Good,' retorted Rocco.

'Oh,' said Santoro. 'Where are you going to?'

'Corner shop.'

'Here in Cassiatorre?'

'Yes. Move next week.'

Rocco shook his head. 'That's crazy,' he said. 'There's not enough custom to keep a shop going six days a week.'

'Seven,' quipped Chen. 'Open seven days.'

'Well, that's exciting news, Signor Chen,' said Santoro. 'I hope the move goes well and that the shop is a great success. Eh, Rocco?'

Rocco muttered under his breath, 'Crazy idea.'

*

At the section of the market where most of the clothes were sold, a tall, slim, sunburned young Englishman, holding two bags full of fruit and vegetables, waited patiently in the shade of an umbrella while his new wife shopped for underwear from the multicoloured selection on offer.

She tossed her shoulder-length brown hair back and called to him, 'These prices are incredible.'

He smiled.

'There's only so much underwear that you can wear, Sue,' he said. 'We might have to buy another suitcase.'

Handing the stallholder another handful of slips, she replied, 'Andy, these colours match clothes that I already have. Don't worry, they'll roll up to almost nothing.'

Sue paid and took the bulging bag from the vendor. 'Look,' she said, squeezing it tightly between her arm and her side. 'They squash to hardly anything.'

Andy kissed her, transferred both of his bags to his right hand, and took Sue's hand in his left.

'Oh, we didn't see that stall,' Sue cried, pointing. 'Let's have a look.'

Tucked behind sellers of fresh flowers and house plants, in a corner of the carpark, was a stall selling fresh, dried, and preserved fungi.

Jars of truffle paste, bottles of truffle oil, truffle flavoured dried pasta, and packets of mixed dried porcini were neatly stacked on upturned, wooden tomato boxes. In the centre of the stall, however, were some fresh mushrooms the size of golf balls, resting on a bed of lettuce.

'What are those?' Sue asked in passable Italian.

'They're called ovoli or Caesar's mushroom,' replied the seller, a bent old man with a complexion like tanned leather. 'Very delicious and highly prized, but expensive.'

'How do you cook them?'

'We shave them over salad and eat them raw.'

The stall holder picked up a handheld metal tool that had a fine blade with an adjustable gap.

'We use this,' he explained, showing how the gap could be closed or opened by turning a screw.

'You can use it for truffles or bottarga, too. Look.'

He picked up one of the mushrooms and rubbed it along the device, sending paper-thin slivers onto the lettuce. He picked up two leaves, dripped two or three drops of olive oil onto them, added a sprinkle of salt, and held them out.

'Here, try it.'

Andy and Sue took the sample and tasted it.

'Wow,' said Andy. 'We have to get some of those to go with the salad we already have.'

'Can you find these locally?' Sue asked.

The seller put about a dozen into a brown paper bag.

'If you know where to look and what to look for,' he said with a smile.

'What about the shaving tool, where can I buy one of those?' asked Andy.

'Try the Chinese guy, or the man next to him. Between them, they sell everything.'

CHAPTER FOUR

The two men stood on opposite sides of the upturned car.

'What the hell are you doing here, Sergio?' Moretti ignored forensic protocol and gripped the sides of the smashed window.

'I've missed you, too, Dino,' said the doctor. 'Yes, it's good to be back, and I'm very well, thanks for asking.'

He moved around the front of the car, past Moretti, put down his medical bag, removed his latex gloves, and held his hand out to Cristina.

'Dr Sergio Vanni,' he said 'Pleased to meet you.'

Cristina shook Vanni's hand.

'Ispettore Cristina Furlan,' she replied. 'What are you doing here, Dr Vanni?'

Vanni removed his metal-rimmed glasses and cleaned them on the tail of his shirt that he wore outside of his trousers, lifting it enough to reveal a flat stomach.

'Mere coincidence,' he said. 'This guy and the chasing police car overtook me. I saw the crash and came to see if I could help.'

Cristina turned to defer to Moretti, but her boss walked away in the direction of the traffic police.

She looked back at Vanni as he was putting his glasses back on. They slightly magnified his cornflower blue eyes.

She switched on her phone. 'I'll record this, if you

don't mind,' she said.

'No problem. I guess you want me to tell you what happened.'

'Start with the car chase.'

He scratched his short-cut white hair.

'I wouldn't have called it a car chase,' he clarified. 'This car – and for the purposes of this recording, I am referring to the red Fiat that overturned and crashed into an olive tree, killing its only occupant – was being driven erratically and excessively fast, given the twisting nature of the road and the presence of other vehicles. It was being followed by a State Police traffic car with two officers inside. They were travelling at a speed matching the Fiat's. The Fiat overtook me on a bend and was still on the other side of the carriageway when a vehicle approached from the other direction. The driver of that vehicle swerved sharply and performed an emergency stop, bringing his car safely to a stop in a controlled manner.' He glanced to the side. 'This car, however, continued straight on, rose onto the verge at full speed, clipping olive trees as it continued, before it hit that tree stump.' Vanni pointed. 'At which point it flipped over and was airborne briefly, before coming finally to rest when it collided with an olive tree. The following police vehicle overtook me, too, but when they saw the oncoming vehicle, they pulled over back in front of me and stopped. I had to brake sharply, but I stopped safely, too.'

Cristina tilted her head to one side and raised her eyebrows.

'Did you get a look at the driver? How did he seem?'

'I first saw him in the rear mirror. He was singing or shouting wildly, throwing his head from side to side in time to very loud music.'

'You said that you went to see if you could help,' said Cristina. 'What did you do, exactly?'

'I took my bag and climbed up to where the car was. I reached in and switched off the engine to silence the deafening music, and I checked the driver for a pulse. There was none. The deceased man was covered in blood which I am certain was a result of the collision. I observed that emesis had occurred, so I looked closely at the vomit. Let me show you.'

Cristina followed Vanni around the front of the car. He crouched down at the smashed side window.

'Look,' he said, pointing to the vomit on the deceased man's clothing. 'You see those bits of partially digested food material. They're mushroom, to be precise. If my guess is correct, it will be shown to be *Amanita muscaria*, fly agaric.'

'Your guess?' queried Cristina.

'Yes. My guess is that the deceased man ingested the mushrooms, experienced mild psychotropic effects such as elation, but then got into his car. While he was driving, the effects reached their peak. That would explain his shouting, singing, erratic driving, and the vomit.'

'Excuse me, Dr Vanni,' said Cristina, her curiosity piqued, 'but what sort of doctor are you?'

Vanni smiled.

'I'm a doctor who has an interest – both professional and culinary – in fungi,' he replied.

Cristina stopped the recording and put her phone away.

'I hope you don't mind me asking again, Dr Vanni, but what are you doing here?'

The doctor looked down the slope towards Moretti and the others.

'Coming home,' he said pensively. 'I used to live and work in Maghicchio as a family doctor, but I moved to Rome and studied, trained, and worked there for over fifteen years. I decided it was time for a change.'

'From the job or the city?'

He glanced at her and laughed.

'You can be very direct, Ispettore,' he said. 'I suppose that comes with the job.' He looked back down the slope again. 'Both. The city is unbearably hot and sticky in the summer, and I needed a change from the smog and the crowds.'

Now Cristina laughed. 'And you come home to this.'

She followed his gaze down towards the road and watched the officers gathering evidence. Moretti stood on the verge, talking into his phone.

'You and Commissario Moretti know each other.'

Vanni hesitated a fraction. 'We were best friends once.'

Cristina dismissed the urge to press for details. She changed the subject.

'So, are you retiring, or are you looking for a job here?'

'No, I'm not retiring,' he replied. 'When I said I was coming home, I meant more than relocating here. I'm returning to the job that I loved best – being a family doctor in a small rural community. I've bought into the practice here in Cassiatorre. I was supposed to be house-hunting today.' He looked at his watch. 'Is there anything else you need to ask me, Ispettore?'

Cristina pulled out a card.

'Not at the moment, Doctor Vanni, but since you reached into the car, you'll need to report to the Questura for fingerprinting. If anything else occurs to you, you can reach me on that number.'

Vanni took her card and put it into his wallet. 'In that case, I'll head off to my appointment with the estate agent.' He took out his card and gave it to Cristina. 'And if you need to get in touch, my number and email are there.'

'Thank you.'

'And Ispettore,' Vanni said, holding out his hand again, 'it's Sergio.'

They shook hands and he left for his car.

Cristina watched him go and saw how Moretti turned away as he approached. She tucked Vanni's card into her pocket and walked down to join the commissario.

'I called Carlo in Maghicchio,' Moretti said. 'To reassure him that we've spoken to a couple who said that his guys were not to blame for the accident.'

'He'll be relieved.' She held up her phone and waggled it. 'I've also got a recording of Dr Vanni's account.'

'Right. That's that then. Let's head back to the Questura.'

Back in the car, Cristina broke the awkward silence between them.

'Interesting character, Dr Vanni.'

'Hmm.'

She paused, waiting for more. Moretti remained silent.

'He's interested in mushrooms.'

Still nothing from Moretti.

'He thinks that the deceased man had ingested fly agaric mushrooms and was driving under their influence, and that's what caused the crash.'

Her seat was further back than Moretti's, and although she looked sideways at him for a reaction to the news, his expression didn't change.

Cristina drove in silence for a little.

'He's moving to Cassiatorre,' she said brightly. 'He's going to be part of the medical practice in the town.'

Moretti's eyes squeezed shut, and his moustache moved in a way that let Cristina know his mouth had tightened.

'Shit,' he said with a gasp. 'That's all we need.'

Cristina thought about it for a moment, then slowed and stopped the car off the road at the entrance to one of the farms and switched off the engine.

Moretti turned to look at her. 'What are you doing?'

She inhaled deeply.

'Sir, it's obvious that there is something between you and Dr Vanni,' she blurted. 'He told me that you were once best friends, and that's clearly not the case now.'

Moretti opened his mouth to speak, but Cristina continued.

'I have to say that I found him both helpful and professional. His recorded account of what happened would be enough on its own to exonerate the traffic officers without the other witnesses, but he did more than that. He suggested how the whole accident could have happened. I'm uncomfortable with this atmosphere, and I had to stop and let you know.'

Moretti looked at her and nodded.

'Sergio and I were best friends, Cristina. Did he tell you what happened to change that?'

'No.'

She saw his focus change to a point over her shoulder in the distance.

'This isn't the time or place to talk about it, Cristina,' he said. 'It's bringing back memories that I'd buried.'

She could feel that her face had reddened. 'I'm sorry, sir.'

Moretti now looked back at her. 'Don't apologise, you've done nothing wrong. It was unexpected, that's all. I will tell you sometime, but not now.'

'Okay, Commissario.'

He turned to face front again.

'I'd like you to deal with this case, Cristina,' he said. 'I don't want to have anything to do with Dr Sergio Vanni. Ever.'

*

In the cool shade of the vine pergola attached to the refurbished eighteenth-century farmhouse, Andy and Sue laid the table for lunch. With a view down across the valley's rolling hills to Lake Trasimeno, their mood in the holiday rental was a peaceful, restful contrast to their busy lives in London. They had risen early and walked for several kilometres before showering and walking into Cassiatorre for breakfast and a visit to the market.

The air was already hot enough for the cicadas to begin their ratchety serenade from the line of holm oaks that bordered the property.

An olivewood platter of mixed salami and cheeses sat in the middle of the table, beside a basket holding fingers of rosemary and olive oil focaccia. At the end of the table, Sue placed a vase with some lavender spikes that she had cut from the garden, adding a solitary sunflower that she'd bought from the market.

Andy cut the foil from a bottle of local red and twisted in the corkscrew, folding down its arms to extract the cork.

'It's a real cork, not plastic,' he called into the kitchen. 'How's the salad coming?'

'It's ready for your final touch,' Sue replied, emerging from the cool. 'Wow, it's even hot under the shade.'

She laid the large majolica bowl of mixed salad leaves onto the table.

'That looks lovely, darling,' said Andy, reaching for his phone. 'I'm sending photographs back to the guys in the office. Everyone's jealous.'

He took half a dozen shots from different angles, with blurred Tuscan backgrounds and different lighting effects.

'Enough,' Sue said, ruffling his hair. 'Let's eat. I'm

starving.'

Andy exchanged his phone for the metal slicing tool that he'd bought. Resting on top of the salad were the Caesar's mushrooms. He carefully took them off and put them on another plate.

'I'll toss the salad first,' said Sue.

She drizzled some local olive oil over the leaves and tossed them with her fingers. 'Now go.'

Andy picked up one of the egg-shaped mushrooms, held the shaver over the salad leaves, and sent a stream of thin ovoli shavings over them.

When he reached for the fourth mushroom, he asked, 'How many of these do you think we should use?'

Sue shrugged, wiping her hands on a piece of kitchen paper torn from a roll. 'I don't know. The guy knew that there were only the two of us.' She poured them each a glass of wine. 'Let's use them all while they're fresh.'

Andy grinned.

'You're crazy. This is the most expensive salad I've ever made.'

Sue picked up a sliver of mushroom, held it between her lips and kissed him, letting him nibble the free end.

'But I'm worth it,' she said.

CHAPTER FIVE

Moretti left Furlan talking to Alfiero, the desk officer at the Questura, and went directly to his office. He closed the door behind him, crossed to the other side of the room, opened the French windows, and stood out on the little balcony that overlooked the main square. He took out a small cigar and lit it eagerly, sending a large puff of pale blue smoke into the convection current that rose up the side of the building.

Since his wife Maria continued to find work in the south and had all but separated from him, his smoking was no longer restricted to a furtive one cigar a day. So, he had fixed an aluminium ashtray to a corner of the wrought iron railing of the balcony.

Sergio bloody Vanni. Why had he come back?

The spiralling up-draught lifted a swirling cloud of dust and multicoloured confetti from a recent wedding past his balcony, the confusion of coloured shapes echoing his thoughts. He closed his eyes to the dust and emitted a single ironic laugh.

Behind him, the knocking on his office door brought him back to the present.

'Are you in here, Capo?' Santoro asked as he entered, leaving the door open.

Moretti took one last puff and stubbed out the cigar.

'Out here, Gennaro,' he called back into the room. He

took out a small plastic container and removed a single filmy breath sheet, letting it dissolve in icy mintiness on his tongue as he stepped back into his office.

Gennaro Santoro sat in one of the chairs in front of Moretti's desk without waiting for his superior and smiled broadly. He glanced at the date circled on Moretti's desk calendar and jabbed his thumb at it.

'Looking forward to the new arrival next week?'

Moretti half shrugged. 'We'll see. Did you manage to find anything out?'

'Nothing. I asked a good friend up north, and all he did was laugh and say that they were always referred to and known by their initials – CC.'

Moretti shook his head.

'CC. Is that all? I don't know what we pay you for, Agente Santoro.' He sat at the desk. 'How was the market today?'

'Oh well,' he said with a grin, 'I did defuse a potentially dangerous international incident.'

Moretti smiled and settled back in his chair. 'Tell me all about it.'

'It was nothing, really, Capo. I stepped in to calm down Rocco and Signor Chen, who were arguing over nothing at all. They have a little flare up from time to time, but this should be the last one.'

'Oh?'

'Yes. Chen's moving. He's opening a shop, apparently.'

'Will he sell enough to be viable?'

'That's what Rocco said,' exclaimed Santoro. 'Chen seems to think so.'

'When's the move?'

'This week, I think. Oh, and did you know Bar Roma has been sold? Rocco says it's some more Chinese people.'

'Yes. I met them this morning. Three generations. The old woman had her luggage stolen from the railway station.'

'Oh no.'

Moretti looked up when Cristina appeared at the door. 'Come and join us, Cristina,' he said. 'Gennaro was updating me on the weekly market.'

She looked puzzled but sat next to Santoro. 'I've had a call from the traffic police,' she began.

It was Santoro's turn to look puzzled.

'About the road traffic accident this morning,' said Moretti. 'Go on, Cristina.'

'The deceased has been taken away for a post-mortem, they're in the process of recovering the car, and the road is open again, although there are still officers directing the traffic and making sure there are no rubberneckers.'

'Why were—'

'Why were two detectives summoned to a traffic case?' Moretti interrupted Santoro. 'Carlo wanted to be prepared in case his officers had caused it.'

'So, what—'

'Cristina can fill you in on the details later, Gennaro,' Moretti interrupted again. 'Anything else? I feel that I need to get out of the office today.'

Santoro shrugged. Cristina placed a message pad sheet on Moretti's desk.

'Just this,' she said, sliding it across to him.

Moretti picked up the sheet. 'Someone has broken into a barn.' He burst out laughing. 'Great,' he said, slapping both thighs. 'Just what I need. Santoro, come with me as back-up. Let's crack this case before CC, the new Vice Questore, gets here on Monday.'

The three detectives stood, and Moretti headed to the door. Gennaro grabbed the message from Moretti's desk and exchanged a baffled look with Cristina as they both followed him. Cristina turned towards her office while the men left the Questura and headed out into the square, Santoro half running, half walking, to catch up with Moretti.

Moments later in Moretti's car, Santoro spoke. 'Capo, I hope you don't mind me saying, but you're acting a bit oddly.'

Moretti's hands tightened a little on the steering wheel. 'Sergio's back.'

Santoro turned to read Moretti's face. 'Vanni?'

'The same.'

'Ah.'

Santoro looked out of the side window and stayed

silent until they reached the crash site where the traffic policeman signalled them to slow down. The mangled red Fiat was strapped securely on the back of a transporter, ready to move off. Incident tape still surrounded the olive tree, the stump, and the place where the car left the road. The forensics team had gone.

When the traffic officer recognised Moretti's car, he stopped the oncoming traffic to let the commissario pass and saluted him as they drove by.

'Do you know this place?' Moretti asked.

Santoro read the address from the message sheet.

'No, but I'm sure we've both eaten their beef. The farmer's name is Buina. He's one of the best Fiorentina producers in the whole of Valdichiana.'

They headed down from Maghicchio and continued to the lowest part of the wide valley, along narrowing country roads until they turned into a dirt road and followed it to the farm, where their arrival was met by the usual barking of farm dogs.

Both detectives got out. Santoro crouched and fished out a bag of pork crackling that he broke and shared among the dogs.

Moretti grinned. 'I don't know how you can carry that stuff around in this heat.'

'Ziplock bags and zero interest in fashion,' replied the agente. 'But worth it when you work in a town surrounded by farms.'

'Over here.'

The detectives looked in the direction of the shout and saw a farmer standing in the doorway of a large structure whose steel framework supported a white corrugated roof.

The barrel-chested farmer wore a red, checked shirt and grubby denim dungarees. His dark complexion of a man who spent every day outdoors contrasted with the white of his thin horseshoe moustache. 'Over here,' the man repeated. 'This is where they tried to break in.'

The two detectives joined him, and Moretti held out his hand.

'Signor Buina, I'm Commissario Moretti and this is Agente Santoro.

'Moretti, like the beer?'

'Like the beer,' said Moretti, shaking the farmer's hand. Although roughly the same height, Moretti could hardly close his hand around the farmer's great, calloused paw.

Santoro had the same problem, and surreptitiously shook his crushed hand before reaching for his notebook.

'Look,' said the farmer, pointing to a chain. 'This has been cut through.'

Two sturdy metal handles lined up where the barn's tall sliding doors met in the middle. On the ground beside them was a hefty chain, protected by a plastic sleeve attached to a large, solid padlock.

'They used bolt-cutters to cut the chain,' said Buina.

Moretti picked up the weighty chain and padlock. 'What's inside the shed?'

Buina slid one of the doors open.

'My entire herd of prizewinning Chianina cattle,' he said. 'Including my stud bull Hercules.'

The door opened onto a wide, concrete corridor, flanked on either side by galvanised steel pens, through which the large white cattle stuck their heads to feed from the fodder piled tidily in front of each. In the middle of one side, in a larger pen than all the other animals, was a huge white bull.

Moretti passed the chain to Santoro, who placed it back on the ground as they followed Buina inside.

'Much cooler inside,' observed Moretti, tilting his head back to take in the huge space.

Buina pointed to the roof apex.

'It's offset so that hot air can escape, while cooler air enters from the sides.'

They arrived at the stud bull's pen. Buina scratched Hercules' head between his horns. The animal's massive shoulders were head high.

'This is my pride and joy,' he said.

'How much is a beast like this worth?' Moretti asked.

'With his pedigree and past performance, I'd estimate his lifetime earnings at about seventy thousand euro,' said Buina. 'Just look at the balls on him.'

Moretti and Santoro tilted their heads to look at the

bull's impressively large scrotum.

'He's insured for a hundred thousand,' continued Buina.

Santoro scribbled the numbers down.

'Do you think the ones who cut the chain were after Hercules?' Moretti asked.

Buina grinned.

'No, Commissario. Hercules tolerates me because he has known me since birth. I'm the one who feeds him and looks after him. If you approached him without me, he'd be very dangerous. He could easily kill you.'

'Why do you think they tried to break in, and what stopped them?' quizzed Moretti.

'There are motion sensor security lights and cameras under the eaves,' Buina replied. 'My guess is that the lights came on and they ran off.'

Moretti smoothed his moustache with finger and thumb. 'So, you don't know what they were after?'

'Nope.'

Moretti looked at the walls of the shed. They were made of prefabricated, reinforced concrete slabs to a height of two metres that left plenty of space above for air to circulate.

'Why didn't they climb over the walls?'

'Would you climb over a wall into the pen of a bull? I don't only mean Hercules, Commissario. If you got into a pen in the dark with any of these guys, it wouldn't end well for you.'

Moretti looked at the stubby horns of the feeding animals. 'I see what you mean.'

'Do you have any enemies, Signor Buina?' asked Santoro.

The farmer's eyes narrowed. 'What do you mean?'

'Anyone who'd want to harm you or your animals?'

Buina immediately held down his middle two fingers with his thumbs and jabbed the index and pinkies downwards to ward off the evil eye.

'Everyone has enemies,' he said. 'You can't be in the business of producing prime beef without attracting jealousy or even hatred from your competitors.'

'Anyone in particular?'

Buina repeated the gesture and spat on the floor. 'If I had to name anyone, it would be Nardelli. He has a bull stud ten kilometres from here.'

Moretti exchanged a look with Santoro and held out a card to the farmer.

'Thank you, Signor Buina. If you think of anything else, please get in touch.'

*

Something about Dr Sergio Vanni's recording made Cristina curious, so after transcribing his focused, almost breathless account of the accident on her PC, she did an internet search for him on her phone. Her intuition was right. The way he had given his account of the accident was honed from years of expert witness testimony in court. She also found that the man who had left Maghicchio as a family doctor was now an eminent forensic pathologist. Cristina closed her phone. That discovery presented her with two problems. The first was simple curiosity. Why did Vanni not tell her that he was used to working in accident and crime scenes? The second problem was bigger. She didn't know if Moretti knew and, given the commissario's reaction earlier, whether she should be the one to tell him.

CHAPTER SIX

Sue woke up with a stiff neck. Her shoulder was tucked under Andy's armpit, and her head lay on his shoulder. Tender and romantic, but very awkward. She moved her head back slightly and found it a more comfortable position on the pillow with his arm under her neck. From here she could watch him breathe, his nostrils flaring almost imperceptibly with each inhalation. Her arm was across his chest and her leg was bent across him. He was warm, hot even, to cuddle into. How could he generate so much heat? His eyes moved under his lids. Dreaming. She felt his penis move against her leg and smiled. It became harder, and she giggled silently, fearful that her movement would disturb his sleep – but eager to take the consequences if it did so.

Outside the open shutters, this little part of Italy – for a whole week their little part of Italy – was coming awake. Cockerels, dogs, and car engines. The sun streamed in, hot already, and swifts raced past, dark screaming sickles.

Andy was right. Married felt different. They'd been a couple for five years and two months, and in that time had lived together for three years, seven months, and four days. Now they'd been married for three days, and it did feel different. He was the one to insist that they got married; she'd been fine with the way things were. She smiled again. Andy had surprised her in the middle of the little neighbourhood Italian place they frequented, by kneeling before her – in front of the whole restaurant – and proposing. When she accepted, the owner and the entire staff came to their table clapping, popping a bottle of Franciacorta as they arrived, and filling their glasses with bubbles. Then the whole place joined in the applause. A couple of the other diners even took photographs or videos. Who knew where they were posted? She didn't care. She lifted her fingers, and the ring caught the light.

Sue suddenly felt hungry and the need to pee. She gingerly detached herself from Andy and got up, standing briefly in the full sun streaming in the bedroom window, and enjoying its warmth on her skin – on her belly. She'd share her secret with Andy next week when they moved to Sorrento for the second part of their honeymoon. Meanwhile, she stretched then padded to the toilet.

Her rising must have woken him. She heard his footsteps heading to the kitchen and the sound of the Moka being dismantled, filled, reassembled, and clunked onto the stove. Three clicks from the piezo and the gas roared. He had the same little ritual at home in London.

She finished up and joined him in the kitchen. He was standing naked at the counter, arranging tiny cups onto tiny saucers. She pressed herself against him and wrapped her arms around him, her cheek between his shoulder blades. He stretched his arms behind him and placed his hands on her bottom, pulling her into him.

'I don't know who you are, Signorina,' he said without turning, 'but we'll have to be quick before my wife sees us.'

Sue squeezed him then let go, spanking him on the rear.

'Oi!' he yelped, as he turned and grabbed her in a hug. 'That hurt.'

He kissed her.

'Oi!' Sue yelped. 'Go and shave. Your beard is tearing my face.'

He pecked her on the lips and broke off to pour the coffee while Sue went back to the bedroom. She returned wearing pants and a t-shirt.

'What's the plan today?'

Andy passed her a cup of strong black coffee.

'Well, I thought that we could go for a long walk,

maybe in the hills, work up an appetite and take it from there. I'd also like to find a phone signal and check my messages.'

'Sounds good,' she replied. 'What about breakfast? I'm starving.'

'We'll stop in one of the bars for a cornetto and cappuccino on the way.'

'We can buy some water, too. It's roasting outside.'

'Okay, but we should be fine if we stay under the trees.'

Half an hour later they had showered, dressed, and packed a small daysack with a map of the area, energy bars, wipes, tissues, a little first aid kit, mosquito repellent, after-bite, and a clean pair of pants in a plastic bag that Sue always insisted on carrying. You never knew when you might need them.

On the way, their phones picked up a signal and pinged repeatedly. By the time they had walked the short distance to Cassiatorre, the bells of Santa Lucia were ringing for Mass. They approached Bar Italia as the faithful drained their cups and sauntered off to church.

'Let's sit here,' Sue said, pointing to a table outside.

'I'll go and order. What kind of pastry would you like?'

'A custard one, please.'

Andy waited at the counter while the owner served the man with a huge walrus moustache who had come in ahead of him. Then he ordered for Sue and himself in his faltering Italian. The owner smiled and told him that she'd bring it outside.

A young boy appeared from nowhere and tidied away the crockery and wiped down Sue's table. She thanked him, and the boy gave her a lopsided grin.

Andy reappeared. 'She's bringing it out,' he said, then sat under the shade of the large umbrella while Sue settled in the full sun.

She took the map out of the daysack. 'Show me where we're walking today.'

Andy opened the map fully, then folded it down to show the hillside nearest town.

'Somewhere in this area,' he said, indicating vaguely on the sheet. 'I'm not particularly bothered, as long as we can relax and get a bit of exercise.'

Carla came with their breakfast, and they cleared the map away.

Sue bit hungrily into the pastry.

'Mmm,' she said, her mouth full. 'This is wonderful. Why can't we get anything this good back home?'

Andy smiled.

'Italians care about food, Sue. It's that simple.'

Mouth stuffed and chewing, Sue leaned back and caught the attention of the young boy, signalling that she wanted another pastry. He went inside and his mother came out to check.

'Could I have another one of these, please?' Sue asked in Italian.

Carla nodded and turned to Andy. 'And for you, sir?' she asked in English.

'No thanks,' Andy replied in Italian.

Carla disappeared to get the pastry while Sue and Andy checked their phones.

'Just some work stuff, 'said Andy, switching his phone off. 'I'm going to say that we were out of signal the whole time we were here.'

Sue patted his hand.

'I've missed a flurry of calls and messages from my girlfriends. They all want to know how the honeymoon is going.' She scrolled down and giggled. 'Also, some very rude questions about our wedding night that I'm not going to reply to.'

Sue made short work of the second pastry when it arrived.

Andy chuckled and rose. 'You were hungry. I'll go and pay.'

'Don't forget the water.'

Shortly after, now with two small bottles of mineral water in the net pocket of the daysack slung over Andy's shoulder, the young couple headed out of town, along a winding road to the wooded hills.

Sue traced their progress on the folded-back map.

'I think we're here,' she said, pointing. 'If we come off this road and take that trail to our right, we'll be able to walk up through the trees to the ridge.'

'Lead on, MacDuff,' said Andy.

'You just want to look at my bum.'

'Guilty as charged.'

Sue led them off onto the dusty trail that meandered through the trees. Swallowtails and sulphur yellow butterflies fluttered and glided in the dappled shade, while lizards rustled to escape in the dry leaves as they approached. Although their path was undulating, the steepness of the slope gradually increased, and both were breathing heavily.

'There's a stream ahead, Andy. I'm going to cool my hands and splash my face.'

Sue sped up and fell to her knees at the edge of the stream.

'It's warm,' she squealed. 'Hot, almost.'

Andy caught up with her.

'I'm stopping for a drink,' he said. 'Want some?'

'Yes, please.'

Sue picked up a dry twig, stripped the bark, and twisted her dark hair back and up, holding it in place with the twig. 'That's better.'

Andy handed her a bottle of water. 'We'll share this one,' he said.

She gulped thirstily.

'I love watching you do that stuff,' he said.

Sue wiped her arm across her mouth. 'What, drinking like a sailor?' She passed the water back.

'No, the way you can simply fix your hair up using a random stick.'

She stood on tiptoes and kissed him.

'Silly.' She turned. 'Let's go.' She strode off, leaving him still sipping the water.

'Wait,' he called after her.

'Come on, slowcoach.'

'No, wait, Sue. Come back.'

She turned and grinned. 'Andy, if this is a trick…'

'Look,' he said, pointing to a shady patch.

'I can't see. What is it?'

'I've spotted some of those mushrooms we had last night.'

Sue skipped down towards him. 'Are you sure? Where?'

They crouched over the little cluster of ovoli.

'That's them right enough,' said Sue.

'I'm not so certain.' He took out his phone. 'Let me check.'

He found the photos that he had taken the day before and they looked at them together.

'That's definitely them,' announced Sue. 'Pass me the daysack.'

She fished around inside, brought out her spare pants, and removed them from the plastic bag.

'We can put them in this,' she said triumphantly.

They collected eight of the mushrooms, wrapped them in paper tissue, popped them into the plastic bag, and spent a few minutes searching the surrounding area in case there were more.

'I'll cook us mushroom risotto tonight,' she said.

'If you're sure they're okay,' said Andy.

Before Sue could reply, her phone rang. 'It's an online call,' she said.

'Who from?'

She laughed. 'Everyone, it looks like. Hello, you lot. I'm on honeymoon. What do you think you're doing?'

A chorus of tinny voices issued from the phone.

Sue nodded in the direction of the thermal stream, and the couple returned to it. She kicked off her sandals, sat on the grassy bank, and dangled her feet in the warm water.

'Where are you?' asked one of the callers.

'Paradise,' she replied to a chorus of Ohs. 'We're in the middle of a wood, halfway up an Italian hillside, I'm waggling my toes in a warm stream, and we've foraged some mushrooms for tonight's dinner.'

She discerned Andy's name from the cacophony, so she touched the screen to flip the camera around.

'There he is.'

Andy gave a little wave.

Another noisy chorus.

Sue flipped the camera back.

'Tell us your plans,' said one. 'You kept everything secret before you left.'

'How's the weather?' asked another.

'Never mind the weather, how's the sex?' chipped in a third.

Andy made a walking signal with his fingers. Sue gave him a thumbs up.

'We're in a little town in southern Tuscany.'

'Ooh.'

'We're planning to visit Siena, Florence, and Orvieto.'

'Sounds lovely.'

'Can I come?'

'How's the sex?'

General laughter. Sue ignored the comment and continued, 'Then next week we're going to the Amalfi Coast near Sorrento, to lie on a beach, although we'll probably visit Pompei and other touristy stuff.'

'Ooh.'

'Well jel.'

'So, are you having sex?'

More laughter.

'Who's that?' Sue asked. 'Is that you, Phillipa?'

'Yes.'

'How many are there of you, anyway? My screen is too tiny to see.'

'About ten of us.'

Sue noticed that Andy was now kicking the dead leaves.

'Look, girls, I'm losing the signal. I have to go now. Bye.'

Sue smiled and switched off to a raucous chorus of Byes, Cheerios, and Have fun.

Andy began climbing to join her.

'Wait there,' said Sue, pulling on her sandals. 'I'll come to you. I've had enough. Let's go back to where we don't have a signal.'

He waited until she arrived, then wrapped an arm around her waist. Sue slipped her hand into the back pocket of his jeans, and they walked like that back to the asphalt road.

'So,' he said. 'Mushroom risotto tonight. How can we work up an appetite?'

Sue took her hand out of his pocket, spanked him again, and they made their way back to their rental.

CHAPTER SEVEN

Moretti arrived at the station a little earlier than usual, picked up his messages from Alfiero at the desk, and headed along the corridor. He was unsurprised to see that Cristina was already in her office. He put his head round the door.

'Good morning, Cristina. Any news?'

'I've been here for an hour and seen nothing.'

'Santoro?'

Cristina looked at her watch. 'A bit early yet, although he did tell me that he was going to make a special effort today.'

Moretti heard a noise behind him and looked back along the corridor. Santoro was hurrying lopsidedly to join them.

'Am I late?' he puffed at the door of Cristina's office.

She smiled. 'Why don't you both come in?'

Santoro made to step forward, but Moretti stopped him.

'I think it's best if CC sees us hard at work in our own offices,' he said.

Santoro agreed, and the two men left Cristina. Moretti patted Santoro's back as they parted.

Since Vice Questore Innocenti had been forced to accept early retirement in the spring, an interim Vice Questore, Rossi, had been appointed. But he had suffered from a prolonged bout of ill health that meant the department had sustained a break in the line of command. None of that had affected the detectives' day-to-day work. If anything, they had become more efficient. Without the need to generate reports that contributed to the Crime Resolution statistics, they'd had more time to spend solving cases.

Moretti's mobile buzzed along his desk. He picked it up and read the message.

Meeting in my office now. CC

He got to the door of his office at the same time as Cristina and Gennaro reached theirs, sharing variations of the same puzzled expression. They spoke in whispers as they approached the door of the Vice Questore's office.

'Didn't you see CC arrive, Cristina?' Moretti asked.

'No,' breathed Cristina. 'And Alfero at the desk said nothing when I passed him.'

The three arranged themselves in order of rank outside the door. Moretti knocked.

'Enter.'

The detectives exchanged looks of surprise. CC was a woman.

Moretti opened the door and held it for Cristina to enter, followed by Santoro, and stood in the space left between them in front of the new Vice Questore's desk. The seats that were usually there had been removed to the side of the room. Seated behind the desk with fingers steepled was a short, heavy-set woman of about fifty, with neat, short black hair and no make-up. Her very large, dark eyes, framed with naturally long lashes, scanned each of them from head to toe in turn before fixing on Cristina.

'I am CC Montanari,' she announced in the distinct accent of Bologna, and pointed to a chunky brass nameplate at the front of her desk. 'You are Ispettore Furlan, Commissario Moretti, and Agente Santoro.' She tapped a stack of files with a coloured leaflet on top on the desk.

'I came in yesterday evening to get an idea of what you've been working on.' Her eyes moved from one to the other as she rested her hand on the files. 'And it's clear that there have been some successes.' Now she looked at Cristina. 'Clearly there is talent here, but there is a lack of structure, organisation, and accountability. That is something that I will say more of shortly. But first, tell me what cases you are working on currently.' She addressed Cristina. 'Ispettore Furlan, you begin.'

Cristina hesitated in case she had meant for Moretti to go first.

'Come on, Ispettore.'

With the tiniest of movements, Moretti pushed his elbow against her arm.

Cristina cleared her throat.

'There was a fatal car crash on Saturday. A tourist was killed.' Cristina sensed the imminent interruption and continued quickly to prevent it. 'Normally this would be a case dealt with by our colleagues in Traffic, but because it involved a high-speed pursuit, their commissario asked that we attend the scene and conduct some preliminary investigations in case the actions of his officers were called into question.'

CC smiled at Cristina.

'Have you reached any initial conclusions?'

Cristina shifted her weight slightly.

'It's thought that the tourist was under the influence of drugs – psychotropic mushrooms, to be precise. Samples of vomit and blood have been collected by the forensics team and a post-mortem is being conducted.'

CC nodded. She opened her phone with her middle fingerprint. 'Good. Very good. What was the name of the commissario who called you?'

Cristina kept her eyes on CC but turned her head and shoulders a fraction towards Moretti.

'The commissario's first name is Carlo, Vice Questore Montanari,' she said. 'I don't know his surname, and it was Commissario Moretti that he called.'

CC made a note in her phone.

Moretti inhaled, ready to supply the surname.

'Commissario,' CC began, flatly, without looking up. 'What are you working on?'

Moretti paused to make eye contact – there was none

– then began to give his account in the broadest Tuscan accent.

'I investigated a report of a stolen trunk. An old woman, Chinese, and newly arrived in Italy, had left it unattended for a short while at the station in Maghicchio. Its whereabouts are unknown, but I'm still working on it.'

Montanari did not look up and Moretti began to feel annoyed.

'We also received a report from a nationally important supplier of quality beef that an attempt had been made to enter premises housing his entire prizewinning herd of pedigree Chianina cattle. In particular, he was concerned for the safety of Hercules, an extremely valuable stud bull whose progeny command very high prices.'

CC's head was still down. Moretti's annoyance grew to anger.

'The owner invited me and Agente Santoro to witness for ourselves. And indeed, even though neither the agente nor I are experts in this field, we were both very impressed by nature's generosity in bestowing the bull with testicles of prodigious dimensions, weren't we, Agente?'

Moretti held his hands out, palms facing each other – one at chest height, the other waist height – to demonstrate – a gesture wasted on Montanari whose attention was fixed on her phone.

'I'll leave it to Agente Santoro to confirm and to supply details of the value of the bull from the extensive note he recorded at the time.'

The Vice Questore still did not look up. Moretti felt on one side Cristina tighten her arm close to her to create a gap between them, and on the other side the silent heaving of Santoro's shoulders.

'The owner then showed us the attempted point of entry to the locus,' he continued dryly. 'To wit, the large sliding doors situated to the east of the property. Said doors had previously been secured by what appeared to be a heavy-duty security chain made of a steel alloy. The chain, according to the owner, had been severed by bolt-cutters – although he offered no evidence of this. We enquired if the owner suspected anyone, but he was unable to furnish us with any reliable information in that regard.'

Moretti stopped.

Now CC looked up. 'You're telling me that a cowshed was broken into, Commissario,' she said with a smirk.

'Yes, Vice Questore.'

'And that it took *two* of you to investigate?'

'Yes, Vice Questore.'

Montanari sighed. 'This is how things will be from now on,' she said firmly. 'One detective, one case. Each of you will take separate assignments and follow them through, unless it's a major investigation, when you will be permitted to work together. There'll be no more of this handholding and time wasting with two of you going to the same incident. That way we'll have greater efficiency, and it will introduce a deal of accountability that has been lacking up until now. I'll also get to see quickly who is performing well and who is slacking.'

She looked at Moretti.

'Commissario Moretti, you will take over the fatal car crash case from Ispettore Furlan and add that to your cowshed investigation, which you will now pursue without the assistance of Agente Santoro.'

Moretti held up a finger.

'Ah,' he started, 'there's a complicating circumstance which means I can't take over that case, and there's the matter of the stolen luggage.'

CC glared at him. 'Well, uncomplicate it, Commissario. It's your case now. And as for the missing luggage, forget about that.'

She turned and spoke directly to Santoro for the first time.

'You will fill in Crime Resolution proformas for each of the cases in these folders, Agente,' she said, tapping the bundle on her desk. 'That will let me draft a report on what state I found the station in when I arrived. Everyone will be able to see how my new initiatives improve the ratings. When you finish, you can file the folders then come to me for some other duties.'

She shoved the folders over to Santoro, who gathered them up into his arms.

When she turned to Cristina, her tone softened.

'I understand that you transferred here only a few months ago, Ispettore. So, as one newcomer from the north to another, I'm assigning you to fill me in on how things work here.'

Cristina opened her mouth to speak.

Vice Questore Montanari continued, 'You'll work closely with me, and the first thing we'll tackle is this annual festival.' She took the coloured leaflet from the corner of her desk and held it up. 'What do you know about it?'

Cristina gulped. 'Almost nothing, Vice Questore Montanari,' she replied. 'Maybe Commissario—'

Montanari raised a hand to stop her.

'The commissario will be busy with his cowshed.' She addressed Moretti and Santoro. 'Gentlemen, that's all for now. I have things to discuss with the Ispettore.'

Moretti and Santoro left.

The Vice Questore waited until they had gone. 'Bring over a chair, Ispettore.'

Cristina did so and sat down. 'May I speak, Vice Questore Montanari?'

'Yes, and call me CC when the boys aren't here.'

'Well, CC, I'm unfamiliar about the arrangements for the Disfida. It's an important event locally. Visitor numbers increase, and it is essential for the local economy that it's a success. I'm sure that Commissario Moretti would do a much better job.'

'I'm sure he thinks that, too,' CC replied flatly. 'You and I will find out together. It'll give us a chance to get to know each other better. When I read over the files last night, it was obvious that you bring a valuable contribution to this Questura, but you don't always get the recognition. That's the problem with shared investigations; the senior officer gets the credit. My way of working will change all that.' She slid the pamphlet to Cristina. 'Ask Moretti how this works. I imagine that there is some liaison between the State and Municipal Police and the Carabinieri. It can't be too difficult. So, find out and report back to me.'

'Yes, Vice Questore… CC.'

Montanari smiled.

'Don't worry, you'll get used to it.' She gestured towards the pamphlet. 'Make a note of the contact details and dates. The mayor wants a meeting – supposedly to discuss the plans for the policing of the Disfida. I think that the more likely reason is that he wants to see for himself who has been appointed to Vice Questore of Police.'

She leaned back in her chair and Cristina took that as a signal to go, so she stood and made to move the chair back.

'Oh, leave that. I was just making a point.'

'Very good, CC. I'll get on this right away and get back to you with my report as soon as I can.'

'Today,' said Montanari.

'Today,' confirmed Cristina.

*

Despite another clear blue sky, it was not a good start to the day for Sue. She'd expected to feel a little sick in the mornings, but this was much worse. The gurgling which turned into low, crampy pain that made her leap out of bed and race to the toilet – a race that she barely managed to win – was the prelude to what seemed to be the complete evacuation – from both ends, often simultaneously – of the entire contents of her alimentary canal.

Her day worsened considerably minutes later when Andy ran into the property's only bathroom, clutching his stomach, while unstoppable watery diarrhoea fell out of her. They both shared a look of panic as he took the only course open to him and sat next to her on the bidet. His lower half transformed itself into a fetid volcano that erupted violently, explosively, and noisily, into a receptacle not designed for – and which therefore magnificently failed at – receiving and safely retaining waste matter. Sue's bare leg was splashed by collateral damage, but the biggest casualty was the tiled floor whose pattern was obliterated in part by the geyser that issued from between Andy's splayed legs and in part by the vomit that he, then she, added to the mess.

CHAPTER EIGHT

Moretti followed Santoro out of CC Montanari's office and tapped him on the shoulder when they reached his office. Santoro turned round, and Moretti nodded his head sideways towards the open door. Santoro nodded and both men entered the room. Moretti let the agente pass and plonk the pile of filing onto his desk, then closed the door quietly and sat opposite him.

'Well, Gennaro, what do you think of our new Vice Questore?'

Santoro patted the pile of folders. 'Doesn't like me much, does she?'

'I don't think she likes either of us.'

'Are you planning to do anything about it, Capo?'

Moretti rubbed the nape of his neck.

'No. I'm going to get on with whatever comes my way, do my own thing, tell the Vice Questore as little as possible, and if I need your help, I'll still ask for it. I can't think of the number of cases we've worked on together, and your contacts have proved invaluable.'

Santoro smiled and produced a bag of seeds from his pocket.

Moretti raised his brows.

'My new diet, Capo,' Santoro explained. 'Sunflower seeds. High in fibre and high in vitamin E. They're more of a detox, really, but I was getting nowhere and bored with the last one.'

'Remind me what that was again.'

Santoro had tossed a handful of seeds into his mouth, and he crunched them as he spoke. 'The artichoke diet.'

'Ah. I see how that could get a bit samey after a while.'

Santoro finished chewing and swallowed before continuing. 'You said that Sergio's back,' he ventured. 'Is that for good?'

Moretti leaned forward, both elbows on his desk, and smoothed both sides of his moustache simultaneously with his middle fingers before interlocking his fingers and resting his hands on the desk.

'Apparently. Cristina told me that he's joining the local medical practice and looking for a house.'

Santoro prepared his next mouthful of seeds. 'Did Cristina say anything else about him?' He sucked the seeds from the palm of his hand.

'No. What do you mean?'

'She searched for him on the internet.'

'And?'

'He's not only a family doctor.'

Moretti rolled his eyes. 'Gennaro, what the hell is he?'

'He's a top forensic pathologist.'

'He's a what?'

'A pathologist.'

Moretti paused, leaned back, and folded his arms.

'That explains it,' he mused, exhaling loudly. 'I read Cristina's transcription of his statement from the car crash. It read like an expert witness testimony in court.' He shook his head. 'Why in heaven's name would he come back here?' He searched Santoro's face for an answer. 'It doesn't make sense. There are only memories here. Tragic memories.'

Santoro reached into his bag of seeds.

Moretti held up his hand.

'No, Gennaro.' He opened a drawer, took out a small bottle of water, and passed it to the agente. 'Rinse your teeth. They're covered in sunflower seed shrapnel.'

'Sorry, Capo,' he said, putting the seeds away and reaching over for the bottle. He opened it and swooshed his teeth. 'Better?'

'Better,' replied Moretti.

Santoro capped the bottle then clapped his hands. 'Maybe you can use him to your advantage, Capo.'

Moretti furrowed his brows deeply. 'Gennaro, you don't understand.'

Santoro sat forward, brows arched and wide-eyed.

'Vanni was at the heart of the only case that I didn't solve,' Moretti said solemnly. 'The only case in my entire career. Why would I want to work with him when I find it impossible to be in the same room as the man?'

'Capo, you said earlier that you were – what was it? – going to do your own thing and tell the new Vice Questore as little as possible. Vanni can help you do that.'

'Gennaro, I must be incredibly slow today, so I'll stay quiet and let you explain it to me.'

Santoro shifted excitedly in his seat.

'You can go to Vanni for forensic help either before, or instead of going to the local pathologist in Maghicchio. He can give you information off the record. In other words, without Vice Questore Montanari finding out about it through official channels.' He clapped his hands again. 'You can investigate what you like, get expert help, and the fact that you don't like Vanni is a perfect cover. Nobody will suspect you two of working together.' He picked up the water and gulped it.

Moretti hooked a thumb under his chin and smoothed his moustache with his index finger, first left, then right.

'You know, Gennaro,' he said warmly, 'that's why I'm going to miss working with you. You have a knack of coming up with totally insane, yet genius ideas.'

The agente's face broke into a broad smile.

Moretti smiled, too.

'It's just your diet ideas that are totally insane. Period.' Moretti stood. 'Now, if you'll excuse me, you can take your filing off my desk and get to work. I have to see a farmer about a bull.'

Santoro stood, too, and collected the bundle of folders into his arms. Moretti passed him and held open the door.

'See you later, Gennaro. And thanks.'

A few minutes later, Moretti was on his way to the

Nardelli farm. Having the car to himself gave him time to consider Santoro's suggestion. He smiled. His old friend's plan could work – if only he could stomach it. Since Cristina seemed to be the new Vice Questore's favoured one, she could do nothing other than confirm his reaction on first meeting Vanni at the car crash, or that he asked her to take over the case. His biggest problem was that the case he so desperately wanted to solve, and the one where he could not ask for Vanni's help, was the murder of Sergio Vanni's parents.

He turned off the main road onto a dirt track that led to a large farm, next to one of the side channels of the main canal that collected and controlled the level of the water in the valley from Lake Trasimeno as far as Arezzo. The fields around the farm buildings were green, kept watered even in times of drought by the extensive system of irrigation pipes that drew water from the canal and fired it from cannons in huge arcs over the crops.

Moretti's arrival was announced by the farm dogs, and two men appeared: one wearing the farmers' unofficial uniform of checked shirt and dungarees came from the house; the other, wearing jeans and a heavy metal t-shirt, from a barn. They converged to meet him.

'Commissario Moretti,' he called. 'Which of you is Signor Nardelli?'

The older man replied. 'We both are. I'm Ignazio, and this is my son Beppe. How can we help you?'

Moretti turned to take in the whole view.

'It's some place you have here: lovely house, big barn, and huge cowshed.'

Beppe Nardelli spat on the ground then squinted at Moretti's silhouette in the strong sun. 'We also have a big red tractor if you'd like to sit on it.'

Ignazio turned to his son. 'Go and finish your chores, Beppe.' Then to Moretti, 'I'm sorry, Commissario, I'm afraid my son has little or no respect for authority.'

Beppe scuffled off, whistling tunelessly, sending up little dust clouds with each step.

'How can *I* help, Commissario?'

'We had a call yesterday from a neighbour of yours, a Signor Buina. He has a cowshed similar to yours, and someone had cut the security chain.'

Nardelli shook his head. 'And Buina said that we had done it?'

Moretti studied his face. 'Not in so many words, but I wondered if you had maybe suffered the same attempt.'

'Come with me and see for yourself, Commissario.'

Both men walked to the cowshed.

'It's similar to Buina's – maybe a little older,' observed Moretti.

Nardelli grabbed the chain and tugged it.

'Intact,' he said, producing a keychain from his pocket that was attached by a long cable to his belt. 'Here, I'll open up so you can look inside.'

The farmer slid open the tall doors to reveal a shed almost identical in layout to the one Moretti had seen the day before. Large white cattle were feeding from mangers, and in the place that corresponded to the position of Buina's bull, Hercules, was an even more massive animal.

'Jupiter,' said the farmer proudly.

'Wow,' gasped Moretti. 'He's huge. I don't even come up to the top of his shoulders.'

'One of the biggest on record.'

'Tell me this. Is there a reason that your prize bull is in this place in the cowshed? Signor Buina's was in the same position.'

Nardelli sighed.

'Buina is a good farmer with good stock, but he has always been jealous that I rear bigger, better animals that command better prices, both at stud and in the market. He came here a couple of years ago to find out what my "secret" was.'

'And did you tell him?'

'Commissario, I showed him around the place and told him there was no secret – only that I've bred a good line of cattle. He has a good line, too, but it wasn't enough. So, he tore down his old cowshed and had a new one built exactly like this one. As you saw yourself, he's even laid it out the same way.'

'So, as far as you're concerned, the two set-ups are identical?'

'Not identical, Commissario. We use our own fodder and grain, which is replenished every day with the different feed materials – fodder, maize, barley, flax, and a little dried alfalfa. We rigorously screen it so that there's no clover, for example, which could kill the beasts. Jupiter, here, is the exception. We keep his feed separate in these bins beside his pen, because we have to adjust his diet, depending on the time of year, if he has to service cows, or we're harvesting semen from him.'

Moretti screwed up his face. 'Harvesting semen? You do that?'

Nardelli laughed. 'Of course. Every breeder does. We sell Jupiter's semen all over the world. It's harvested by electroejaculation.'

Moretti winced and shifted his feet. 'Don't go into detail.'

Nardelli smiled and continued. 'Then the semen is extended and put into a carefully balanced solution of glycerol that protects it when it's put into straws and frozen.'

'How valuable is Jupiter?'

'To me, he's probably worth about a hundred thousand euros, but his straws sell for over two thousand euros each so I've insured him for half a million.'

Nardelli's son Beppe appeared at the entrance to the shed, carrying a phone. 'Dad, it's a customer. He wants to talk to you personally.'

Nardelli looked at Moretti. 'Excuse me, Commissario, I have to take this.'

'No. Thank you, Signor Nardelli, it was very helpful.'

The men shook hands and Moretti followed Beppe out into the courtyard.

'Excuse me, Beppe, could I have a word with you?'

The young man stopped and turned. 'Yes?'

'Your father was telling me all about how the cattle are raised and so on. Fascinating. Are you continuing in his footsteps?'

Beppe's hands were deep in the pockets of his low-slung jeans. 'Pah! Not me. He comes in every night smelling of shit.'

'Yes, I suppose that's a downside,' agreed Moretti. 'So,

tell me, what do you do?'

Beppe's chin jutted out and he folded his arms. 'I run my own business.'

'Oh? From here?'

Beppe jabbed a thumb over his shoulder. 'Yes. From that barn.'

'So, it's still agriculture then?'

Beppe tutted his impatience. 'Mushrooms. I grow them in the dark and feed them bull shit.'

Moretti wondered how closely that statement might relate to his own relationship with the new Vice Questore.

'I know you must be busy, but could I possibly see how it's done?' he said, mustering up every gram of charm. 'Since I'm here anyway.'

Beppe sighed loudly. 'I suppose so.' He turned and shuffled off again, hands in pockets, while Moretti followed.

The musty, fungal smell was obvious as soon as they entered the cool, airy, but windowless barn. Beppe went to the first of several large containers and shone the light from his phone inside. Moretti looked down. Hundreds of white domes were emerging from the dark substrate.

'*Agaricus bisporus*,' said Beppe. 'Growing on straw, old stucco from demolished walls, and bull shit.'

'Do you sell them direct from here or to retailers?'

'Both. Are you interested?'

'Yes, but tell me, what are these?' Moretti had turned and was pointing at the large bags hanging from the rafters.

Beppe shone the light on them.

'Oyster mushrooms,' he said. 'These nearest are *Pleurotus pulmonarius*, the Summer Oyster; the sulphur yellow ones over there are *Pleurotus citrinopileaus*, the Yellow Oyster; and in the winter when it's cooler, I grow *Pleurotus ostreatus var. columbinus,* the Blue Oyster.'

Moretti nodded his approval.

'Impressive, Beppe,' he said. 'You sound like a mushroom expert. How did that start?'

Beppe returned to the first container and picked two handfuls of white mushrooms and placed them in a paper bag.

'When I was a kid, I went looking for porcini and truffles with Dad.' He glanced at the cowshed. 'That was when he had more time. And he had a great dog, could find truffles anywhere.'

He handed Moretti the paper bag.

Moretti put his hand in his pocket. 'How much do I owe you?'

Beppe waved his hand. 'A free sample, Commissario,' he said. 'I'll charge you next time.'

The young man turned and shuffled off before Moretti could shake his hand.

He called after him. 'Thanks, Beppe.'

CHAPTER NINE

Moretti drove back up the winding road from the valley towards Cassiatorre. He'd decided not to return to the Questura but instead to go straight home and do what he'd told Santoro. He was going to do his own thing, and that meant cooking mushroom risotto and digging out the old case files from the murder of Vanni's parents.

Once inside, he placed the bag of mushrooms on the counter, opened the fridge, took out a vacuum-stoppered bottle of white wine, and poured a large glass. By now he was used to the house being silent. What he had not yet come to terms with was the almost complete absence of traces of his wife, Maria. No food in the fridge, everything exactly the way he left it, no lingering perfume, no long hairs on the floor or shower tray. And most of all, no-one beside him in bed.

He took off his jacket and hung it over the back of a dining room chair, left the glass behind in the open plan kitchen, and climbed into the loft. Being careful to avoid the heavy beams that supported the terracotta roof tiles, he went directly to his archives and straight to a banker's box that held the Vanni files. He grabbed the cut-out carrying handle and pulled it to him, breaking a large cobweb in the process. He blew then wiped the dust from the heavy box before carrying it downstairs to the kitchen and dumped it on the dining table.

He rinsed the dust from his hands under the tap and dried them before glugging some wine and returning to the box. Taking a deep breath, he closed his eyes, exhaled slowly, removed the lid, and planted his palms on the table on either side of the open box. He then leaned over it to inhale air and memories that had been locked away for eighteen years.

He stayed like that until he became aware of the pulse in his neck, then straightened up and began to unpack, carefully positioning the files, folders, and photographs over the whole surface of the dining table. With the empty box on the floor underneath the table, Moretti stepped back, picked up his glass, and raised it to the memory of Vanni's parents, repeating the vow he had made in their home almost two decades earlier.

'I will find out who is responsible,' he intoned solemnly. 'I promise.' Moretti drained his glass, refilled it, and raised it again. 'I promise that I'll find whoever stole your grandmother's trunk, Signorina Cao. I refuse to have two unsolved cases on my record.'

He took another large gulp and began preparing the risotto. When it was ready, he stood at the table, bowl in hand, eating risotto and surveying the case files below him. He stopped from time to time to make a note on a pad on the counter, so that by the time he had finished eating and tidying up, he had a list of the people that he wanted to interview again – the Vannis' neighbours, their nurses and carers, the gardener, and Sergio Vanni himself.

He sat at the table and began reading the files in more detail, adding notes beside the names on his pad. Then he shook his head and scored out all the names except Vanni's. He was the only one who'd be sure to remember events from so long ago. Beside him on the table, his phone buzzed, and Maria's face appeared on the screen. He accepted the video call.

'Hello, Dino,' she said brightly. 'Have you time to talk?'

Moretti propped his phone open. 'Hello, Maria. Yes, of course. You're looking well. The climate must suit you.'

She fanned her face with her hand.

'I'd forgotten how hot it gets down here,' she replied. 'How are things?'

Moretti arched his brows. 'The new Vice Questore started today.'

'Oh, what's he like? Is it a he?'

Moretti grinned.

'Well saved, Maria. No, CC Montanari is a woman,' he said. 'Or at least, part woman. The other part is maybe dragon.'

His wife laughed. 'Good. You lot need a shake-up.'

'How's your case going? It must be almost over now.'

'That's why I'm calling. It's turned out to be rather more complex than anyone previously thought.'

Moretti noticed her eyes dart somewhere off screen – somewhere up and off to the right, as if she were looking at someone standing behind her phone.

'Oh? That doesn't sound good.' He knew where this conversation was going and decided to get there quicker. 'It sounds like you'll have to be away longer than you originally planned.'

Her expression relaxed instantly.

'Yes. Exactly. I'm sorry. I knew you'd understand, Dino.'

He could feel her relief.

'So, is there anything you need me to do?

Now she looked embarrassed.

'Dino, could you forward my mail. I hate to ask, but I don't think there'll be too many opportunities to pop home to visit.'

He kept his voice bright. 'Of course, Maria, that makes sense. You need all your spare time to focus on winning the case.'

The smile on her face was tight, awkward, forced. It was a smile that he had seen her use in court when addressing a judge or a jury while extolling the virtues of a client whom she knew was guilty. She inhaled as if to speak, and Moretti suspected that she was about to end the call.

'You'll never guess who's back in Cassiatorre,' he interjected.

He could see that he had caught her off guard.

'Who?

'Sergio Vanni.'

He couldn't read her reaction; except he knew that behind her dark eyes her mind was working hard to compose a reply and congruent facial expression.

'Oh. Was it for a visit or something else?' She was fishing for his reaction.

'No. He's moving back here permanently. He's joining the town's medical practice and is buying a house here.'

'In Cassiatorre, not Maghicchio?'

'Apparently. I've only heard second-hand.'

Now Maria's expression was of genuine concern.

'How do you feel about that, Dino? I know how important that case was to you.'

'Still is, Maria. The new Vice Questore has ideas about controlling which cases I'm assigned, so I've decided to reopen the Vanni case. Look.' He touched the screen of his phone to swap cameras. 'I've brought down all the old case files. I was reading through them when you called.'

'Dino—'

'Hang on, Maria.' He switched cameras again so that she could see his face – and he could see hers. 'Okay, go on.' He managed to catch her looking beyond the phone again.

'Dino, I want to give this proper attention, but I'm tired tonight. Can we pick it up later?'

Moretti was now certain that there was someone else in the room with his wife. He desperately wanted to ask her outright, but he didn't want her to have to lie. More than that, he was afraid to hear the truth – about who was with her, and about her relationship with Vanni before he left for Rome.

'Absolutely,' he said, aiming to strike a balance between upbeat and understanding. 'I have to push on with this. There's so much of the detail that I've forgotten.'

That last sentence was a mistake. He saw on Maria's face that she knew it was a lie.

'Thanks, Dino. I'll call soon.'

'Goodnight, Maria. I love you.'

Too late. She had ended the call.

Moretti continued looking at the empty screen even after it went black, then he sighed, got up and poured another glass of wine, and studied his notes. No matter the starting point, no matter from whose perspective he looked at the case, his thoughts led him to one of two places – a dead end or Sergio Vanni. Eventually, exhaustion – emotional rather than physical – forced him to bed. But not to sleep.

Memories floated around him like wraiths that he could not banish, because he needed to transport his present self, equipped with all the experience and clarity of thought of twenty-five years of police work, back to that time. The relationships of that time – his friendship with Vanni, and his infatuation with Maria – had no doubt clouded his thinking, so it had to be an impersonal self that revisited the facts. His role now would be as dispassionate observer rather than the participant that he felt himself to be back then.

His phone buzzed on the bedside cabinet behind him. He twisted round and grabbed it, hoping that Maria had got rid of whoever had been with her.

'Commissario?'

Moretti slumped.

'Cristina. Is everything okay?'

'I'm sorry to disturb you so late and at home, but I need to tell you something.'

Moretti swung his legs round and sat up on the edge of the bed. 'Go ahead, I'm listening.'

'While I was reporting back about the arrangements for the Disfida to Vice Questore Montanari this afternoon, I saw a note on her desk.'

Moretti rubbed the sleep from his eyes. 'You mean you snooped, Cristina.'

He heard a nervous laugh.

'Not really, it was the only thing on her desk. It was upside down, but I managed to read the gist of it.'

'Go on.'

'It was something about you not following Vice Questore Innocenti's orders. The note wasn't signed.'

His stomach knotted.

'Cristina, one thing you'll learn in policing is that anonymous letters come in all the time. In fact, the further south you go, the more it happens. It's a daily occurrence in Sicily. But thanks for letting me know, I appreciate it. See you tomorrow.'

'Good night, Commissario.'

'Good night, Cristina.'

He put the phone down, rubbed the nape of his neck, and picked up the card that Cristina had given to him, then sent a message before getting up and going to the kitchen. He resisted the temptation to sit at the case files, and instead took a small cigar from his jacket and stepped outside to smoke it.

Lights twinkled in the valley below him, and the hills on the far side were black against the inky blue sky. He stubbed the cigar out after three puffs, preferring instead to breathe in the warm, humid night air, as if the peacefulness of the scene could inoculate him against his inner turmoil.

*

Between them, and in the face of the worsening severity of the abdominal pain that left them both weak and sore, Sue and Andy began the Herculean task of cleaning the now bloody vomit and diarrhoea off the floor and walls of the bathroom.

'I've checked all the kitchen cupboards, there's no more kitchen roll,' Sue called through the door to Andy.

'We're out of toilet paper, too,' he groaned. 'I'm having to use a facecloth right now.'

'I don't need to know that, Andy. I'm going to have to use the towels.'

'Use whatever you have to.'

'Is there no-one we can call?'

'Even if we had a phone signal, we don't have the proper insurance,' he replied. 'Not for this. I'm really sorry.'

Eventually every towel was soiled in the process, cleaned in the washing machine, and hung to dry over towel rails, radiators, and the top of the shower cabinet.

They opened every window in the house in an unsuccessful attempt to purify the air. The undilutable odour of skatole that no amount of bleach, disinfectant, or plug-in air fresheners could cover, emanated from the house and attracted an army of invaders. The couple's only defence, for which they thanked every god, were the insect screens fitted to each window. Scores of large, dark flies, some iridescent green or blue, crawled over the screens searching for a way in.

CHAPTER TEN

Moretti lay in that state between sleep and wakefulness. He and Maria were walking together, hand-in-hand, in the Valley of the Temples in Sicily. She rested her head on his shoulder and wrapped both arms around him, eyes closed, smiling, head tilted up to the warm sun.

His phone buzzed on the cabinet beside him, and he fought to hang onto the dream. Unwelcome consciousness took over, and his mind began to prepare for the day. He sat up, rubbed his eyes, and picked up his phone. A message from Maria, giving him the address where she wanted him to forward her mail.

He rose, went to the kitchen, filled the Moka, then Googled her new address. Zooming into the satellite image, he discovered that it was a large property on a hillside overlooking the sea. He poured the coffee, sat down, and sipped it as he zoomed out and explored the surroundings – residential properties, a bar, restaurant, small beachfront hotels. He preened his moustache, first left then right. She was in the sort of place that they'd always talked about retiring to. He sighed, drained his cup, finished getting ready, and left.

'Good morning,' he announced as he entered Bar Italia.

As usual, the three gossips – Rosalia Seccavigne, Fausta Racano, and Donatella Luchia – pretended to ignore him but leaned towards the counter where Carla had his pastry ready for him.

Carla's mouth and eyes smiled at him.

'Good morning, Commissario,' she said, handing him the pastry. 'What a lovely morning.'

The ordinariness of her greeting shocked him out of the dark mood that had been building since Maria's call the previous night. He picked up his cappuccino, sipped it, and wiped the froth from his moustache.

'Yes, it is, Carla. It's a lovely morning.' He turned to the gossips, held up his cup, and nodded. 'Ladies.'

'I hear the new Vice Questore has arrived,' said Carla.

Moretti turned to face her and bit into his pastry. He chewed it and took another sip before replying.

'Yes. CC Montanari is her name.'

The gossips leaned a little closer.

'A fine police officer,' he continued. 'Cassiatorre is lucky to have someone of her experience and standing. I'm certain that she'll make great improvements to public safety, and we all are looking forward so much to working with her.'

The gossips resumed a vertical posture. Carla shook her head and laughed. Moretti finished his breakfast, paid, and left.

He stopped at the front desk of the Questura to pick up his messages. Head down, Alfiero handed them over.

'Lovely morning, Alfiero,' Moretti declared.

Alfiero looked up at him. 'She said when you arrived I was to tell you that she wants to see you right away.'

'Wonderful news. Thank you, Alfiero.'

Moretti walked off jauntily, leaving Alfiero, too, shaking his head. He knocked on the Vice Questore's door and entered without being told.

'Good morning, CC,' he said, smiling. 'It's alright to call you CC, isn't it? Alfiero gave me your message.'

Montanari glowered up at him. 'Commissario Moretti, I have only arrived, and I've already received a complaint about you.'

'Oh dear,' he said. 'I'm sorry to hear that. Sounds serious. I'd better sit down for this.' He crossed to the side of the room and sat on one of the chairs beside the wall. 'Sorry, should I bring this chair over?'

Montanari's hands were on the desk, fingers interlaced.

'I've also taken the time to read the report that my predecessor, Vice Questore Innocenti, wrote on you.' She brought a manila folder from a desk drawer, placed it in front of her, and tapped it as she spoke. 'A very full report.'

Moretti held up a finger. 'Once removed,' he said.

Montanari furrowed her brows. 'What?'

'Once removed,' repeated Moretti. 'Vice Questore Innocenti was your predecessor once removed. Vice Questore Rossi, the interim Vice Questore, was your predecessor.'

Montanari responded coolly. 'Can we both agree that Vice Questore Innocenti was the last substantive holder of this post?'

'Yes.'

'Can we therefore both agree that he was, in fact, the substantive predecessor?'

'Yes.'

'Can we both agree that to save further time, we will refer to Vice Questore Innocenti as my predecessor from now on?'

'Yes.'

Montanari opened the file, took out the letter, and held it up.

'Let me read this, Commissario. *To whom it may concern, I wish to bring to your attention the conduct of Commissario Dino Moretti. While suspended from duty he travelled south and continued with an investigation, during which time he fraudulently represented himself as a serving police officer, claimed travelling and subsistence, and acted in direct contravention of orders given to him in person by Vice Questore Innocenti. He was subject of a disciplinary enquiry and was brought up on criminal charges.*' She returned the letter to the file. 'Well?'

'Who wrote the letter?'

'It's signed *A seeker of Justice.*'

'You mean it's anonymous.'

'What do you have to say, Commissario?'

Moretti looked at her blankly. 'What would you like

me to say?'

CC narrowed her eyes. 'It matches very closely the report that Vice Questore Innocenti, my predecessor, wrote about you. Don't you think that odd?'

Moretti slapped his thigh.

'Ah. I see what you're getting at. You think that Vice Questore Innocenti wrote an anonymous letter, signed it as *A seeker of Justice,* and you want me to investigate. Is that it? Well, we have some very able IT technicians who can put the letter and former Vice Questore Innocenti's report through some software that will analyse the text and find if there is a match in the style.'

Montanari steepled her fingers.

'Commissario Moretti, you are demonstrating the exact characteristics ascribed to you in this report. Let me be clear. What I want from you now is a line-by-line explanation or rebuttal of the contents of the letter. Now, what do you have to say?'

Moretti used finger and thumb to smooth his moustache.

'Vice Questore Montanari,' he began in a solemn, measured tone, 'I have a lot to say on the matter.' He touched his pinkie and began counting on his fingers. 'First of all, I am registering my strong objection to you placing an anonymous letter in my file, which is supposed to contain facts not fiction. I am happy to confirm this objection in writing if that is what you wish. Second, I would caution you not to give credence to anything written by a man who was sacked for corruption about the officer who discovered that corruption. The so-called report written by Vice Questore Innocenti should not form part of my official record either. Third, my journey south was in response to a nationwide appeal for the whereabouts of a missing child and his mother who were fleeing the Mafia. I found them, persuaded them to come back, returned a substantial sum of money to the bank, and helped prevent Mafia infiltration into both the local business and political communities. Fourth, I made the journey entirely at my own expense, claiming neither travel nor subsistence. Finally, I was not the subject of disciplinary charges, nor was I brought up on criminal charges.' He sat back and folded his arms. 'Does that answer your question?'

Montanari pursed her lips, paused, then removed the letter and Innocenti's report from Moretti's file.

'Thank you, Commissario Moretti. I admire the sort of initiative that you used in this case, and as you already know I am in favour of officers taking personal responsibility for their actions. I like clear accountability. But not following orders, despite the circumstances, is a very serious matter. Yes, things worked out well this time, but what if circumstances had been different and the Mafia had followed you to the mother and child, killed them, and you, and seized the money? No, Commissario Moretti, I still have questions, and I will keep a close eye on how you conduct yourself to ensure that you are always acting in accordance both with the strict letter of the law and my instructions. Now, is that clear?'

Moretti unfolded his arms.

'As mountain air,' he replied. 'If there is nothing else, Vice Questore Montanari, please excuse me I have to get on.'

'Remember what I've said, Commissario Moretti.'

He smiled, rose, and left.

Along the corridor, he saw Gennaro, who beckoned him into his office.

'Good morning, Gennaro. How are you today?'

Gennaro studied his face. 'How are you, Capo? Alfiero told me where you've been.'

Moretti patted Gennaro's shoulder.

'Vice Questore CC and I had a full and frank exchange of ideas.'

Santoro leaned towards him. 'And?'

'And nothing. That's it. Now, if you'll excuse me, I have to see a man about a mushroom.'

Moretti left the bewildered agente and headed out into the square, looking down the gentle slope to Bar Italia. At a table outside, a man raised a hand and waved. Moretti raised his hand to acknowledge and walked down.

Dr Sergio Vanni left some money on the table and crossed the road to join him. Neither man held out a hand to shake when they met.

'Good morning, Dino. I got your message. How can I help?'

'I need to get some details about the car crash, Sergio.'

'Sure. Do you want me to come to the Questura or shall we sit outside the bar?'

'Neither. Let's walk.'

They fell in step and took the mountain road out of the town so that they'd be less likely to meet anyone.

'You said in the statement you made to Ispettore Furlan that you suspected the driver was under the influence of fly agaric. Well, forensics have confirmed that guess.'

'Okay.'

'You also said that the driver was behaving oddly. Can you be more specific?'

'Dino, he was yelling and singing at the top of his voice. I mean, I heard his music before I saw him. He'd already been sick when he overtook me. I don't know what else to fill in, but here is what I think happened. He'd eaten the mushrooms, had a mild buzz, and gone for a drive. While driving, the full effect hit him, and he vomited but he continued driving, being more and more badly affected as the toxin entered his system. He lost control of the car, either because his coordination was affected, but equally probably because he was hallucinating and wasn't able to understand and process the information around him with respect to his speed, the presence of other vehicles, and the consequences of leaving the road. It looked like death was instantaneous from the crash. If I had to guess, I'd say a broken neck, although there was blood where he hit his face on the dash or steering wheel.'

Moretti nodded.

'That's more or less what the forensics report said.'

'The only thing that I don't have an answer to is where the tourist got the mushrooms. You'd really have to know someone who knew about mushrooms to find them at this time of the year.'

They walked on in silence for a short while as Moretti considered what Vanni had said.

'Dino, you could have asked me all this with a message. What's the real reason that you wanted to meet in person?'

Moretti stopped and turned to face Vanni.

'Sergio, it's been almost twenty years.' He tried to fathom the intense blue eyes. 'We were like brothers back then.'

Vanni's lips parted, and he inhaled but stayed silent.

'No news, no contact, nothing,' continued Moretti. 'It's as though you dropped off the earth. What happened?'

'What happened was, I had to get away after all the stuff about my parents' death.' He took off his glasses and cleaned them on a tissue. 'I found a job in Rome but was still restless, so I threw myself into studying forensic medicine, and I retrained as a forensic pathologist. That's what I've been doing for the last ten years or so.'

Moretti noted that Vanni was avoiding eye contact.

'And now?'

Vanni put his glasses back on and looked up at Moretti again.

'And now I'm back here. I've had enough of dealing with the worst of humanity. I need to be doing something that can make a difference – to work with the living, to help people, to bring life into the world.'

Moretti nodded. 'That's *what*, Sergio. You still haven't told me *why* you went away.'

Vanni smiled. 'Always the detective, Dino. The short answer is Maria chose you over me.'

'And the long answer?'

Vanni placed his hand on Moretti's shoulder. 'That will have to wait for another time.'

CHAPTER ELEVEN

Cristina caught Moretti as he returned to the Questura. 'Commissario, can I have a word?'

Moretti beckoned her outside, and they stood at the fountain in the square.

'First of all, how did things go with CC?'

Moretti smiled.

'Better than they might have, if you hadn't called me about the letter,' he replied. 'Thanks. I think that after our little exchange, she and I both know where we stand. How can I help?'

Cristina shot a glance up at the Questura behind him.

'It's about the Disfida,' she said. 'I haven't a clue about it, and CC wants me to be the liaison with the community groups and keep her abreast of any developments. You can't be seen to help, so who can I go to?'

Moretti threw back his head and laughed. 'Oh, you're going to love this, Cristina.'

She looked puzzled.

'There's a person who knows all about the tradition, its history, what's involved, and who does what.'

'Good,' she exclaimed. 'That's what I need. Who is it?'

'You've met him before.'

'Even better. Who is he?'

'Signor Ettore Erpicone.'

Her jaw dropped. 'Please tell me you're not serious.'

'I'm very serious. He was one of the group who revived the tradition back in the fifties. Do you remember him?'

'How could I forget him? I interviewed him in the spring when we were on the missing boy case. He's probably – no, he's definitely the most objectionable person I've ever met.'

Moretti chuckled. 'Well, he's your man. Have fun.'

She watched Moretti turn, stride off, and leave her. She was sure he was still laughing.

Ten minutes later, she turned onto the dirt road that led to Erpicone's farm. When the buildings came in sight, however, she didn't recognise them. Where before things had been ramshackle, rusty, and run down, there was now order, tidiness, and repairs had been done. The farmhouse roof and gutters had been fixed, and its walls had been painted.

She remembered the little pack of farm dogs that barked their welcome to her car, and they obviously remembered her because they kept further back than the first time she had visited. Their barking alerted Erpicone, though, and the short, squat farmer appeared at the door. Cristina prepared herself for the worst.

'Ispettore Furlan,' he called. 'Good to see you. How can I help you?'

Cristina did a poor job of disguising her surprise.

Erpicone laughed. 'Yes, Ispettore, I can see you now.'

'So, you've had the cataract operation?'

He held out his hand and they shook. 'Yes, both eyes. Come in.'

He led the way inside. The cool interior was as clean and tidy as on her last visit. Erpicone noticed her surveying the room.

'I still get a woman to come and clean for me, and she brings some food, too, although I've started cooking for myself again and I do my own laundry now.'

'I'm sorry to gawk, Signor Erpicone, but it's all so different.'

He smiled.

'You mean that I'm so different, Ispettore. Please sit. Can I offer you anything – water, coffee? I'm making some for me.'

She sat on the sofa. 'Coffee would be great, thank you.'

He filled the Moka and sat facing her, hands stretched out. 'No shakes,' he said. 'I've cut down on my drinking.'

Cristina shook her head.

'I'm stunned at the difference, Signor Erpicone,' she blurted, then quickly covered her mouth with her hand. 'Oh, I'm sorry, that was so rude. Please tell me what happened.'

'Let me get the coffee.'

He brought back two cups and sat opposite her.

'As you know, I was arrested in the spring for passing on Etruscan artefacts for sale. As part of the deal to avoid a prison sentence, I had to agree to several things. First, I was ordered to give properly paid employment to the immigrants who had been working here. They'd all been given a cash reward for finding the Etruscan tomb, and some of them used it to travel on to other countries. Five of them, including Yusuf, decided to stay here, and they used their money to buy shares in this farm.'

'Goodness.'

'They're now part-owners of the farm. So, all the work you see, Ispettore, was done by them. The barn has been made into comfortable living quarters, but they have plans to build a small house each, when profits allow. The farm is thriving.'

He paused to sip his coffee.

'I also had to agree to have my eyes done.' He stared into the small cup. 'It was the best thing ever. When I regained my sight, I saw my life as clearly as my surroundings again.' He swallowed hard. 'I know my wife killed herself, Ispettore. I was deluding myself. But since I've faced facts – and stopped drinking – my life has been transformed.' He looked up at Cristina. 'I want to apologise to you for the dreadful things I said when you were last here.'

Cristina put down her cup.

'I'm glad that things are working out for you, Signor Erpicone. I said some unkind things to you, too. Let's forget them and move on.' She inhaled, sat up, and smiled. 'What can you tell me about the Disfida?'

Erpicone slapped his thighs and stood. He went to a

sideboard and collected a photo album which he handed to Cristina.

'These are photographs of the Disfida going back to the fifties.'

She leafed through the album. Each of the thin, sticky, board pages was covered by transparent plastic and held two or three photographs – black and white at the start of the album, changing to colour part of the way through. They showed people dressed in medieval costumes, flag bearers, and, uniquely, archers on horseback firing at targets.

'The embroidery work in these costumes is amazing – so detailed.'

Erpicone chuckled. 'The costumes are about the only historically authentic part of the festival.'

'How do you mean?'

'When tourism started to take off in the fifties, the local council decided to host an event to get its share of visitors. We already had flag waving and processions like lots of other towns, but we could see that places like Siena and Arezzo could attract huge numbers to the Palio or the Giostra.'

Cristina smiled.

'Our tradition is different,' she said. 'The women dress in traditional white blouses and embroidered bodices over long skirts. The men wear hats decorated with feathers, waistcoats, scarves, and knee-length trousers over white stockings.'

'The contrada outfits are based on Renaissance costumes,' explained Erpicone. 'Women research old paintings, drawings, and archives, and come up with the designs that are then made and embroidered. But the competition itself is fake. There was never any tradition of horseback archery in this area – perhaps not in the whole of Italy.'

'Then why choose that?'

Erpicone sat back into the sofa and grabbed his elbows in a sort of hug.

'Well, lots of towns had archery competitions. Lots of towns had riding competitions. We decided to put them both together and have a competition of horseback archery – and that's how the Disfida of Cassiatorre was born.'

'That's amazing,' Cristina gasped. 'It looks like a lot of organisation. How long does it last?'

Erpicone smiled proudly.

'We set it all up and take it all down in six days. Wednesday and Thursday to build everything, Friday and Saturday for practice and heats, and Sunday for the final. Everything comes down on Monday.'

Cristina reached the end of the album and returned to the beginning. 'It sounds exciting. I'm looking forward to seeing it.'

'It's become very important to the local economy. It's one of the reasons that so many tourists come to Cassiatorre in the summer.'

She closed the album and handed it back to Erpicone. 'The new Vice Questore has appointed me liaison. So, tell me, what exactly do you need me to do?'

Erpicone scratched his stubble.

'You personally, Ispettore, nothing really. But we need to make sure that there is a sufficient police presence for safety, more than anything else. We cordon off the overflow carparking on the open field. Some of the locals might grumble, but that's all. The Traffic Police will have barriers up to reduce the speed of vehicles in the area, and the Municipal Police will make sure that the stallholders all have permits.'

'Stallholders?'

Erpicone turned to one of the more recent photos, held it up, and pointed. 'A mock medieval village is built around the competition area. Look.'

The photograph showed a neat collection of circular and rectangular tents, decorated with scalloped or castellated valances. Bunting was strung between the tents, and every tent had an X-frame, refectory-style table in front of it to display goods for sale.

'In the old days, some of the townsfolk used to sell local wine and cheese, and there was always porchetta.' Erpicone shook his head. 'Now it's become more commercialised, with traders from outside the town selling almost everything.'

'So, the ones in tabards and tunics are the traders.'

'Yes. The ones in the fancier costumes represent their contrada in the processions.'

Cristina took back the album and looked more closely. 'It looks like they're selling beer and burgers.'

'Beer, burgers, hot dogs, lampredotto, local honey, dried herbs and spices, confectionery, toy swords and shields, toy bows – it's like the weekly market, times ten.'

'What happens when the crowds go home at night?'

'Each stall holder packs everything away inside their tent and secures it with rope until the next day.'

'What about theft?'

Erpicone laughed. 'Ispettore, the food is put into locked fridges, the beer is in kegs with the dispensers removed, and as for the confectionery and toys, who's going to steal that stuff?'

Cristina laughed, too, then produced a card from her pocket and rose to leave.

'Signor Erpicone, it's been both a pleasure and an education,' she said, holding out her hand. 'If there is anything that you need from me, please call me direct on that number.'

They shook hands and Erpicone led her to the door.

'You should check out the municipal museum for more information, or the different contrada headquarters to see costumes, bows, and arrows from past years.'

'I'll do that. Thank you.' She weaved past the dogs to her car and drove off with a final wave to the old farmer.

Instead of returning to the Questura, Cristina headed away from Cassiatorre and left on the next dirt road that led to the Rosati farm. She followed it to where it split, and a new road had been made. She turned off and parked on the short grass, near to where a large billboard had been erected with photographs and details in three languages of the newly excavated Etruscan tomb. The sound of her tyres on the uneven surface brought a figure out of the tomb. Tall, slim, with almost black skin, he approached smiling broadly.

'Hello, Yusuf,' she called. 'How are things?'

They shook hands.

'Ispettore, how good to see you,' the man replied in

perfect Italian. 'Have you come for a sneak preview?'

'I was in the area, and I thought I'd take the opportunity to see how work was going.'

Yusuf waved his arm in the direction of the entrance. 'Why don't you come and see for yourself?'

She followed him to the brick-lined narrow entrance that sloped gently down into the tomb. A soft light automatically came on when the sensor picked them up.

'Wow, this is amazing,' she said, turning to take in the whole space. 'The wall art is so fresh – like it was painted yesterday.'

One wall was covered in depictions of dancing women, faces in profile, with ornate hairstyles held in place by clasps and pins. Some wore laurel wreaths. Another wall showed bare-torsoed men wrestling, fighting, or bearing weapons.

'All of the artefacts have been repaired where necessary, identified, catalogued, and made into a new display in the museum in Cassiatorre.'

'When is the official opening?'

'In a couple of days, but we are ready. There will be a ceremony here, followed by a tour of the inside of the tomb, then everyone will go back to Cassiatorre to visit the museum and have a drinks reception.'

Cristina placed her hand on Yusuf's shoulder.

'I'm happy for you, Yusuf I visited Signor Erbicone, and I'm still recovering from the transformation.'

Yusuf laughed.

'So are we. But it's good to see how he has embraced so much change.'

'Have any of his children visited him since his eye operations?'

Yusuf looked at the floor and shook his head.

'That's a very sore point for him. The only contact he has had is a series of lawyers' letters challenging the sale of shares of his farm to us. His children think that they are being cheated out of their inheritance.'

'He didn't mention any of that to me.'

'He wouldn't, but it preoccupies him.'

'I'll keep it in mind. Thank you, Yusuf, and good luck with the opening.'

CHAPTER TWELVE

On his way into Bar Italia, Moretti passed the table where the three gossips – Rosalia, Fausta, and Donatella – sat, minding everyone else's business.

'Good afternoon, ladies.'

To his surprise, they responded.

'Good afternoon, Commissario,' they chorused.

He smiled, entered, and scanned the contents of the glass counter as he approached. Carla's broad smile welcomed him as ever.

'Twice in the one day, Commissario. Bar Italia must be doing something right. What can I get you?'

'I'll take a slice of Margherita and one of the panini, please.' He pointed at a bread roll whose rounded top was marked with a grid to resemble a corn cob. 'What's in the *pannocchia*?'

'Speck and Emmental,' replied Carla.

'I'll take that as well.'

'I'll warm them both, shall I?'

'Just the panino, please. I'll eat the pizza now. And I'll have a glass of Crodino.'

Carla picked up the slice of pizza in a serviette and handed it to him, then placed the roll in a ridged toaster and closed the lid. He was already munching the pizza when his drink arrived on the counter.

'Busy morning?'

He nodded, finished chewing, and swallowed.

'Just the usual.' He spoke a little louder than necessary and turned a fraction so that the three women whose choice of summer table outside, directly in front of the door, could hear better. 'Just keeping the streets of Cassiatorre free from crime so that the townsfolk can sleep safely in their beds at night.'

Carla laughed, and a sudden memory of her kiss after the meal they had shared returned and caught him unguarded. He coughed and sipped the cool drink.

Carla looked concerned and stretched out to touch his wrist. 'Are you alright? Is the pizza okay?'

'Everything's okay, Carla. I was talking and eating at the same time.' He cleared his throat. 'A bit went down the wrong way, that's all.'

As usual, the three women outside had stopped talking so that they could eavesdrop. Rosalia and Donatella sat sideways on and could use peripheral vision trained and developed over decades to observe what was happening inside the bar without having to turn their heads. Fausta, whose back was to the bar, deployed a small makeup mirror that she always carried in her bag for the express purpose of covert surveillance in exactly this situation.

Carla noticed, smiled, and removed her hand, giving Moretti the merest eye flick in their direction.

He understood perfectly and changed topic. 'And soon Bar Italia will be the only bar in this part of town.'

'So I believe,' replied Carla. 'It's so sad. Bar Roma had their century anniversary only a couple of years ago.' She collected his warm panino out of the toaster and brought it to the counter. 'It's the same old story, children don't want to keep the family business on because the hours are so long. Nobody wants to take on a bar, because you have to refurbish and build up a clientele. I don't know what'll happen to this place if Gigi doesn't want to take it over when he's older.'

Moretti's phone buzzed. He switched the roll to the other hand and brought it out.

'Moretti… When? Okay, I'm on my way.'

He stuffed the roll between his teeth and held it there

while he dealt with his phone and his wallet.

Carla handed back his change. 'You'll get indigestion.'

'Occupational hazard,' he replied, grabbing a serviette, and stepped out into the bright sunlight.

'Oh, Commissario,' began Rosalia, 'do you have a moment?'

Moretti wiped his moustache with the serviette.

'Of course. How may I help?'

Rosalia leaned towards him. 'It's these…' she paused and lowered her voice, 'Chinese.'

'Chinese?'

'Yes. They're taking over.'

Her two companions nodded.

'Taking over?'

'Yes, Commissario,' chipped in Fausta. 'First it was the market stall, then a corner shop, now a restaurant. And I've heard that a Russian is buying the Castello.'

'Never mind the Russians, it's the Chinese I'm worried about,' mumped Rosalia.

'Oh, I see,' said Moretti. 'Haven't you ever bought from Signor Chen's stall?'

'Yes, we all have,' interjected Donatella.

The others gave her a reproachful look.

'Well, we have,' she insisted. 'He has the best prices.'

'There you are then. All that's happening is that Signor Chen is changing from a stallholder to a shopkeeper, so you will all be able to enjoy his prices on six days a week instead of one.'

'But what about the restaurant?' Rosalia whined. 'All that foreign muck. It's not right.'

'Foreign muck?'

'Yes, noodles and such.'

Moretti scratched his head.

'Signora Seccavigne,' he said kindly. 'You do know that Marco Polo got the idea for spaghetti from China, don't you?'

Rosalia's jaw gaped. Before she could add anything else, Moretti bowed his head a little.

'Ladies, I must go on a matter of great urgency. Good afternoon.' He strode off, munching the remains of his lunch, leaving a chorus of tuts in his wake.

He arrived at the farm beside the canal in less than half an hour and was met in the yard by Nardelli, the farmer, brandishing a chain in the air.

'There you are,' he shouted. 'Look at this. He's gone.'

Moretti looked past Nardelli to the open door of the cowshed.

'Tell me what happened, Signor Nardelli.'

'I told you,' fumed the farmer. 'Jupiter has been stolen.'

He thrust the chain at Moretti. 'This was Buina,' he accused. 'Has to be. He's eaten up by jealousy. I'm going there to confront him.'

Moretti held up his palms to placate Nardelli.

'Signor Nardelli, no-one is going anywhere until you show me inside the cowshed. I need to see where it happened.'

'See where it happened? You know damn well where it happened. You were here only yesterday. He's stolen my bloody bull.'

Moretti took the chain.

'Show me his pen, Signor Nardelli,' he said firmly.

The farmer opened his mouth to speak, but instead turned and marched off to the cowshed with Moretti in tow.

'Look,' he shouted. 'That big empty space used to hold a prize-winning, pedigree bull. Now there's only his shit.' He motioned to open the pen.

'Stop. There may be prints or DNA on the gate. Step back, please.'

Nardelli did as he was told, while Moretti crouched and examined the area.

'When I said there was only his shit, I didn't expect you to take such an interest.'

'Stay back, Signor Nardelli. There's a partial print of a boot on this particular shit.' The detective stood and scanned the shed. 'Anything else gone?'

'No. Just Jupiter. Look, you're wasting time. Let's go to Buina's.'

Moretti motioned towards the door, then took out his phone and made a call to summon a forensics team. When they were both outside, he studied the eaves.

'No security cameras?'

Nardelli wilted.

'No need,' he mumbled. 'Until now. One of us is always here.'

'Where were you when this happened, Signor Nardelli?' Moretti looked towards the barn. 'And where is your son?'

'I was at a stock auction. I couldn't have been gone more than three hours. I don't know where Beppe is. You should be searching Buina's place, Commissario, he's behind this. I can feel it.'

'I will, Signor Nardelli, but I'd like to speak with Beppe first. You're sure he's not in the house?'

'I'm certain. I've tried calling him but there's no answer.'

'Okay, the forensics team will arrive shortly. Stay out of the cowshed until they tell you it's alright to go back in.'

'I'll stay indoors and keep trying Beppe,' he said dejectedly.

'Signor Nardelli, what will you do if we can't find Jupiter? Can you continue?'

The old farmer wiped his palm over his mouth.

'I can get by, but not much more. I've a small batch of frozen straws in the freezer, so I can sell them on. My number two bull was supposed to succeed Jupiter in two years. He'll have to start work earlier than planned.'

'Really? If the number two bull has to start serving cows two years early, maybe that makes him a suspect,' Moretti joked darkly.

The farmer looked hotly at Moretti, paused, then his face contorted, and he let out a howl of laughter.

'Makes him a suspect,' he repeated, clapping his hands. 'Makes him a suspect.' He walked off to the house, laughing and shaking his head.

'Let me know when Beppe's back,' Moretti called after him.

He got into his car and drove to the Buina farm. When he arrived, the farmer was nowhere to be found, but his dogs surrounded the car. Moretti searched around the buildings and peered inside the house, followed by the little pack of barking dogs. He tried the door of the cowshed, but it was locked securely with a new padlock and an even sturdier chain. He walked to the side of the building, jumped up, and looked at the upper edges of the concrete slabs that formed the side walls. There was a layer of broken glass cemented along the top to deter people from pulling themselves up.

He continued round to the back of the building and found a tiny hole. He peered through. There was certainly one large bull inside, but not two. He straightened up and rubbed the back of his neck. He'd had enough of the dogs barking around his legs, so he wrote a note and stuffed it in the front door of the farmhouse before driving off, chased by the victorious guard dogs.

On the drive back up to Cassiatorre, Moretti's thoughts shifted from the stolen bull to the stolen luggage, and he became steadily angrier at the idea that the other passengers had failed to help an old woman with trunks that were probably heavier than she was. He decided that instead of returning to headquarters he had to visit the family and update them with his lack of success.

He parked in the square, walked the short distance to Bar Roma, and knocked on the glass door

An Na opened it.

'Moretti,' she said brightly. 'Have you found the trunk?'

He sighed. 'No. I'm sorry, but I'm still working on it.

She opened the door wider and stood back. 'Come in, Moretti.'

Even in the space of one day, they had managed quite a transformation. A new, smaller counter had been installed near the door, with a touchscreen ordering system on top. The floor was completely covered in dust sheets, as were the square tables and chairs stacked at the far end of the room. There was a smell of fresh paint from the warm red walls. The ceiling, which had been stained by a century's worth of cigarette smoke, was now a fresh cream colour.

Zhao came out to see who was talking and busied himself removing the plastic sleeves from the chair legs while his daughter spoke to Moretti.

'I spoke to the railway staff and the witnesses, but they could not add anything useful. We have CCTV footage of the trunk disappearing in the crowd, but not of it leaving the station. As I said, I haven't given up.'

An Na translated for her father's benefit.

'I was wondering what was inside the trunk. It would help me greatly if I knew what I was looking for.'

'It is part of our family's fortune. Not a great fortune, perhaps, but all we have. My grandmother brought her most valuable possessions in the trunks. There were items of gold, silver, jade, ivory, and jewels that we planned to sell to help pay for the work in our restaurant.' She paused as an unreadable emotion passed across her expression. 'My father has had to make other arrangements to permit us to open on time. Please continue to search, Moretti. I trust you.'

Moretti swallowed.

'You have my word,' he said solemnly. 'I will do everything in my power to find and return your grandmother's possessions.'

'I believe you, Moretti.'

*

In their holiday rental a few kilometres outside of Cassiatorre, Andy's convulsions woke Sue. She opened her eyes enough to see – even with her blurry vision – that his pallor had become yellow. She knew that was bad, but she had none of the mental faculties nor physical resources to do anything about it. Her head ached and her skin tingled. The sheet below her was drenched in sweat.

She laid her arm across his chest.

CHAPTER THIRTEEN

Montanari's summons brought the three detectives together in her office. They stood in rank order in front of her desk, with the Vice Questore craning up to look at Cristina.

'Bring the chairs over,' she snapped.

Seated, it was more comfortable for her to maintain eye contact.

'Today is a big day,' she began. 'I have received an invitation to the official opening of the new Etruscan tomb.' She held up a gold-edged card. 'Places are limited, owing to the prestigious nature of the event, and because it's important to limit the number of visitors to the tomb at any one time. The mayor and other important dignitaries will be there, so it's a chance for the department to make a good impression.'

Moretti cleared his throat.

Montanari ignored him.

'I haven't had an opportunity yet to meet many of the significant local figures, so I will need someone to introduce me to them. Cristina, that will be you.'

Cristina stiffened. 'Vice Questore Montanari, I have only been here a few months. Perhaps Commissario Moretti or Agente Santoro would be better placed. They know everyone.'

Montanari swatted Cristina's reservations away like a

troublesome fly.

'Even better,' she replied. 'If the boys already know them, it will be a chance for you to become better acquainted with the local movers and shakers, too.'

Moretti cleared his throat again.

Montanari glared at him and read from a flyer.

'After the opening and tour of the interior of the tomb,' she continued, 'guests will then be transported to the museum for an inaugural visit to the new exhibition, followed by a drinks reception.' She looked up at Cristina. 'Cristina, I'll come with you in your car so that we don't have to wait for the transport.'

Moretti cleared his throat a third time.

'Commissario Moretti,' snapped Montanari. 'What exactly is wrong with your throat?'

'I was listening carefully to what you said about the prestigious nature of the grand opening and the limited number of tickets, and I was wondering how Ispettore Furlan was going to get inside.' He paused. 'Or was it your intention that she should drive you there and wait in the car?'

'She'll be with me,' retorted the Vice Questore. 'Of course she'll get in.'

Moretti leaned forward and pointed at the flyer.

'I admire and commend your confidence, Vice Questore Montanari, but I think you'll see at the bottom of the page that it says that entry is strictly limited to ticket holders only. It's in bold text, so I rather think they're serious.'

Montanari examined the flyer, and her mouth tightened. 'How could you possibly…'

Moretti held up a gold-edged card of his own.

'Ispettore Furlan is welcome to use my invitation.' He paused. 'If you think there might be any doubt.'

'That's very generous of you,' seethed Montanari.

Moretti handed Cristina the invitation.

'Not at all. After all, as you said yourself, Vice Questore, I don't have to make a good impression with the other guests and I have other investigations that I'm pursuing.' He turned to Gennaro. 'Agente Santoro, did you receive an invitation?'

'I've still to check my mail, Commissario,' he replied, po-faced. 'But if I have, I'm afraid I'll have to decline. Today is also the grand opening of Signor Chen's shop, and I thought I'd go there.'

'Perhaps you could give our apologies, Ispettore,' offered Moretti.

'Enough.' Vice Questore Montanari brought the meeting back to order. 'This meeting is over. Let's all get to work.'

The three detectives returned the chairs to the wall and left.

'Thanks for the invitation, Commissario,' said Cristina.

'Don't mention it, Cristina, I'm popping down there anyway. I just won't go inside the tomb. How about you, Gennaro?'

'Not me. I was serious about visiting Chen's shop.'

'Well, I'd best be on my way if I want to get a parking space,' Moretti said. 'See you there, Cristina.'

He headed straight for his car and drove down the hill then turned off onto the dirt road which now had a brown tourist sign indicating the Etruscan tomb. Instead of going to the tomb, however, he drove straight on and stopped at the Rosati farm. He waved to the boy playing in the yard and parked in the shade.

'Hello, Mario, how are things?'

The barefooted boy, dressed in shorts and a t-shirt, smiled, waved, and came to greet him.

'Great, Commissario.'

They shook hands.

'How's your mum?'

Mario tilted his head to one side.

'Today's a bit difficult,' he replied. 'A mixture of excitement and sadness, I think. Would you like me to fetch her?'

Moretti ruffled the boy's unkempt hair. 'Yes, please.'

He ran off towards the farmhouse door. 'Mamma. A visitor.'

Moretti's gaze followed Mario to the building from where, only a few months before, the boy had seemingly vanished, impossibly, from the locked farmhouse.

A slim woman with short, neat black hair appeared at

the door wearing one of the floral print, cotton crossover housecoats that all Italian women wore to do housework. She wiped her hands on her sides and smiled.

'Commissario Moretti, how are you? Can I offer you something?'

'I'm fine, Signora Rosati,' he replied. 'No, nothing, thanks. I thought I'd pop by to see how things were.'

Chiara Rosati nodded in the direction of the tomb. 'You mean with the grand opening today?'

He grinned. 'Yes, I suppose so.'

She indicated a bench in the shade against the wall of the house, and they sat down. Mario was investigating something in a hedge across from them.

'I got my invitation, but I'm not going. How about you?'

'I was invited, too, but I gave my invite to Ispettore Furlan.'

She looked in silence beyond the open yard to where the tomb had been found.

'It's too soon,' she said softly. 'Just a few months since Domenico's funeral.' She placed her hands on her knees, fingers intertwined. 'I still miss him so much,' she breathed. 'Even though I have Mario, the house seems so empty without Domenico. I keep turning up reminders in odd places.'

The sliver of guilt that twisted in Moretti's heart from his daughter's disappearance was joined by another caused by Maria's move to work in the south. And he inhaled reflexively, and audibly, before he could control it.

Chiara turned to look at him.

'I understand what you mean,' he said.

She studied his face and replied, 'I believe you do.'

Mario's yelp as he found a praying mantis changed the atmosphere.

'Look,' he whooped, running towards them. 'It's a beauty. Can I keep it?'

He held the bright green insect in his open palm at his mother's eye level. 'Ow! Its spiky claws are digging into me.'

'I think that answers your question,' Chiara replied.

'Put it back where you found it so that it can find some dinner.'

'Okay.'

He ran off back to the hedge, cupping the insect.

Both adults smiled.

'Do you think Domenico would have gone to the ceremony?'

Chiara watched her son gingerly placing the insect back on a twig.

'I'm not sure. He liked to keep himself to himself. I don't know. Maybe.'

'Well, if you were to ask me – which I know you aren't – I'd say that you should go. Both of you. To honour the memory of Domenico, who found this place for you all in the first place.'

She rubbed an arm. 'It's late. Mario takes ages to get ready.'

'There's plenty of time, and you can be there in a couple of minutes.'

'I'm not sure.'

'Look, why not do what I'm doing? I'm going to see the mayor cut the ribbon, but I'm not going inside or to the thing afterwards. The tomb was on your land, after all. What do you say?'

She straightened up and nodded.

'You're right. I'll do it for Domenico.' She stood. 'Mario, come here. We need to get ready quickly We're going to the opening of the tomb.'

Mario cheered and did a crazy flailing jump in the air as he ran towards them.

Chiara held out her hand.

'I'll see you there, Commissario.' They shook. 'Thanks.'

Despite his detour, Moretti was still one of the first to arrive at the level, grassy slope that was the new carpark. The sprawling juniper bush that had hidden the immigrants' entry point to the tomb had been cleared, along with other shrubs, to increase access for vehicles. He turned and reversed into a spot that would allow him to leave easily.

Five very slim black men appeared from the tomb

entrance, smartly dressed in short-sleeved shirts and light-coloured trousers. The tallest of them held up his hand and waved.

'Good morning, Yusuf,' Moretti called. 'Everything ready?'

The men crowded round Moretti, shaking hands, smiling, and exchanging quips among themselves in their own language.

'Good to see you, Commissario Moretti,' said Yusuf. He turned to his friends and nodded.

'Good morning, sir,' they chorused in Italian. 'How are you?'

Moretti laughed.

'I'm very well, thank you. How are you enjoying being shareholders in a farm?'

Yusuf held up his hands. 'Wait, Commissario. That's beyond them. I'll translate.'

He relayed Moretti's question and summarised their simultaneous replies.

'They are eternally grateful; they love it; they will work hard and prove that it was worth taking a chance on them; they will remember the mayor for supporting them and your wife for representing them forever.'

Moretti grinned.

'Will your wife be coming to the ceremony today?'

The grin froze on Moretti's face. 'No, she is working on a complex case in the south and can't get away unfortunately.'

'Please send her our regards.'

'I will.'

One of the men spoke to Yusuf and gave him what looked like a tangle of plastic thread.

Yusuf passed it to Moretti. 'The men found this hung between some trees in a far corner of Erpicone's farm.'

Moretti took the ball and unravelled a piece.

'It's a mist net,' he explained. 'Poachers use them to catch migrating songbirds. They're illegal in Italy, if not the whole of Europe now.' He held his hand behind the mesh. 'Look, it's so fine it's almost invisible to birds. But this isn't the season. Where did they find it?'

Yusuf translated the answer.

'It must have been left over from last year.'

'Yes,' said Yusuf. 'There were a few dead birds trapped in it. The men cut them out and buried them.'

'Please ask them to let me know if they see any strangers on the farm. I'd like to catch these poachers.'

The arrival of three cars ended their conversation. The men went off to their positions, and Moretti returned with the net to his car and sat inside with the window down. Over the next few minutes, the carpark filled, and a small crowd assembled near the entrance to the tomb. Cristina and Montanari arrived right before the mayor's car. Cristina recognised Moretti's car and raised her fingers a little as she walked past. Montanari was preoccupied with speaking to the mayor.

Among the last to arrive were the Rosatis. Moretti flashed his lights and Chiara parked beside him. She was dressed in a grey linen jacket and white blouse over a knee-length black skirt. Mario wore a clean shirt, shorts, and sandals. There clearly hadn't been time to tame his hair. They stood between his car and theirs.

Across the carr park at the entrance, someone tested the microphone.

'You should go over,' Moretti said, getting out of his car. 'You've come this far, go and hear properly.'

'This is far enough,' Chiara replied. 'I'd never been to this part of the property when Domenico was alive, and now that we've sold it, it doesn't feel like it was ever ours. I'll stand beside you, if that's alright.'

Mario looked up at her, and she smiled. 'On you go, Mario, you can report back to me.'

'Thanks, Mamma. I'll get right to the front.'

He ran off and wriggled his way through the crowd.

'Good morning, and thank you for coming here today, ladies and gentlemen,' began Mayor Donati. 'We Tuscans are proud of our Etruscan heritage, and I am honoured to be standing here today to open what preliminary research has already shown to be a very significant and historically important find – an almost intact tomb.'

Applause.

'Before I declare it officially open, I would like to thank

the builders and ground staff who prepared the area. I would like to thank the museum staff for organising the research and restoration teams, and mounting the exhibition that we will shortly be inaugurating. I also want to pay tribute to the hard work and dedication of the men who first excavated the tomb in such a way as to cause minimal damage to the friezes and artefacts. Some of them are here today.'

Applause.

'Yusuf now works between this site and the museum, and his comrades are part-owners of the farm next door. As you will remember, I put championing their human rights for asylum at the heart of my successful election campaign.'

'Oh, get on with it, Achille,' called someone in the crowd, provoking laughter.

'Alright, alright, but I also have to thank Signora Rosati for agreeing to sell the land to the town.' He scanned the crowd but couldn't see her. 'I hope to thank her again personally later, but without further ado,' he turned to receive a huge pair of scissors from Yusuf, 'I declare this Etruscan tomb open.' Mayor Donati cut the tricolour ribbon to general applause.

Moretti felt his phone buzz. He took it out and looked at the screen. *Unknown caller.* He raised a finger and walked away from Chiara.

'Moretti. Who is this?'

'Dino, it's Sergio. I'm with Gennaro. He's collapsed at Chen's shop. I have to go.'

CHAPTER FOURTEEN

Moretti arrived outside Chen's shop and tried to make sense of the scene. Outside, his ashen-faced friend Santoro was being hoisted, strapped to a trolley, into an ambulance. Inside, a throng of shoppers were filling wire baskets full of goods chosen from a labyrinth of tall, metal shelving displaying electrical and household goods as well as Chinese ornaments

He went to Santoro's side. The neck brace made it impossible for the man to turn his head, so Moretti placed his hand on Santoro's arm.

'Gennaro, it's Dino. You'll be fine, don't worry. You'll be well cared for.'

Santoro's eyes were closed, and he made no response.

'Excuse us, Commissario,' one of the paramedics said brusquely. Moretti stood back and watched as Santoro was secured in the ambulance and then whisked rapidly, and noisily, away.

Only when Santoro had disappeared around the bend did Moretti turn and notice Vanni looking in the front window of Chen's shop.

Vanni noticed Moretti's reflection.

'Good prices, Dino,' he said casually. 'This place will do really well.'

Moretti came to Vanni's side, shoulder touching the shop window.

'Thanks, Sergio.'

Vanni continued to look at the wares on display.

'It's Chen you should thank. When Gennaro collapsed, he put him in the recovery position and ran to the practice to fetch help. We called the ambulance, and I came to deal with Gennaro.'

'What is it? Do you know?'

Vanni turned to face Moretti. 'It looks like a TIA, but they'll check him at hospital and make sure.'

Moretti furrowed his brows. 'That's a transient something or other?'

'Transient Ischaemic Attack – a mini stroke. I gave him aspirin as a precaution against a full-blown stroke, but it's impossible to say what damage has been done and what the short- or long-term consequences will be until they've done tests. His blood pressure was a little high, and he's overweight, but they'll do blood tests and perform an ECG and an MRI scan.'

'How did you—?'

'Get your number?' Vanni smiled. 'Gennaro had it on his phone.' He dug into his trouser pockets. 'He also said to give you his keys.'

'Thanks. I'll go round to his place and pack a bag.'

'Leave it for a couple of hours to give the hospital time to do the tests.'

Moretti's phone buzzed. 'Cristina?'

'I've just heard about Gennaro, Commissario. How is he?'

'Okay, I think. Hold on, I'll pass you to Dr Vanni.'

He gave his phone to Vanni, exhaled deeply, and looked down the road to where the ambulance had last been seen while the doctor answered Cristina's questions.

Vanni handed back the phone. 'The Ispettore wants a word with you.'

Moretti nodded his thanks, took the phone, and walked away from Chen's shop. 'Cristina?'

'That's terrible news. Poor Gennaro.'

'If Vanni's right, he'll be okay.'

'How are you, Commissario?'

Moretti arched his brows and pushed out his bottom lip.

'CC has us working on our own now, so I imagine I won't notice the difference.'

'I don't believe that. You two are close.'

Moretti was about to reply when Cristina interjected, 'Commissario, I'm sorry, I can't talk. The Vice Questore needs a lift back to the museum.' She hung up.

Moretti looked behind him. He was ready to ask Vanni the question that had been incubating in his mind – a question that he did not want to know the answer to – but Vanni had already returned to the practice. The thought struck Moretti that all the people who had been significant in his life – his daughter, Sergio, Maria, and now Santoro – were no longer there, and he felt oddly and suddenly alone.

'Excuse me, Commissario.'

Two shoppers were exiting Chen's shop, carrying bags and boxes. He moved aside and walked to his car. His phone buzzed again.

'Moretti.'

'Commissario, it's Nardelli. Beppe's returned. He's locked himself in his room and refuses to speak.'

'I'm on my way.'

*

When Moretti arrived at the farm, he found the farmer standing at the front door, arms folded, having blocked in his son's car front and back with a tractor and trailer.

'I take it your son is still here, Signor Nardelli.'

'I wasn't taking any chances. He still hasn't spoken with me.'

'May I try?'

The farmer stood aside and opened the door. 'Be my guest. Top of the stairs, second left.'

Moretti stepped inside. One wall of the entrance was covered in rosettes which Nardelli's bulls had been awarded over the years. The greatest number by far had been won by Jupiter.

He called up, 'Beppe, it's Commissario Moretti. I'm coming up.'

There was no reply, and Moretti climbed the stairs and stood outside the bedroom door. He listened then knocked.

'Beppe, I need to speak with you,' he said quietly. 'Now, that can be here or at the station. It's up to you.'

'Where's my father?' Beppe's voice was muffled.

'As far as I know, he's still outside, guarding the door.'

'Shit.' There was movement inside the bedroom.

Moretti leaned towards the door and held his breath to hear better.

'Can our talk remain between us?' Beppe's voice was quieter now and just on the other side of the door.

Moretti dropped his voice to almost a whisper.

'I can't promise that, Beppe,' he replied. 'But if you haven't done anything illegal, I can stay here and help to smooth things over with your father.'

'Shit. You better come in then.'

Beppe opened the door and let Moretti into his tidy bedroom. He moved a bundle of folded clothes from a chair onto the end of his bed. 'You can sit there.'

Moretti sat down while Beppe paced up and down.

'He'll kill me,' he said, rubbing the palm of his hand with his other thumb.

'Beppe, sit down,' said Moretti firmly. 'He's more preoccupied with losing Jupiter. If he was going to kill you, he'd already have done it, cut up your body, and buried it.'

Beppe stopped and gaped at the detective.

'Sit down. You're making me dizzy. Tell me what happened, from the beginning.'

Beppe sat on the bed opposite Moretti. 'I haven't done anything illegal, so this can stay between us, yes?'

Moretti pursed his lips and counted on his fingers.

'Beppe, I'm guessing that this is going to involve a girl, drugs, a car, gambling, or all four. It certainly won't be the worst thing I've ever heard, and the quicker you tell me the sooner it'll be sorted.'

Beppe turned to look out the window in the direction of the cowshed, clutched his hand and ran his thumb up the inside of each finger in turn.

'I knew that Dad was going to the stock auction, and I thought that he was going away all day so I reckoned that I could meet my girlfriend.'

'Go on.'

'Dad doesn't know about her, and if he did, he would be raging.'

'Why raging?'

'She lives in the town, and she wants me to go and live with her.'

'I'm still not seeing why your father would be raging.'

'Dad wants me to follow in the family tradition and inherit the farm. She doesn't want me to inherit the farm. She loves travelling, and managing a farm doesn't allow that – it's a full-time job. She wants me to give it up and tell Dad.'

'What do you want?'

Beppe looked at Moretti. 'I don't know. She's right, though. Running a farm is all-consuming.'

'Why didn't you answer your father's calls?'

Beppe looked at the floor.

'When he called the first time, we were… I was busy. So, I switched my phone off. Then when I put it back on again, I saw that he'd messaged me to say that Jupiter was missing. I knew that I'd get the blame because I was supposed to be here keeping an eye on things.'

'So, you thought the best thing would be to stay away and not come home?'

'I panicked. I know how much it means to him. It's his whole life. He and my grandfather had been breeding Chianina bulls for years, and Jupiter is by far the best.'

'I know. I saw the rosettes downstairs.' Moretti leaned forward and his dark brown eyes fixed Beppe. 'Beppe, I have to ask you, did you have anything to do with Jupiter's disappearance?'

'No,' he replied immediately.

Moretti smoothed his moustache. 'Okay,' he said, sitting back again. 'Tell me more about this young woman. Does she have a name?'

'Bea.'

'How did you and Bea meet?'

The young man smiled. 'We bumped into each other – literally. I was delivering a selection of mushrooms to one of the restaurants in Maghicchio, and she was on her phone, not looking where she was going, and she walked right into me.'

'Oh?'

'Yes. The bags fell. Mushrooms rolled everywhere. She apologised and helped me collect them back into the bags, then she asked if she could buy me a coffee to make up.'

Moretti smiled. 'Love's young dream,' he said. 'Fate works in mysterious ways. Tell me, when did this fateful meeting happen?'

'Three weeks ago.'

'Ah, so the fire of passion burns strongly.' He slapped his thighs. 'Very well, Beppe, I don't think I need to speak to your father about this. But I think that you should. He needs to know that you're sorry. Your relationship with him, no matter what you decide to do about your future, is more important than Jupiter.' He stood. 'Okay?'

Beppe hesitated.

'Okay?' repeated Moretti.

'Okay, Commissario.'

'Do you want me to be here, or shall I see myself out?'

'I'll come down with you and tell him myself. You don't have to stay.'

Signor Nardelli was still guarding the front door when Moretti opened it.

'Well? Anything? You were up there long enough.'

'Beppe wants to have a chat with you. I'm satisfied that he was not involved in Jupiter's disappearance.'

'So, what am I meant to do?'

'Number one, listen to your son. Number two, be patient. We're working on it. Number three, look out your insurance policy, just in case.'

'And that's it?'

'For now, yes. As soon as we know any more, we'll be in touch. If you hear anything, call immediately.'

Nardelli's grumbling followed Moretti until he reached his car and drove off. A glance in his rear mirror saw father and son face-to-face on the doorstep.

He decided to go to Santoro's house and call the hospital from there, in case he had to pack a bag.

When he opened the door, he was surprised to be met by a sleek black cat with a white patch between its eyes. It greeted him by rubbing the side of its head against his leg and kept pace with him as he walked to the kitchen, nimbly weaving itself between and around his legs like a champion dancing the Argentine Tango in such a way that neither of them was impeded nor tripped.

'Are you hungry?' The cat sat with its tidy, little round paws together and looked up at him. 'I didn't know that Gennaro had a pet.'

Moretti emptied and cleaned the milk bowl then poured fresh milk from the fridge. He searched the cupboards and found some cat food, opened a tin, and measured half of it out into the other bowl on the floor. The cat was interested, but its curiosity about Moretti outweighed its hunger and thirst. It chaperoned him from bathroom to bedroom as he looked for toiletries, pyjamas, and underwear, and a bag to put them in.

He sat on the end of the bed and called the hospital.

'It's Commissario Moretti about Gennaro Santoro. He was admitted with a suspected TIA. What can you tell me about his condition?'

'Are you a family member, Commissario Moretti?'

'I understand why you're asking. I'm his friend and work colleague. All his family are in Puglia. I'm phoning from his home, and I need to know if I should bring in the bag I've packed.'

'One moment and I'll check.'

The cat joined Moretti on the bed to add weight to his argument. Moretti stroked it between the eyes. It closed them and pressed against him.

'We'll be keeping Signor Santoro overnight for observation and for us to complete tests. You can bring in the bag and leave it at reception.'

Moretti began to form a pointed reply but thought better of it.

'Thank you for your help,' he said and ended the call. 'Well, she wasn't very helpful,' he explained to the cat.

The cat was indifferent. It separated from him and stretched out, claws apparent, and yawned, eyes tightly closed, tongue pressed to the floor of its mouth, tip curved upwards. Then it dropped silently off the bed and padded through to its supper.

CHAPTER FIFTEEN

A little crowd formed around the trestle table in the square. A slim, young woman wearing black trousers and a traditional tailored top in scarlet and gold silk was offering samples of food. Fanned out beside the little pots were menus written in Italian and English. She smiled and nodded as she explained what each sample was, switching comfortably from Italian to English, according to whom she was speaking.

Donatella, Rosalia, and Fausta stood to one side, watching spoonfuls of food pass from pot to mouth without incident.

Carla waited until it was her turn and took the sample offered by the smiling young woman.

'I'm Carla Marino,' she said cheerily. 'I own Bar Italia across the road behind me. I'm very pleased to meet you.'

The young woman returned her smile. 'I'm Cao An Na,' she replied, holding out her hand. 'It is my pleasure.'

Carla tasted the food.

'Mm, it's delicious,' she enthused, then turned to the three onlookers and called, 'You should really come over and try this. You'd like it.'

Fausta lowered her brows, Rosalia shook her head, but Donatella nodded and left the others to join the loose queue.

'Come up here, Donatella, the others won't mind,'

said Carla, addressing the little crowd behind her.

Donatella joined her and took one of the samples from An Na, dipped half of the plastic spoon into it, and touched it against her tongue.

'Oh, fragrant,' she exclaimed. 'And warm.' She ate what was on her spoon and quickly finished the rest. 'Thank you very much. Did I hear your name was Ciao Anna?'

The young woman smiled at her. 'You heard and pronounced it perfectly. Would you like to try a different sample?'

While An Na passed Donatella another little pot, Carla picked up one of the menus and scanned it.

'Look, I must get back to the bar. Would you like me to take some of your menus so that customers can see what you have on offer?'

'Thank you. That's very kind of you.'

Carla took the bundle of menus from An Na.

'Not at all. Thank you,' she said. 'Your food is delicious. When do you open?'

'Tonight.'

'I'm sure it will be a great success.'

Donatella nodded and gave a thumbs up to Rosalia and Fausta, waving them over, but they refused the invitation and followed Carla back to Bar Italia where they took up position at their usual outside table.

Corrado and Mauro, two members of the Hunting Association, timed their arrival to coincide with the last of the free samples.

'Thank you, Signorina,' said Corrado. He and Mauro stood eating the food while An Na cleared everything away into bin bags, until the last of the others had left. 'We were wondering if we might speak to your father.'

An Na stopped her tidying and wiped her hands on a paper towel. She looked at the barrel-chested bear of a man.

'What would you like to speak to him about?'

'It's a delicate matter,' said Mauro quietly.

She folded her arms. 'In any case I will have to be there to translate, so you can tell me.'

'It's the Disfida,' said Corrado.

'The Disfida?'

'The summer festival. The central part is a horseback archery competition between the four contradas.'

An Na shook her head and continued to put things away.

'Too busy,' she said. 'The restaurant opens tonight. I must get back to help prepare.'

'At least let us help you carry things back,' said Corrado. 'You'll get back quicker if we do.'

She looked from one to the other and nodded.

'You,' she looked at Corrado, 'take the table.' Then to Mauro, 'You bring the black bags, and I'll take the menus.'

Corrado picked up the table as if it were a ring binder, and they followed her to the former Bar Roma and looked up at the new sign. The Chinese characters **吃飽** and the name **Chībăo** stood out in red against a gold background.

'How do you say that?' Mauro asked.

An Na pronounced the name.

'Cibo? That's the Italian word for food,' Corrado said. 'How clever.'

An Na shook her head. 'You can leave these things on the floor inside. I'll deal with them. Thank you.'

'Signorina, we really are serious about wanting to speak with your father,' insisted Corrado. 'It could be good business.'

An Na placed the menus on the counter and leaned the table against it. She grabbed all the black bags.

'Wait here.'

She disappeared through a door at the back of the restaurant and returned moments later with her father. He was dressed in chef's whites, and had a large apron tied around his waist.

'This is my father, Zhao Yu. You have five minutes,' she said, indicating a table. 'Please sit down.'

'We represent the Girolamo Contrada. The Disfida began in the 1950s,' began Mauro.

Corrado put his hand on his friend's arm. 'We only have five minutes.' He looked at Zhao. 'The owners of

Bar Roma used to sponsor a horse and rider in the Disfida. And in return, we would hold our committee meetings here, our contrada meetings, our contrada meal, and another one if we won the competition. We want to know if you would like to continue this tradition.'

An Na translated. Her father studied the men, then spoke.

'My father wants to know how much money it costs to sponsor a horse and rider, and how many people come to each of the events that you mentioned.'

Corrado and Mauro looked at each other.

'Each of the four contradas has someone skilled in horseback archery. We pay their time and for the upkeep of the horse for two months, which is about the time they need to practise for the competition. I'd have to ask or guess-timate how much that would cost.'

Signor Zhao looked interested when An Na translated.

'As far as the benefits to you are concerned, I can be very specific. We have six committee meetings a year, with eight on the committee. We have three contrada meetings, with an attendance of twenty-four. The contrada meal usually has about eighty, and if we win, that can be doubled. So, it's potentially quite a benefit, particularly because the meetings happen outside of the tourist season.'

An Na relayed the figures to her father, and they had an animated exchange that ended with her nodding to Zhao.

'My father thanks you for bringing this proposal to us. It is something that he will consider carefully. It is our intention both to promote our restaurant and to become established in the community, and this may be a way of achieving these goals.' She took a pad and pen from the counter. 'Please write your names and a contact number, and we will get back to you when we have arrived at our decision.'

They wrote down the information that she had requested.

'Time is not on our side, Signorina,' said Corrado, sliding the pad back. 'We have other potential sponsors to speak to.'

An Na studied the names on the pad and placed her hands on her lap.

'Corrado,' she said with a smile, 'if you had other potential sponsors to speak to, that is where you would be now, instead of here. My father has said that he must give your proposal consideration. That he will do, and we will contact you.' She stood. 'Now, if you will excuse us, we must finish preparing for our opening night. I do hope that you will come and bring all your friends.' She held out her hand, shook theirs, and ushered the dazed Italians back out into the street.

She closed the door behind her and went to the kitchen to find her father.

'What do you think, Father? It would certainly give us a presence in the community.'

Her father was shaving cooked duck into thin slices, using a cleaver whose large, square, Damascus steel blade looked like watermarked silk.

'I think we can't afford it,' he said without looking up. 'We're overstretched as it is, and with the loss of your grandmother's luggage, we have nothing to sell to keep us going until we have sufficient customers to become solvent.'

An Na stayed silent and admired his finesse with the blade.

'We don't even know who these people are and if they can deliver their side of the deal.'

'Maybe I can help with that, Father,' she said, occupying herself with stacking plates ready for warming. 'I can call Moretti.'

'The walrus who hasn't found your grandmother's trunk?'

'The detective who gave me his promise that he will keep looking for grandmother's trunk.'

'That doesn't help with the cash flow.'

She stood by him and rested her hand gently on his shoulder. 'I know, but at least it will help us decide whether it's worth considering. I trust him.'

Her father made a noncommittal sound in reply, and she kissed the side of his head.

'Enough,' he said in a mock gruff voice. 'I'm busy.'

An Na collected the message pad and went to the family apartment above the restaurant, found Moretti's card, and dialled the number.

'Moretti.'

'Moretti, it's An Na. Can you spare me a minute of your time?'

'Of course. Is it about the luggage?'

'No. Another matter.'

'How can I help?'

'Two men came to ask for sponsorship for a horse and rider in the…' She read her notes from the pad. 'The Disfida? They said they represented a contrada. Their names are Corrado and Mauro.'

'Ah yes, the previous owners of Bar Roma used to sponsor the contrada. They are genuine, and what they say sounds true enough. It's up to you whether you want to involve yourself with them and the Disfida. It might bring in business. I think they held all their meetings in Bar Roma.'

'Thank you, Moretti. That confirms what they said. I will speak with my father.'

'Tonight is when you open, yes?'

'Yes. Will you come?'

'Do I need to book?'

'No, we don't know how many will turn up, but I will reserve you a table in any case.'

'For one.'

'For one. I'll see you tonight.'

An Na picked up another cell phone from a lacquered table and took it downstairs.

'Moretti says we can trust these men, Father. I've brought the phone.'

Her father stopped, wiped his hands on his apron, and searched her face. 'Are you sure?'

She nodded.

'This is what I am sure of,' she said, putting the second phone into his hand. 'I am sure that Moretti is telling the truth. I am sure we can trust these men, and most of all I am sure that you are a wonderful cook, and that people will love to come here and eat.'

Zhao pressed speed dial and explained the situation

to the person who answered, listened, then gave his daughter the phone.

'They have to talk about it.'

He resumed his preparation while An Na busied herself in the restaurant ensuring that every table was ready. Several minutes later the phone rang, and she rushed back to the kitchen and passed it to Zhao. He answered and signalled for a pad and wrote down a long list. When the call finished, he handed An Na the list.

'I hope you know what you're doing,' he said.

She read the list and exhaled deeply. 'Leave it to me, Father.'

Her next call was to Corrado.

'Hello?'

'Corrado, my father is still considering your proposal. It has a certain appeal for us, but it demands that we lay out money before we have even opened for business and recouped our outlay.'

'I'm sorry, the timing could have been better, but the date of the Disfida is fixed every year.'

'My father says that his decision will be influenced by how serious the contrada is about making our restaurant the base for its meetings, and all the things you described.'

'Oh, we are very serious.'

'Good. In that case we can expect a big turnout of the contrada at tonight's opening meal.'

Corrado laughed.

'I'll take care of it. Just make sure there is plenty to eat.'

CHAPTER SIXTEEN

Moretti had no sooner finished speaking to Gennaro at the hospital and reassuring him that his cat had been fed, when his desk phone rang.

'Moretti.'

'Can you take this call, Commissario?' asked Alfiero. 'Something about a bull.'

'Put it through… Moretti.'

'Oh, Commissario, I didn't need to speak to you, I wanted to report a bull.'

'That's quite alright. Who am I speaking to, please?'

'Signor Costantini. I stay in Castiglione del Lago, at Lago Trasimeno.'

'A lovely spot. Thank you for calling. Now, what can you tell me about this bull?'

'I was driving back from Montepulciano along the back roads when I saw it. It's big, Commissario. In fact, it's huge. A white Chianina bull.'

'Can you tell me where you saw it?'

Moretti wrote down the detailed directions then grabbed his jacket and left. He found the spot twenty minutes later. The bull was grazing alone in a grassy field with a short rope through its nose ring. Moretti called Nardelli.

'Signor Nardelli, it's Moretti. I've found what I think is Jupiter. I need you to come and identify him.'

He gave the farmer directions then called forensics and waited in his car.

When Nardelli arrived, his son Beppe was with him, and they had brought a livestock trailer. Without greeting the detective, the two men climbed into the field and approached the massive animal. Moretti followed them. Beppe held the rope while his father ran his hands over the animal.

Nardelli screamed as Moretti joined them.

'The bastards!' he shouted, pointing to the bull's scrotum. 'They've castrated him.'

Moretti bent to look under Jupiter.

Nardelli sank to his knees, cupped, and lifted the empty sac. He patted the ox's flank and sobbed. 'He's nothing but butcher meat now.'

Nardelli was too upset to speak, so Moretti stood beside Beppe.

'How is that even possible?'

'It's not difficult,' Beppe replied. 'It can be done with a local anaesthetic into the testes while the bull is standing up.'

Moretti unconsciously squeezed his knees together. 'Do you think a vet did it?'

'It wouldn't even need to be a vet. You could do it.'

Moretti felt his scrotum contract. He looked down between the animal's legs.

'No. I couldn't,' he grimaced. 'But it's the sort of thing that another farmer could do?'

'Anyone who's watched a vet performing the operation could do it. You only need to be able to put the bull where it can't move about, and have anaesthetic, a syringe, and a scalpel. Ten minutes.'

Nardelli senior was back on his feet, stroking Jupiter as he came towards them.

'Is Jupiter otherwise alright?' Moretti asked.

'Other than having the most expensive balls in the Valdichiana cut off, I suppose he is,' the farmer replied. 'I'll get him home and call the vet to check him.'

He slapped Jupiter's thick neck and took the rope from Beppe. He pulled up the animal's head and leaned into its flank to get it moving.

'Come on, boy. Let's get you home. Get that gate, Beppe.' He turned back to Moretti. 'If I find out who did this, I'll do the same to them. Without the anaesthetic.'

Moretti watched them leave, then scanned the grassy field for clues. Nothing but grass and piles of excreta that matched Jupiter's bulk. He walked from one pile to the next until he saw something. There was a partial, cleated boot print in what he estimated was a day-old heap. He photographed it with his phone then shoved a stick in the ground beside it and waited in his car until forensics arrived.

'Don't bother putting on the full Tyvek suit,' he called to the officer. 'I want you to dust the gate for prints and make a cast of a boot print in a shit.'

The crime scene officer lifted a cantilever case out of the boot of his car and followed Moretti to the stick.

'This is becoming a regular thing with you, Moretti,' he quipped. 'We've more to do than examine shit all day.'

'You wouldn't be so chirpy if you knew what happened,' Moretti replied grimly. 'Just take the sample and compare it to the one that you took from the farm the other day. Message me if they're the same.'

'Will do.'

'Thanks.'

*

Moretti drove to the Buina farm to be met as usual by the farm dogs. Their barking brought Buina out from the cowshed, and the red-faced farmer came striding over to Moretti's car.

'Good,' he said. 'I was about to call you. 'I had a crazy call from Nardelli, threatening to cut my balls off and the balls of every bull in my shed.'

Moretti held up his palms. 'Slow down, Signor Buina. Did you read the note I left in your door, asking you to call me?'

'The one about Nardelli's missing bull? Yes, but it had nothing to do with me. I don't know anything about it.'

'As you've discovered, Signor Nardelli is very upset – too upset for me to ask him how someone would go about castrating a bull. Would it be alright if I asked you, as another beef farmer? I mean, how difficult is it? Do you need special training and equipment? Where can you do it? I guess you need some kind of sterile room, like an operation theatre.'

Now it was Buina who held up his hands.

'First of all, it's not that difficult. Anyone could do it, and you don't need any fancy rooms or equipment. Ideally, for a castration, you would ask a vet. The bull is injected with anaesthetic into its balls, then the scrotum is cut, and the balls are taken out, ligatured, and removed one at a time, cauterised with iodine, then the cut is stitched up and treated with iodine.'

'That sounds very complicated. Have you ever done it?'

'Commissario, you must remember the Chianina breed was bred as a draught animal, so every farmer used to convert his bulls to oxen. To answer your question, yes I have, to save on vet bills. But only with much younger animals.'

'How do you keep the animal still?'

'What you need is a contraption called a squeeze chute that holds the bull securely in place. Every stock farm has one for routine examinations and veterinary treatment. Mine is in the barn if you want to see it.'

'That won't be necessary, thanks.'

Buina shook his head. 'It's a terrible thing,' he said gravely. 'I can't imagine how I'd feel if it happened to my bull.'

'When I asked you to call me, I was going to ask where you were during the time that Jupiter was stolen.'

Buina made a cackling noise.

'Commissario Moretti, you've established that I have the know-how to castrate Nardelli's bull – in other words, the means. You've probably jumped to the conclusion that Hercules has now become the top stud bull in Valdichiana. You might have been going to ask what this would do to the value of Hercules and his semen – so I have a motive. Your last question was to confirm if I had the opportunity. Just like in all the detective stories I've read. Well, I'm sorry to disappoint you, but I was with my bank manager in Maghicchio, then I took a prospective client to lunch at the trattoria across from the pharmacy. You can check for yourself.'

Moretti turned to his car.

'I will, Signor Buina, if only to rule you out. But I'm still interested if you hear anything, or even if something occurs to you, no matter how unimportant it might seem.'

*

Moretti drove back to the Questura, where Alfiero warned him by touching an index finger just below his eye. Moretti nodded. His phone rang the moment he reached his office.

'Moretti.'

'Can you spare me a minute, Commissario?'

'Certainly, CC, I'll be right in.'

He walked to the end of the corridor, knocked, and entered without pausing. 'Good afternoon, how can I help you?'

'Take a seat. I want to talk to you about the men who work on the Erpicone farm.'

Moretti held up a finger. 'Part-own.'

'What?'

'Part-own,' he repeated. 'The immigrants part-own the Erpicone farm. They bought shares in the farm with the reward they had for finding the tomb.'

Montanari ignored him and brought a letter from her drawer. 'This came today.'

Moretti sighed. 'Let me guess, another anonymous letter?'

Montanari read the letter aloud.

'To whom it may concern, I wish to bring to your attention the fact that the immigrants who were at the opening ceremony escaped from police custody. It may be interesting to ask Commissario Moretti how that happened.'

She looked at him. 'Well, what do you have to say, Commissario?'

'It's shorter than the previous one – and factually inaccurate.'

Montanari leaned closer. 'Inaccurate, how exactly?'

'It says that there were immigrants at the ceremony. In fact, there were Italian residents of Somali and Ethiopian origin present. As to the circumstances of their arrest, escape, and surrender, all the details are contained in the documents that you asked Santoro to file. I refer you to those, and I stand by everything that is written in them. Oh, and Santoro is recovering in hospital, by the way. I spoke with him earlier. Can I be of further assistance, Vice Questore?'

Montanari stiffened.

'Don't try to provoke me, Commissario,' she hissed. 'You'll come off worst.'

'Thank you, I'll remember that.' He rose. 'Can I go now?'

She dismissed him with her hand, and he returned to his office where he phoned both the bank and the trattoria.

Satisfied that Buina's alibi held up, he packed up and walked to the new restaurant. A queue, comprised of locals and tourists in equal measure, stretched from its door to the square. He made his way to the front and greeted An Na, who was handing out cards telling the customers when to return. He peered past her into the restaurant and saw that every table was full of diners studying the menu.

'It's still early. I'll come back later or another night,' he said.

'No, Moretti. I promised you a table, and there is one left. Go inside and turn to the left. I'll be with you shortly.'

Inside, he stopped at a table of four.

'Well, Corrado, you must be keen for the sponsorship.'

'And to taste the food, if I'm honest.'

Moretti found his table for one and settled down to read the menu.

*

Cristina met the owner of the rental property in the parking space outside it. The woman sat on the grass, curled up, holding her knees to her chest.

'Signora Cioli, you called the police. I'm Ispettore Furlan. It's me you spoke with on the phone. What's happened, exactly?'

Signora Cioli looked up only as far as Cristina's knees.

'I can't go back in there,' she said hoarsely.

Cristina looked across the garden. The front door was open. 'May I go inside?'

The woman nodded and hugged herself more tightly to her knees.

Three metres from the open door, the smell assailed the detective. She paused to put on her Latex gloves and covered her mouth and nose with a handkerchief. Cristina stepped into the kitchen where the floor was strewn with plastic bottles and flagons of cleaning products. Every cupboard, and the door of the washing machine, was open.

She tiptoed along the short corridor to the bathroom next, where the stench was intensely more foul than before. Soiled towels and bedlinen were heaped in the shower cubicle and laundered ones hung over the cabinet.

Finally, Cristina entered the bedroom and saw the young couple lying in bed, the woman's arm across her partner's chest. She retraced her steps back outside, removed the handkerchief and gulped in the clean air, then called the ambulance, the forensics team, and Doctor Sergio Vanni.

CHAPTER SEVENTEEN

Moretti helped Santoro into the car.

'Capo, there's no need to fuss. I can do this myself,' he said. 'I'm not an invalid.'

'Just get in and fasten your seatbelt, Gennaro.'

Moretti made sure Santoro was organised before getting in and setting off. 'Are you alright to come back to work?'

'The doctors said that I should have a couple of days off, then I'll be fine to return. It's Friday today, so I'll be back on Monday.'

'I guess you'll have to take things easy.'

Santoro sighed.

'I have to make major changes to my lifestyle,' he complained. 'I can't drive for a month, I have to eat tons more fruit and vegetables, give up all the stuff I like, and follow a diet and exercise plan that they've drawn up. I'll probably have to work from a desk now, too.'

'No more carrot sticks or seeds, then.'

'No, it's what they claim is a balanced diet, but I don't see how it can be if all my favourite foods have been cut out of it – and small portions.'

'Ah, in that case you maybe don't want to hear about my meal last night.'

'Not in the new Chinese place?'

'The same. It was incredible. They did a tasting version

of their menu – smaller portions than normal, to let customers sample everything – but it all added up to a banquet. The flavours and different spices were out of this world. It'll do well.'

'Capo, I'm sure it was wonderful, but can you stop now? I'm getting hunger pangs listening to you.'

'Very well, I'll change the subject. You didn't tell me you had a cat.'

Santoro chuckled. 'Poirot? I've had him for ages. Thanks for taking care of him. So, what have I missed at work?'

'Where do I begin? There's been another anonymous letter to Montanari, about the immigrants escaping last year.'

'What? Someone's got it in for you. Any ideas? Do you think it's Innocenti?'

'I don't know, Gennaro, but please don't be concerned – I'm not. Then there's Nardelli's bull. First stolen, then found castrated.'

Santoro drew his knees together. 'Who'd do a thing like that?'

'Nardelli's convinced it was Buina, but he has an alibi.'

They arrived at the outskirts of Cassiatorre.

'Is there anything that you need from the office, or shall I drop you off at home, Gennaro? I'm going to the Chinese restaurant again.'

'Come on, Capo, you said you'd stop it. Drop me at home, please. I need to throw out all my unhealthy food and buy healthy stuff.'

Moretti grinned. 'I'm not going there to eat. I've been asked to attend a meeting between the owners and the contrada.'

'Which contrada?'

'Girolamo.'

'Oh, that's right, the previous owners hosted their meetings.'

'And sponsored their rider, too.'

'Well, have fun. And if you do get offered something to eat, don't tell me about it.'

Moretti parked outside Santoro's place. He waited until his friend was out of the car, opened the passenger window, and said, 'Say hello to Poirot for me.'

Santoro waved him off, and he drove to the centre and parked beside the square. He checked the time then crossed to Bar Italia, nodding to the three women sitting at their usual table as he passed.

'Good morning.'

'Good morning, Commissario,' replied Carla from inside. 'What can I get you?'

'An espresso, please.'

She turned to the machine, measured and tamped down the coffee, then placed a saucer and spoon on the counter in front of him.

'Did you go to the grand opening of the restaurant last night?'

'I did.' He grinned and half turned for the benefit of the eavesdroppers outside. 'It was mobbed. The food was amazing.' He turned back to face Carla. 'I told Gennaro, and he was salivating.'

Carla placed the small cup on the saucer. She looked concerned. 'How is he?'

'He'll be fine, but he has to make big changes to his lifestyle.' He swirled the coffee, inhaled it, and finished it in three short sips. 'Did you know Gennaro had a cat?'

'Poirot? Yes, of course. Didn't you?'

Moretti grinned. 'No.'

He put a euro on the counter. Carla picked it up and rang off a receipt.

'Maybe you're not as close as you thought you were,' she joked.

He wiped his moustache on a serviette then smoothed it with his index finger, first left, then right.

'No, clearly not. See you later.'

He crossed the square and turned the corner to the restaurant. The door was slightly ajar, so he knocked it.

'It's Moretti. May I come in?'

An Na appeared.

'Yes, Moretti, come in. You are the first to arrive.' She led him to where three tables had been pushed together. 'Did you enjoy the food last night?'

'Signorina Cao, it was quite unlike anything that I've had before. I loved every mouthful. How long did you remain open?'

'The last guests left a little after midnight, then we had to clean everything away for a couple of hours.'

'And there was only you serving tables?'

'Yes, but last night was an exception, Moretti.' She looked up. 'Ah, here are the others.'

She met the new arrivals at the door and brought them to the table. 'Please be seated, and I will bring my father.'

An Na returned with Zhao, and they sat at the top of the table. She placed her tablet on the table in front of her.

'Thank you for agreeing to see us this morning,' began Corrado, to nods from all the contrada representatives. 'I hope that you saw from last night's attendance how serious we are about this partnership.' He paused while An Na translated. 'Speaking for us all, I also want to thank you for the wonderful food we enjoyed. It is such a change from our Tuscan diet, but quite delicious.' More nods around the table. 'I hope that you have had time, with all of the work that you had to do yesterday, to consider our proposal.'

An Na opened the tablet while translating.

'Yes, my father wishes to confirm the details which, if both parties find agreeable, we will draw up as a contract that we will both sign.'

The contrada members exchanged glances. Corrado spoke for the group.

'Signorina Cao, we haven't been used to having such a formal arrangement in the past. Is it really necessary?'

An Na smiled.

'Corrado, I am sure that the arrangement that you had before worked out well for all concerned. You all knew each other, grew up together, shared a history together, and probably were related either by blood or marriage. We have only recently arrived in Cassiatorre; we do not know each other, have no shared history or even culture. Now, while I am certain that the arrangement will work well, it has always been our practice to make sure that we each know what it is that we are agreeing to, and to put it in writing. What do you say, shall we proceed?'

There was mumbled agreement. An Na continued,

'The Contrada of Girolamo undertakes to do the following: to hold six committee meetings and three contrada meetings, and one annual contrada meal in the restaurant, or in a suitable outside space if numbers exceed the capacity of the restaurant, with a minimum of sixty attending.'

'I think I said eighty for the contrada meal,' clarified Corrado.

An Na nodded. 'Yes, but that was an estimate. This is a contract, and we will expect the revenue which usually attaches to a booking that size. That is why we have reduced the number.'

Corrado looked around the table, and there was general agreement that the conditions were fair.

'Very well, we agree,' he said. 'And for your part?'

'We undertake to do the following: to sponsor the contrada, to host the committee and contrada meetings without charge, to host and provide the annual contrada meal at cost to contrada members, and at a reduced price for visitors and tourists. We also will provide the horse and archer for the Disfida competition.'

Corrado grinned.

'Thank you, but that won't be necessary.' He motioned towards a slim, long-haired young man who raised his hand and smiled. 'We already have our archer and horse. All you need do is to take care of the upkeep of man and horse for two months.'

Zhao looked at his daughter and she translated, then he replied.

An Na translated. 'My father asks when the Disfida is to take place?'

'In two weeks.'

'Well then, he wonders why you would ask that we pay for the upkeep of the horse and rider for six weeks that have already passed?'

Corrado opened his mouth to reply, but An Na spoke first. 'In any case, the argument is irrelevant. The condition that we supply both horse and rider is non-negotiable,' she said softly, but firmly.

'But how can you get someone from China in time?' Mauro asked. 'Even if the animal could be transported here in time, the quarantine laws won't allow it.'

'The horse and archer are not coming from China,' replied An Na. 'They are in Hungary at the moment, competing in a similar competition there.'

The news was met by gasps, the loudest of which came from the slim, long-haired young man.

An Na brought up a video on the tablet and turned it towards the others. 'This is the horse and rider in action.'

The contrada members leaned closer to watch the compilation of clips showing a galloping horse carrying a rider loosing arrows at four targets in front, level, and behind him. As each arrow found its mark, the little audience gasped, then cheered, and finally fell silent. All eyes turned to the young contrada archer.

'Accept the terms,' he said. 'There's no way that I could compete with someone like that. I don't even know how what he does is possible.'

The members beside him slapped his back in appreciation.

'There is one request I would like to make,' he said. 'But it wouldn't be part of the contact.'

'What is the request?' An Na asked.

'I would like to learn from this man when he arrives. Do you think that could be arranged?'

'I will see to it personally,' she replied with a smile, to the loud approval of the company.

An Na turned to Moretti. 'What do you think, Moretti?'

'If both sides feel that they can benefit, then I think that you should go ahead. The only part that I would question, perhaps, is the use of the Chinese archer and horse for what is, after all, a local tradition. Maybe it could be written into the contract that that condition is for one year only?'

'Maybe we should check with Erpicone if having a foreign competitor is within the rules,' added Mauro.

Corrado held up his hands for silence.

'Friends, I strongly suggest that we say nothing of this.' He looked at Moretti. 'There is unofficial betting on the result of the competition, Commissario, that I'm sure you are aware of.'

Moretti shrugged. 'Maybe I should leave now before I hear something that I couldn't in the future deny.'

Corrado stopped, and An Na closed the tablet.

'If we are agreed on the terms, I will draft the contract and you can return here, Corrado, to sign it on behalf of the contrada. My father will sign it and, Moretti, we would be pleased if you could witness it.'

Moretti rose. 'Very well. Call me when everything is ready.' He left them talking about how they could maximise their gambling returns and stepped out into the bright warmth, where he saw a small group of tourists reading the menu in the window.

'What's the food like in there?' one asked.

'Abundant and delicious,' he replied. 'Trust me.'

CHAPTER EIGHTEEN

The receptionist showed Cristina through to Vanni's consulting room and closed the door behind her

'Good morning, Doctor Vanni. You said on the phone that you had some answers.'

'Good morning, Ispettore. Please take a seat. May I offer you something to drink?'

She sat at his desk.

'Nothing, thank you. I'm keen to find out what caused the deaths of the tourists.'

He sat and opened the folder in front of him.

'In a word, mushrooms. They'd eaten a toxic variety. *Amanita phalloides* – the Death Cap, to be precise. And without prompt medical intervention and treatment, death is inevitable, I'm afraid.'

'Where would they get them?'

Vanni leaned back in his swivel chair. 'In any of the wooded areas around Cassiatorre. They're not rare.'

'But why would they pick poisonous mushrooms?'

'It's more common a problem than you might think, Ispettore. When the fruiting body of the poisonous mushroom first emerges from the soil, it looks like the Ovolo of *Amanita caesarea*, Caesar's Mushroom.' He slid two photographs from the folder over to her side of the desk. 'This is the Death Cap, and this is the Ovolo.'

Cristina held a photograph in each hand.

'I see what you mean.' She passed them back to Vanni. 'But I say again, why would they pick poisonous mushrooms?'

'You're right, Ispettore. Why indeed?' He steepled his hands. 'My theory is this. They are English, so their knowledge of fungi was poor to non-existent. The English don't have the same tradition of foraging that we have. The search of their rental property did not turn up a mushroom identification book, so we must ask how did they even know about these mushrooms? My guess is that they bought some from the Saturday market. And that will be simple enough to check. I think there is usually only one seller, and I'm sure he will remember if an English couple bought ovoli.'

'Might they have bought Death Caps from him?'

Vanni removed his glasses and shook his head.

'No. The differences between the two species are obvious when pointed out, but it's something else you can check when you speak to the seller. No, Ispettore, I'm certain that they found the poisonous mushrooms themselves.'

'How tragic.'

Vanni cleaned his spectacles on a tissue. 'Indeed it is, because there's no clue in the taste. In fact, the mushrooms are delicious, and the toxin is not destroyed by the cooking process.'

'What else is in your folder?'

He put his glasses back on and slid the folder towards Cristina. 'That's a draft of the autopsy report.'

Cristina turned back the top page without reading it.

'Did you perform it?'

'No, but I attended.' He smiled. 'I think my colleague was glad of my experience in all matters fungal.'

Cristina slid the folder back. 'So how did they die? I mean the place was a mess.'

'I think the death certificate will show something like hepatic coma. I can go into detail if you like.'

'I'm not sure that *like* is the word I'd choose, but I'm curious to know.'

Vanni leaned back again.

'Amatoxin poisoning follows a predictable path, and

only a small amount of mushroom can be fatal.'

'How small an amount?'

'One mushroom. The toxin is absorbed rapidly and distributed to tissues including the liver and the kidneys. In the liver, the amatoxin enters the cells, where it is attached to other chemicals and secreted as bile back into the gastrointestinal tract and back to the liver again, in a toxic circle known as enterohepatic recycling.'

'Wouldn't it make them sick?'

He shook his head.

'Not immediately. One of the reasons that amatoxin is so deadly is that it is not irritating, and so it goes undetected for a period of between six and up to forty hours – known as the lag phase. If the couple had eaten the mushrooms for dinner, they would have been asleep before they were aware of anything. Then, when the intestinal mucosa are affected, the process moves into the gastrointestinal phase, with a suite of symptoms including nausea, vomiting, abdominal pain, and bloody diarrhoea. That is the phase that caused the conditions that you and the owner found when you entered the house.'

Cristina shuddered involuntarily.

'Shall I continue?' Vanni asked.

'Yes.'

'The gastrointestinal symptoms resolve after a day or so, but by that time the liver and now the kidneys are damaged, and patients will appear jaundiced. Eventually, coma and death follow, preceded by convulsions.'

'My God, how horrible. Could they have been saved? Could they have done anything to save themselves?'

'There is no known antidote, Ispettore, and those who are caught in time usually require a liver transplant.'

Cristina closed her eyes, put both hands behind her head and squeezed her elbows together, blocking her ears. 'I have to call the parents,' she said. 'How in heaven's name can I tell them how their children died?'

'You don't,' said Vanni firmly. 'The written report will be filled with all sorts of medical jargon. All you need do is break the tragic news that they died from mushroom poisoning.'

'Yes. That's all I have to do,' she repeated robotically.

'Break the tragic news that they're dead.'

Vanni closed the folder. 'Is there anything else I can help you with, Ispettore?'

Cristina became focused again and sat up straight. 'No, Dr Vanni. Thank you for your time.'

They stood and shook hands.

'Just one more thing, Ispettore.'

'Yes?'

'The young woman was about six weeks pregnant.'

Cristina hurried out of the practice and back to her car. She clipped on her seatbelt then leaned forward, covered her eyes with her hands, and wept.

The knocking on the side window made her jump. Chen was leaning close to the glass.

'You okay?'

Cristina wiped her face, feigned a smile, and nodded. 'Yes. It's nothing. Thank you.' She sniffed and searched for a tissue. 'I'm sorry if I made you anxious.'

'You sure?'

She blew her nose and smiled for real. 'I'm sure. Thank you, Signor Chen.'

Chen waved and returned to his shop, while Cristina drove off and returned to the Questura.

'The boss wants a word, Ispettore,' said Alfiero. 'You've to knock and go straight in.'

'Commissario Moretti?'

'No, *the* boss.'

'Thanks, Alfiero. Any idea what it's about?'

He shrugged and turned his attention to sorting the mail.

Cristina went to the bathroom to freshen her face, then stepped into the corridor, inhaled deeply, and walked briskly to Vice Questore Montanari's office.

'Good morning, CC,' she said brightly. 'Alfiero said you wanted to see me.'

'My God, Ispettore, what's wrong?'

Cristina opened her mouth, but her throat closed, and she half choked.

'Sit down, Cristina. Take your time and tell me what happened.'

Cristina sat on one of the chairs at the wall. Montanari

poured a glass of water, handed it to her, and sat beside her.

'Thank you, CC.' Cristina sipped the water. 'I'm embarrassed. I've just come from Dr Vanni, who was explaining how the young English couple died. So tragic. They were about my age.'

Montanari looked at a space somewhere across the room.

'We may be police officers, Cristina, but we're still human,' she said quietly. 'Death is never easy to encounter. And neither should it be.' She paused. 'We all have dark memories from our past, but it's the job we do in the present that gives us, and society, hope for the future.'

She moved back across the room and sat behind her desk. 'Bring your chair over.'

Cristina carried the chair and the water over to Montanari's desk.

'Do you have plans for the weekend?'

The question caught Cristina off guard, and she blushed. 'I was going to interview the mushroom seller at the market tomorrow.'

Montanari swatted her reply away. 'One of the boys can do that. I'd like you to come with me to a convention of senior police officers in Florence.'

'Oh?'

'We'll leave early on Saturday morning, attend some seminars, stay over, attend some more seminars, and then get back here for early evening on Sunday.'

'Stay over?'

'Yes, in a hotel. It makes sense. Otherwise, we have to travel back and forth.'

'But won't a hotel be more expensive than travelling?'

'Not if we share a room.'

Cristina felt her stomach flip.

'Share a room?'

Montanari frowned.

'Yes, Ispettore, we'll share a twin room,' she snapped. 'What did you think I was suggesting?'

The ispettore flushed, mind racing.

'I'm not sure why you would take an ispettore to a

convention whose audience is senior police officers, Vice Questore Montanari.'

CC leaned back in her seat.

'Cristina, I'm offering you something that I never had. A chance to meet officers, both male and female, who could be valuable in advancing your career. These people have a network – entirely unofficial, but it exists – that shares information, makes informal recommendations, and gives opinions on rising officers such as yourself. A good impression in this company could save you years of hard work in this pleasant, comfortable little backwater. Now, if you feel that speaking to a mushroom seller is more important, or if you are in any way concerned with sharing a twin room in a rather fine Florentine hotel for a night, then now is the time to tell me.'

'No, Vice Questore… I mean, CC… I only wanted to make sure that you felt I was ready.'

'Good. Moretti can speak to the mushroom seller. Do you want to let him know, or shall I?'

'I'll do it, CC.' She rose to leave. 'And thank you.'

Cristina closed the door behind her, paused, and breathed deeply, contemplating Montanari's motives.

'Been sent to stand outside the headteacher's office?' Moretti quipped, as he appeared at the end of the corridor.

She smiled and joined him in his office. He tossed the mail he had picked up from Alfiero onto the desk.

'How's your day going, Cristina?'

'Pah. Where do I begin? Doctor Vanni gave me the graphic details of mushroom poisoning, Vice Questore Montanari wants me to go with her to some bigwig police do in Florence and stay over in a shared room with her, and I've to tell you to interview the mushroom guy at the market tomorrow. How's your day going, Commissario?'

'Well, the Girolamo contrada can continue to have their meetings in the new restaurant, but their rider is being replaced by a Chinese ringer who's in Hungary competing in some national competition as we speak. But keep that to yourself, it's top secret. Oh, and Gennaro starts back on Monday.'

'How is he?'

Moretti began sorting the bundle of mail. 'Not happy. He has to change his diet and lifestyle. He'll spend most of his time in the Questura, and he can't work with either of us.'

'I'm missing that already, too, Commissario.'

'And me, Cristina. But it is what it is – accountability and efficiency.'

'How was your meal in the new restaurant?'

Moretti continued opening his mail. 'It was really great. Busy, though, because lots of the contrada went.'

Neither spoke for a moment.

'How was Vanni?' Moretti asked. His head was still down, and she couldn't see his expression.

'Thorough, professional, explicit.'

'Good.'

She tilted her head in vain to try to see his face.

'Commissario Moretti,' she began, 'you told me a few days ago that you'd tell me sometime what it was between you and Vanni. Now that he's definitely moved and is working here, I wondered if this was the time?'

Moretti stopped reading his mail and looked up at her.

'Cristina, Doctor Sergio Vanni is at the centre of the only case in my career that I haven't solved.'

'Oh, I didn't realise. What was the case, if you don't mind me asking?'

Moretti hesitated and shuffled the papers on his desk. 'The murder of his parents.'

Cristina gasped. 'Your best friend's parents were murdered? How terrible – for both of you.'

'I thought I had moved on, but with him returning… well, it all came back.' He rubbed the back of his neck. 'I even dug out the old case files from the attic and went over the witness statements and evidence. How crazy is that?'

'I don't think that's crazy at all. I know how important every case is to you.' The thought came into her head and out of her mouth before she had a chance to filter it. 'Do you think that Doctor Vanni had something to do with it?'

Moretti looked steadily at her. 'I know he did, Cristina.'

CHAPTER NINETEEN

Moretti joined the serpentine line that meandered as far as the door of the post office – a rare example of orderly queuing in a country whose citizens preferred to push to the front and form a loose horizontal line. The pace of progress was controlled by a recently installed system of flashing numerals and an automated voice allocating a counter space to the next in line.

The post office staff were seated behind Perspex windows that reached to the ceiling. This afforded them protection from impatient customers and was prompted by an incident in a nearby town when a geriatric had exorcised her frustration at not receiving what she thought was her full pension increase. Blaming the poor functionary for the government's tardiness, she had pulled the ring-pull of a tin of passata like the pin of a hand grenade and thrown the contents of the tin over the man on the other side of the counter to gasps and mumbled comments of the impossibility of ever restoring his shirt to its former pristine whiteness.

That action had resulted simultaneously in increased security for the post office staff and a corresponding loss of privacy for all customers, as all conversations between customer and counter clerks were now relayed through small, but powerful, loudspeakers fixed into the Perspex windows. It was now impossible to conduct business in whispers, and the post office no longer held the confessional-like confidentiality that it once had. The amount of the townsfolk's utilities bills was now common knowledge, as was the destination of every parcel and registered letter, allowing those waiting to be served to speculate on the energy efficiency, bathing habits, and family whereabouts without the inconvenience of striking up a conversation to find out.

So, when Moretti stood in front of window number three in the centre of the Perspex wall to send the large envelope containing Maria's mail, all and sundry found out his wife's new town – the clerk having to read it out to confirm – and that no, he did not think that it would be an arrangement which would be better facilitated with a permanent redirection order.

Fausta Racano, who was next in line to be served, overheard every detail and thought the information so juicy that she forewent her own business to hurry to Bar Italia to let the other two know.

Moretti, meanwhile, followed up on Cristina's investigation and spoke to the mushroom seller at the market, but the conversation only confirmed what Cristina and Vanni had suspected. The young couple had picked the deadly mushrooms themselves.

When he arrived at Bar Italia, Fausta was fanning herself from the exertion of her dash back to her two companions, who shook their heads and tutted as he arrived.

'Good day, ladies,' he said as he passed.

'We'd like a word with you, Commissario,' said Rosalia, holding her lavender bag under her narrow, pointed nose.

'Certainly,' he replied. 'I'll have a coffee and come back out in a moment.'

'Good morning, Commissario.' Carla greeted him holding out a pastry, his cappuccino already prepared and waiting on the counter.

'Thanks, Carla.' He bit deeply into the pastry. His moustache collected a dusting of icing sugar that dissolved and was immediately replaced by the creamy froth of the coffee.

'How is your day so far?' Carla asked.

'Okay, considering that Gennaro won't be back until Monday and Cristina is off on a jolly to Florence for the weekend.'

'So, you're the only thing standing between us and being overrun by criminals?'

He bit his pastry, nodded, chewed, and gulped his coffee.

Carla shook her head. 'You'll give yourself an ulcer if you don't slow down.'

He wiped his moustache clean then smoothed it. 'I don't have time for an ulcer,' he quipped.

Carla leaned towards him across the counter.

'Seriously, Dino,' she said quietly. 'I'm worried about you.'

He looked behind her at the reflection in the gantry mirror and saw that the three gossips were straining to hear, so he dropped his voice, too.

'Thanks, Carla. I'm fine, honest. Things are a bit…' He pondered as he pulled out a ten. '…fluid at the moment.'

'If you need to talk, or a home-cooked meal…'

Their fingers touched briefly as he took his change, and a frisson passed between them.

'Thanks, Carla.' He turned. 'Now, ladies, how can I help?'

'We're very concerned about the way things are going with the Chinese,' Rosalia declared.

'This sounds serious. Let me sit down.' He took a chair from another table and sat facing Rosalia. The other two shuffled their chairs a little to make space. Fausta's tiny dog, whose head poked out of her bag, leaned over to try to lick the new arrival. 'Start from the beginning and tell me everything.'

'It's only that we've heard things,' said Donatella.

'Worrying things,' added Fausta.

'Dreadful things,' breathed Rosalia.

Moretti raised his eyebrows and brought out his phone. 'In that case, you have my full attention. Which of you wants to start?'

They exchanged looks.

'I'll go first,' said Donatella. 'The farmer who sells me some eggs has lost a rooster.'

Moretti bit the inside of his cheek and made a note on his phone. 'His rooster?'

Donatella nodded. 'Yes, his best one.'

'And he thinks that the Chinese have something to do with its disappearance?'

She bent towards him. 'Cockfighting,' she whispered.

'Cockfighting?'

'Yes. They put metal spurs on their heels and make them fight.'

'The Chinese do this?'

'Yes. He saw a programme on television. They bet on the birds, too.'

'Illegal betting,' interjected Rosalia.

'Does the farmer have any suspicions as to which of the Chinese could be involved?'

'Any of them,' Rosalia hissed before Donatella could reply. 'All of them.'

'I see. And does the farmer have any idea where this cockfighting takes place?'

'He heard squawking.'

'Really? Where?'

'He wasn't certain. Out in the country. Not too far from his own place, but there was definitely squawking.'

'Definite squawking,' repeated Moretti, as he added to his notes. 'Did he investigate? You know, maybe look for the rooster?'

'No point,' interrupted Rosalia. 'They eat them – feet and all. I saw *that* on television.'

Moretti frowned.

'He had to put up the price of his eggs because the hens weren't laying as many. I think it must have been the shock of losing the rooster.'

Moretti noted everything, then scratched his short-cut, greying hair. 'This changes the direction of a case I'm working on.' He looked around and dropped his voice. 'His isn't the only rooster to have gone missing.'

The three women nodded in time.

'We'd been of the opinion that a fox was involved, but now, with what you've told me, we'll have to go about our enquiries completely differently.' He looked up and down the road and whispered, 'Please keep this information to yourselves. We don't want to tip anyone off.'

They nodded again.

'Now, what else?'

'I think that Signor Chen is running an opium den from his shop,' Fausta confided. Her dog managed to get its paws up onto the open bag and push itself higher.

'An opium den? Now that really is a serious allegation,' said Moretti, typing into his phone. 'Do you have any proof, Signora Racano?'

'Well, I'm no expert on this, you understand, but I went to the opening of his shop – not to buy anything, of course, just to see what the fuss was about.' They all nodded, Moretti too. 'And there was a funny smell coming from inside.'

'Did you go inside?'

Fausta fanned herself furiously. 'Indeed I did not. I didn't wish to become an opium addict.'

'Quite.'

'And poor Agente Santoro was affected. He must have inhaled the smoke and collapsed.'

'The opium smoke?'

'Certainly the opium smoke,' she replied indignantly. 'What other smoke could it have been?' She closed her fan and pushed the dog back down again.

'Have you ever heard of joss sticks, Signora Racano?'

'No.' She resumed fanning. 'But it wouldn't surprise me if they weren't smoking them, too.'

Moretti turned to Rosalia. 'I guess that you have the gravest news for me, Signora Seccavigne.'

Rosalia tucked the lavender bag into her cuff.

'And you guess correctly, Commissario,' she said conspiratorially. 'It's the new restaurant.'

Moretti brought his hand to his lips. 'Oh, don't tell me,' he said. 'I've eaten there.'

'Birds and cats, Commissario. That's what on the menu, birds and cats.'

'You mean chicken.' He glanced at Donatella. 'Or roosters?'

'Ha. That's maybe what the menu says.'

'And do you have any proof of this?'

'I certainly do. I know that a certain party handed in a mist net – the kind of net used by unscrupulous poachers to catch songbirds. Well, ask yourself, Commissario, who would want to catch little birds to eat?'

'Who indeed. And the cats?'

'I don't have that part of the proof yet, Commissario, but I'm working on it. I've started to keep a note of which cats are in my part of the town, and if any of them go missing, I'll be right back to make a complaint.'

Moretti finished making his notes and switched off his phone.

'Ladies,' he said, standing, 'Cassiatorre is so lucky to have you keeping your eyes and ears open.' He returned the borrowed chair to its table. 'And I know that I can rely on your discretion not to let anyone else into the valuable information you've shared with me today. We don't want to tip them off.' He tapped the side of his nose. 'Our secret.'

'Our secret,' chorused the women.

*

The conference centre was in a six-storey hotel, equidistant between the railway terminal of Santa Maria Novella and the River Arno. Like many buildings of its age and type in that part of Florence, the graffitied external walls hid a grandeur, albeit faded, of past times. The little neighbourhood bars, pastry shops, bakeries, tobacconists, and leather goods shops were now fewer than before, their numbers replaced by kebab shops, franchised takeaways, and places where cell phones could be bought, repaired, or unlocked.

Cristina had driven them both there in Vice Questore Montanari's car, which was now safely parked behind the wrought iron gates of the hotel's carpark. She had changed out of her usual trousers and wore a knee-length black skirt with a crisp white blouse and, unusually, small heels which nudged her height closer to two metres.

She and Vice Questore Montanari were among only seven women in the room of eighty delegates and speakers, and her stunning looks and stature drew blatant stares from some of the leading law enforcement officers in Italy.

Montanari delighted in introducing Cristina as her

protégée to everyone she spoke with, while Cristina delighted in introducing the most leering of her new acquaintances to her firmest handshake.

Most of the men were checked into the conference hotel but, to Cristina's great relief, Montanari had booked them into a different hotel. CC did, however, accept a dinner invitation on their behalf to join another four delegates at a small restaurant off the tourist trail. Cristina enjoyed the food more than the company and was relieved when the four men left before dessert to go on to a nightclub – the invitation to which Montanari refused.

'So, Cristina, what did you think of today?' Montanari asked as their coffee appeared.

'The session on international cooperation was very interesting. I thought that the statistics on people trafficking were horrendous. I hadn't realised that old women were trafficked to work as beggars throughout Europe, and the gang bosses who exploit them are ruthless.'

'Good. I hope that you find tomorrow as interesting.'

They drained their coffee.

'It's still early,' said Montanari. 'Would you like to have something to drink here, or would you prefer to go back to our hotel for a nightcap?'

CHAPTER TWENTY

Moretti stood beside his car in the dappled shade of the forest and checked Vanni's message again.

Meet me in the clearing beside the old monastery in thirty minutes.

The commissario tutted. The message had arrived forty minutes ago; the doctor was late. Moretti puffed on the small cigar he had begun as soon as he'd arrived, in the hope that the tobacco would prepare him for the confrontation he was about to have. He'd decided that this was the time to ask the question that had been gnawing at him for two decades. The doctor's delay was causing him more stress than the nicotine was relieving. He strolled off the track and into the dry, rustling leaf litter and listened to the warm breeze coaxing movement from the heavy branches above him. Down the track he heard a vehicle in low gear winding through the trees, and he returned to his car.

Vanni parked parallel to Moretti, stepped out, and flipped up the sunglasses clipped onto his spectacles. He opened the boot of the car and brought out a stout stick.

'Sorry I'm late, Dino, a last-minute walk-in. I thought Ispettore Furlan was on this case.'

'She is, but she's out of town today. Why did you bring me out here?'

'I planned to be here before you so that I could

explain what I showed Ispettore Furlan. Walk with me.'

The two stepped off the path and onto the leaf litter. Vanni used the stick to sweep the leaves away to reveal the scrubby grass and bare soil underneath.

'Ah, here we are,' he said, crouching at the base of an oak tree. He cleared the leaves away for Moretti to see. 'Look. These are Caesar's mushrooms.' He carefully picked one of the reddish orange mushrooms so that the volva at the base of the stem remained attached, and handed it to Moretti.

'You see, its cap is smooth and unmarked, and it has no distinct smell or taste. Try it.'

Moretti cautiously broke off a tiny piece from the rim and touched it to his tongue.

Vanni laughed. 'It's perfectly safe, Dino.' He picked up another. 'This is the size we usually eat.'

He passed Moretti a white egg-shaped sample. 'It's completely covered in a universal veil.'

Moretti turned it in his hand. 'Yes, I recognise these.'

Vanni passed him a small paper bag.

'Pop them both in there and try not to break them. Good. Okay, follow me.'

Vanni led them off along the slope, stopping every so often before going on.

'Here's what I'm looking for,' he announced. He reached into a pocket and brought out two pairs of rubber gloves. 'Put these on, please, Dino. This one is extremely dangerous.'

While Moretti donned the gloves, Vanni gingerly picked up an older, then a younger specimen in his gloved hands.

'Empty your fungi carefully onto the ground. That's it, leave a space between them.'

Vanni placed the mature mushrooms together, and the two bulbs side by side.

'Tell me the difference between them.'

Moretti knelt. 'The older ones are easy to tell apart. The cap of the poisonous one is the colour of an olive tree compared to the orange of the Caesar's, and its stem is white.'

'Excellent. Now the egg stage.'

Moretti peered from one to the other. 'They're really similar. I don't know if I can tell them apart.'

'Shall I tell you?'

'Go on.'

'The base of the Ovolo is more tapered. The base of the Death Cap is broader.'

'My God, so it is, Sergio. It's obvious when you point it out.'

Vanni produced a pocketknife and cut vertically through the eggs.

'You can see clearly the orange colour and broader cap of the edible mushroom, and the whiter phallus-shaped cap of the poisonous one, as well as the difference in the diameter of the bases.'

Moretti stood and pulled his gloves off by the wrist, taking care to turn them inside out.

'They'd no chance, had they?'

Vanni shook his head and stabbed the blade of the knife into the soil to clean it, before wiping it with an alcoholic wet wipe he tore from a sachet.

'None at all. It's a tragedy. But you see how easy it is to confuse the two mushrooms.'

He removed his gloves and put them, along with Moretti's and the other rubbish, into the paper bag.

They walked back towards the cars in silence. The question was burning its way to Moretti's lips, but Vanni spoke first.

'How's Maria?'

Moretti hesitated. He hesitated because his mind was frantically processing both Vanni's motive for asking and his timing. He hesitated because he didn't know how much to reveal, how much to admit, how much Vanni could possibly already know. He hesitated because he truly did not know the answer, but most of all because he felt that the man who had been his best friend no longer had the right to ask such a question.

'She's working away from home at the moment,' he eventually replied.

They walked on a little farther until Moretti's question rose in his mouth like reflux, and he stopped and grabbed the doctor's arm.

'Sergio, why did you leave?'

Vanni put his hand on Moretti's wrist, and his eyes scanned Moretti's. 'Maria,' he said. 'Maria, and my parents.'

Moretti released his grip and rubbed the nape of his neck. 'Maria?'

'Dino, you must know how I felt about her. We went out together.'

A familiar sliver took a fresh direction in Moretti's heart. 'What?'

'We went out together, and I asked her to marry me. Did she never tell you?'

The sliver divided in two, and each cut its own path. He loosened his collar. 'I can't believe this.'

Memories flashed through his consciousness like a microfiche, and he stretched out his arm to support himself on a tree.

Vanni reached out and placed his hand on Moretti's arm.

'Dino, I left because Maria chose you. The day after I asked her, you asked her, and she accepted. Then you did that whirlwind wedding thing.'

Moretti wiped his brow with a handkerchief. 'She never said,' he said hoarsely. 'I never knew. She never said.'

They stood like that while Moretti brought his breathing under control.

'I have another question for you, Sergio,' he said gravely.

'This sounds serious. Let's sit down over there on the ruins.'

They sat on the crumbling, ivy-covered walls, disturbing a basking lizard that rustled into the foliage. Vanni's hands rested on the wall on either side while Moretti bent forward with his elbows on his knees.

'What happened that night?' Moretti spoke without looking up. 'What happened the night your parents died?'

Vanni took off his glasses and laid them on the wall beside him. He rubbed his eyes, looked around him, and breathed in the peacefulness of the forest.

'I was out of the area. On a date with Maria, actually, so that no-one would see us together and report back to you.' He glanced at Moretti, saw no reaction, and continued. 'My father had dementia by that time, and things were difficult for my mother. So, I organised a home help once a week, and I phoned in between those visits to make sure she was coping. There was no reply when I called. I was anxious and couldn't sleep, so I got up, left Maria sleeping, and went to check on them.'

Vanni wiped his mouth.

'As soon as I entered their place, I could see it had been burgled. There were drawers pulled out, cupboards open. It was a mess. I ran upstairs to check on my parents, and they were both dead. There was a pillow over my father's face. They'd both been smothered.'

Vanni's voice cracked.

'My mother looked peaceful, but my father's pyjama trousers were off. I checked him and found semen on him, on his backside and between his legs. He'd been raped. I was disgusted and horrified, and I panicked. I checked Mum as well. There was nothing on her, so I cleaned Dad, inside and out, put new nightclothes on them, and took away all their pyjamas and bedding. I didn't want any trace of that vermin left on his body. That's why you never found a trace of DNA; I removed it all.'

The two men sat with their thoughts in the stillness of the forest. Two brimstone-yellow butterflies duelled in the sunny clearing beside their parked cars, and a collared dove cooed to its mate somewhere behind them.

'I can't begin to think how that must have felt for all of you, Sergio. I can't tell you how bad I feel that I never managed to find him.'

'I'm not sorry that I cleaned everything up, Dino. The truth is, I didn't want him to be found.'

Moretti whipped round to face Vanni. 'What? You can't mean that. Why ever not?'

'I'm deadly serious, Dino. It was bad enough that it happened, but I didn't want the bastard to admit to raping my father during police questioning. It would have been in all the papers and TV. At least this way my father's memory has some dignity. Surely you understand?'

'Understand? Really, Sergio?' Moretti said hotly. 'You did it for your father? What I understand is that it was more about you and how you would look in the local community?'

'Yes,' he admitted. 'That, too.'

Moretti got to his feet, fists clenched. 'You know it's the only case in my career that I've never solved?'

'No, I didn't. I'm sorry, Dino.'

Moretti slapped the back of his fingers into his palm in time.

'I've agonised over this. Lost sleep over it. Argued with Maria about it. I even got the case files down from the attic, for God's sake. It's been a dark cloud over my soul all this time.'

Vanni pulled a small Ziplock bag from his pocket. 'Maybe this will help.'

Moretti snatched the bag.

'What is it?'

'I also cleaned up my mother. These are the scrapings that I took from under her fingernails. The bastard's DNA is in it.'

Moretti stared at the sample bag, and he instantly realised.

'Shit, Sergio. You know who it is.' His jaw dropped. 'You and your damned forensics training.' He stabbed an accusing finger at Vanni. 'You know who the bastard is.'

Vanni picked up his spectacles and put them on. 'Was, Dino. He died in prison a month ago. That's why I felt that I could come back to Cassiatorre.'

CHAPTER TWENTY-ONE

Moretti sat in his car outside the police lab in Maghicchio until the first of the forensic technicians arrived.

'Good morning, Fabio,' he called, locking his car behind him. 'I've a little job for you.'

The younger man smiled, slipped a small black daysack off his shoulder, and waited until Moretti caught up.

'Good morning, Commissario. You know that the forensics service is understaffed, under-resourced—'

'Unappreciated and overworked. I know,' interrupted Moretti, finishing the sentence that had become Fabio's catchphrase.

They shook. Moretti put his hand on Fabio's shoulder.

'Seriously, Dino, we're processing a mountain of stuff at the moment. Some of the cases go back almost a year, and your new boss is chewing us up to get our analysis and reports done.'

Moretti held up the sample bag. 'It's only a quick DNA check.'

Fabio shook his head.

'I can't, Dino, not this time. The older cases must take precedence, I'm afraid. Look, put it through the official channels and I'll try to expedite it.' He walked towards the entrance.

Moretti nodded and smoothed his moustache with a finger and thumb.

'The older cases take precedence,' he repeated, as Fabio's hand grabbed the door handle. 'Well, in that case you'd better take this.'

Fabio turned. 'Dino, I mean it.'

Moretti's expression hardened. 'Me too, Fabio. This is a sample from a crime scene from over twenty years ago.'

'Twenty years ago?'

'The Vanni case.'

Fabio took the small plastic bag. 'I was a rookie. That was my first investigation.' He turned the bag at eye level. 'The place was scrubbed clean. My first case, and I failed.' He studied Moretti's face. 'Where did you get this?'

'Do me a favour, Fabio, run the DNA through the database and message me when you get the results. Oh, and Fabio, keep this between us.'

Another car arrived in the carpark. Fabio slipped the sample into his rucksack, they shook hands and parted.

Moretti was in the Bar Italia twenty minutes later, enjoying his pastry, cappuccino, and Carla's smile. Her son appeared from the door of the storage area behind the counter.

'Good morning, Gigi,' said Moretti. 'How's the fishing?'

Gigi shot a glance to his mother and smiled his lopsided grin. 'Not so good as springtime, Commissario.'

Moretti chuckled.

'Oh, that's a pity.' He reached into his pocket and took out a handful of loose change. 'Here. Maybe you could save up for some new equipment.'

Gigi took the cash. 'Thank you, Commissario.'

Carla looked bemused and shook her head.

Moretti finished and handed over his usual ten. 'Give the change to Gigi for his fishing fund,' he said, as he turned to leave.

After picking up his messages from Alfiero, Moretti stopped at Santoro's office.

'How are you doing, Gennaro?'

'I'm fine, Capo.' He picked up his phone, tapped the screen, and read, 'I walked here this morning, racking up nearly four thousand steps and three flights of stairs. What have you been up to?'

'Oh, I'll tell you later. Settle in and get organised. What delights has CC for you today?'

'Come in and close the door, Capo.'

Moretti sat opposite Gennaro. 'What is it, Gennaro?'

'I've already met with CC.'

'Oh?'

'Yes, my "Return to Work" interview.'

'Ah, how did that go?'

'More like a "why are you back at work?" interview. She asked all about my family, my plans for retirement, and so on. She's giving me the nudge.'

'How do you feel about that?'

'I'm not ready. I did think about things when I was stuck in hospital, but it's too soon. I haven't made any arrangements, but unless I'm assigned a case that I can get my teeth into, I'll have to go. I can't stand filing and sharpening pencils all day.'

'It could be that CC is anxious about your health, Gennaro. The main thing is to stay well and follow your new regime.'

'You don't believe that any more than I do, Capo. She doesn't want me to die in service.'

'That, too.'

Moretti rose and left, stopping next at Cristina's office. He knocked the door and stuck his head in, but the room was empty, so he continued along the corridor to his own room. He sifted through the papers he'd picked up from Alfiero and stopped at the message about the Chinese restaurant Chībǎo. An Na needed to speak with him personally and confidentially. He left the rest of his mail on his desk and made his way there.

An Na was outside cleaning the windows.

'Moretti, come inside.' She stood aside to let him pass and closed the door behind them. 'Straight through to the kitchen.'

Zhao and her grandmother were there, on hands and knees, shining torches under the units.

'Cockroaches,' said An Na.

Moretti looked blankly at her.

'There are cockroaches in the restaurant.' She spoke like she was addressing a child.

'Do you need help in reporting it to the authorities?'

'You don't understand, Moretti. We scrubbed and steam-cleaned the entire restaurant before we opened. There were no cockroaches. Someone brought them here.'

'Please don't be offended, An Na, but how could you know that?'

She fetched a deep plastic tub from the dry goods store and opened the lid. Several dark brown, almost black, insects were slowly crawling over each other inside. She held it up to his face.

'Look, this is the wrong type.'

Moretti's brows furrowed. 'I'm sorry. The wrong type?'

'The wrong type. Someone brought them here.'

She put the lid on the tub and thrust it into his hands. 'Find who did this, Moretti. We trust you.' An Na shooed him out. 'Now go, Moretti, find the culprit. We have to steam-clean the whole kitchen before service.' She unlocked the door and held it while he stepped out. 'And say nothing.' She closed and locked the door behind him, leaving the bemused detective holding the tub of cockroaches.

Moretti decided against taking the insects to Fabio, given his insistence that he check the DNA. Instead, he sighed and carried the box to Vanni's medical practice. A small number – a mother with her little boy; the rest pensioners, about eight in total – sat on matching wooden chairs in the waiting room.

'Commissario Moretti,' the receptionist smiled. 'How can we help today?'

'I have to see Dr Vanni.'

'Of course.' She handed him a clipboard that had a pen through the spring clip. 'Please take a seat and fill in the details, and the doctor will see you shortly.'

'You don't understand,' said Moretti *sotto voce*. 'I must see the doctor urgently. Immediately.'

The other patients now strained to eavesdrop.

The receptionist smiled. 'Of course, Commissario. Just complete the form first.'

Moretti placed the tub on the receptionist's counter. She noticed the movement inside and her smile froze.

'Call Sergio and say that Dino needs to speak to him

right now.'

The receptionist's smile hardened as she rang through.

'Dr Vanni? Dino says he needs to speak to you right now… I don't know, he won't say… He has a box with something moving in it… No, it's on my counter… Right away, thank you, Doctor.'

She hung up and her original smile returned.

'Dr Vanni said you can go through now. First left.'

Moretti ran the gauntlet of tuts and muttering from the pensioners as he took his tub to Vanni's room.

'Good morning, Dino, take a seat and tell me what I can do for you today.'

Moretti placed the tub on Vanni's desk then sat.

'What I'm about to tell you stays between us, okay?'

'Doctor-patient confidentiality.'

'An Na from the Chinese restaurant called and gave me these.'

Vanni opened the lid.

'She said they're the wrong type, and that someone brought them into the restaurant.'

Sergio slipped on a rubber glove and picked up a cockroach.

'*Blatta orientalis*,' he said 'She's right, they are the wrong type. This is the Oriental Cockroach, an outdoor species. They live in cool, damp places. A kitchen in the summer in Italy is the last place they would be. Someone did bring them.'

'Who the hell would do that?'

'Someone who wants her business closed,' said Vanni. He closed the tub and slid it across to Moretti. 'Now, if you'll excuse me, Dino, I have a waiting room full of patients.'

'What about these?'

Vanni sighed and took the box back. 'I'll kill them and dispose of them.'

'Thanks, Sergio.'

Moretti passed through the glaring and tutting patients in the waiting room. The receptionist didn't even look up.

When he returned to the Questura, Alfiero coughed to get his attention and drew his thumb across his throat to warn him as he walked past.

In the middle of Moretti's desk was a large brown envelope with '*See me. CC*' written in thick, red marker pen. He opened the envelope at eye level and peeped inside. Photographs. He emptied them onto his desk.

'Shit.'

The three photographs showed him kissing Carla in Bar Italia. He slid them back into the envelope and trudged along the corridor to CC's office. He knocked, paused, and entered without being told.

'Good morning, CC. You wanted to see me?'

The Vice Questore had copies of the photographs on her desk, too. She put the lid on her pen and slammed it noisily on the desk.

'Did you look at the photographs, Commissario Moretti?'

'Yes, a moment ago.'

'What do you have to say?'

He shrugged. 'My guess is that they arrived from an anonymous source. Likely the same one as before.'

'But do you admit that it's you?'

'Absolutely, CC. They are photographs of me kissing Carla Marino, the owner of Bar Italia.'

'And did this happen while you were on duty, Commissario?'

'CC, it's not what it seems. The photos were taken in Bar Italia on the day of the funeral of Domenico Rosati, in the spring. The bar was inundated with customers, Carla's helper hadn't turned up, and I stepped in to give her a hand. She was grateful and she kissed me.'

'And you see nothing wrong with a married officer kissing a member of the public while on duty, Commissario Moretti?'

'Vice Questore Montanari, for the record, Carla kissed me. No, I don't see anything wrong with it, and anyway, it's personal.'

'I'm advising you that I'm adding the photographs to your file, along with my comments that in my opinion this counts as another infraction.'

'As you wish, Vice Questore.'

'You can go now.'

'Thank you, Vice Questore.'

His phone buzzed before he reached his office.

'Hello, Maria?'

'Dino, can you talk?'

'Give me a moment.' He closed the door behind him and sat at his desk. 'Now I can. How are you?'

'I'm sitting looking at three photographs of you. You and Carla, to be exact. Would you like to explain what's going on while I'm working away from home?'

'Maria, how did you get the photos? Were they posted?'

'No, Dino, they were faxed. They arrived in the general office fax machine. God knows how many people saw them before they got to me. Now, will you tell me what's happening up there?'

'Nothing's happening. The photos were taken months ago, on the day of Domenico's funeral. You already know about this, remember? Bar Italia was suddenly mobbed, Carla couldn't cope, and I did a spell at the till until the crowds cleared.'

'Domenico's funeral?'

'Yes. Remember the media attention? The town was heaving. It was the day that the immigrants escaped from custody.'

Silence.

'Maria?'

'Yes, I remember. The town was very busy. Look, I can't talk right now, I'm due in court.'

'Okay. Take care, Maria.'

'Dino, I… Never mind. I have to go.' She finished the call.

Moretti stood and opened the door onto his little balcony. He took out a small cigar and puffed it as he surveyed the square. Someone out there was trying to end his career.

Behind him, his office door opened. Santoro entered.

'Give me a break, Capo. I'm working with my window open, and your cigar smoke is wafting in and driving me crazy.'

Moretti took a final puff and stubbed it out. 'Sorry, Gennaro, I was thinking about Vice Questore Innocenti.'

CHAPTER TWENTY-TWO

'Vice Questore Innocenti?' Santoro gasped. 'Why were you thinking about him?'

'Have a look at the photos in that envelope. Sent to Montanari and to Maria.'

Santoro flicked through the photographs.

'Nope. Still don't see the connection, Capo.'

'CC received an anonymous letter about me disregarding Innocenti's orders. Then she gets another anonymous letter about the immigrants escaping custody. Now this. Ask yourself, Gennaro, who was in a position to know these details?'

'Me, Cristina, any of the other cops in the Questura. I don't know. Loads of people.'

'Okay, but which of them had a motive? Which of them had a reason?'

Santoro was mute.

'Innocenti was forced to retire early – and he was lucky to get that,' said Moretti. 'So, his pension took a hit, and without a glowing reference he'll have found it difficult or impossible to get a sinecure on a company board somewhere. He was getting a regular payoff from Ricci, and he would have made a small fortune if the housing development had gone ahead.'

'Look, Capo, while I'm stuck at my desk, do you want me to find out where Innocenti is and what he's doing?'

'That might be useful, Gennaro. Thanks.' Santoro slid the photographs across, and Moretti put them back into the envelope. 'Do you want a guess at the anonymous tip-off I got today?'

'Just tell me.'

'That Chen is selling illegal songbirds out of the back of his shop.'

'Are the birds dead or alive?'

'They didn't say. But the immigrants found a mist net on Erpicone's place. So, there could be something in it.' Moretti tapped the envelope on the desk. 'You know Chen better than I do, Gennaro. What's your feeling?'

'I don't think so, Capo. Chen is a refugee who arrived here from Hong Kong. Some of his family is still there, and the rest is in mainland China. He sends back some money every month – at least, he used to. He's had a huge expense in setting up his shop because he insisted on buying it instead of leasing. The money he saved from his market stall barely paid for the shop, but he didn't budget for the legal fees and taxes.'

'How does he manage?'

'He explained to his family that there would be no money for a while, so they went to one of the local Chinese gangs to borrow some cash in the short term. When the gang found out why his family needed the money, they contacted Chen and offered him a loan. Chen refused, because he knows that you don't just have to pay back the money. His business would have been used as a conduit for drugs and even people trafficking.'

'Thanks for the background, Gennaro. It sounds as if Chen runs a legitimate business.'

'I'm sure he does, but if I was able to, I'd go myself and check. Just to be safe.'

'Okay. I'm on my way.'

'Thanks, Capo, and I'll start looking into Innocenti.' The agente returned to his office.

Moretti put the envelope with the photos in his desk drawer and touched his lips with his fingertips. It wasn't that kiss he was thinking of, but the one at the dinner in Carla's house. He slammed the drawer shut and started off for Chen's shop.

When he arrived, he paced the outside wall of the building before he entered.

'Good afternoon, Signor Chen. I'm Commissario Moretti.' He held up his ID. 'I'm a friend of Agente Santoro.'

Chen was neatly dressed in pressed black trousers and a white short-sleeved shirt. His black hair was parted neatly and held in place by a lightly scented hair cream. Nothing unusual, except for the wide, solid black tattoo that circled Chen's left wrist.

'How is Santoro?'

'He's back at work, thanks to you. It was your quick thinking that saved him from suffering something worse.' Moretti looked along the rows of shelving. 'This is quite a place, Signor Chen. It looks like you sell almost everything.'

'You looking for something, Commissario?'

Moretti strolled down one of the narrow aisles. 'I'm not sure. I heard that you sold birds. Small ones. But I don't know how you could display them on these shelves.'

'No birds, Commissario. You want something else?'

Moretti walked to the end of the aisle and came back along the next one, mentally comparing the number of paces inside to the number he had taken outside the building.

'Is this all your stock, Signor Chen?'

'Everything I have you see.'

'Uh-huh.'

He walked down the next aisle to the back of the shop, followed by Chen, and stopped at a door.

'What's through this wall, Signor Chen?'

'Nothing. Just store.'

'I wonder if I could see inside the store. Just in case there's something that catches my eye.'

'Store is just store.'

'I know, but if I could have a quick look.'

Chen muttered something in Chinese, produced a key, and unlocked the door. 'Commissario, look. Just store.'

Moretti felt the wall for the switch and turned on the light. A very dim energy-saving bulb barely lit up the space. Boxes covered in Chinese characters were stacked to the ceiling. At floor level, one box was opened, and plastic bags containing what looked like dried bark had spilled out.

'What's in these bags, Signor Chen?'

'Medicine.'

'I wonder if I could take a look.'

'Just medicine. You ill?'

'I'm fine, but curious. Is this traditional Chinese medicine? I've never seen it before.' He knelt. 'May I?' He picked up one of the plastic bags. 'What does this cure?'

'Depends on qi.'

'I'm sorry, I don't understand.'

'Must balance qi. This one helps.'

'So, if I take this, I can balance my qi?'

'No. Mix with other medicine.'

'Signor Chen, although I don't know very much about Chinese medicine, I've heard that it uses parts of plants and animals.'

'No birds, Commissario.'

'I believe you, but now that I have seen you have Chinese medicine here, I have to tell the customs authority. They will want to come and check for themselves.'

'Everything legal.'

'I'm sure it is, but sometimes what is legal in one country might not be legal in another.'

'No man's land.'

'What?'

'No man's land. Santoro told me.'

As the light from the bulb grew brighter, Moretti could discern more details of the floor as they emerged from the gloom. A small electric stove sat on a wooden box beside a tidy stack of tinned food, but Moretti was interested in the large navy-blue trunk with a rolled-up mat on top of it which was pushed against the far wall. He pointed at it.

'What's in there?'

'Clothes.'

'May I see, please?'

'Just clothes,' repeated Chen, muttering something

else in Chinese. He set aside the mat and unlocked the trunk. It was full of nothing but clothes, as he had said.

It came to Moretti. 'Signor Chen, where do you live?'

The little man's head dropped. 'Live here.'

'In town? In Cassiatorre?'

Chen pointed to the floor. 'Here.'

'But where did you live before you bought this shop?'

'Apartment in big town.'

'In Maghicchio.'

'Yes.'

'If you don't mind me asking, why are you living here then?'

'Sold apartment.'

'Signor Chen, Agente Santoro told me about your family situation.'

Chen eyed him warily.

'Did you have to sell your apartment to pay for this shop?'

'Money for lawyer and damn government.'

Moretti grinned.

'The damn government is right, Signor Chen. Look, I have to let customs know about the Chinese medicine. But I will wait for a week. So, you have seven days, Signor Chen. Seven days to get rid of the Chinese medicine. Okay?'

'One week.'

'One week, Signor Chen. Please get rid of the Chinese medicine. I don't want you to get into trouble.'

'Okay.'

Moretti led the way back into the shop and Chen locked the door behind them.

'Have you met the other Chinese family who've moved into Cassiatorre? They've opened a restaurant.'

'No. No time for talking. Chen must work.'

'But you have to eat, Signor Chen. You must make time to eat.'

'Chen good cook.'

'Well, all I'm saying is that there's another Chinese family here now. Who knows, you might need someone to talk to, or for you. The daughter, An Na, speaks Italian very well.'

Chen acknowledged the comment with a nod.

'Oh, and one last thing,' said Moretti at the threshold. 'Move your sleeping mat, stove, and trunk, and don't tell the customs people that you live here.'

On his way back to the Questura, Moretti saw Cristina and Signor Erpicone in the distance. They were engaged in a conversation that included pointing, nodding, and shrugging. He was glad, as he reached them, to see that there was plenty of smiling involved as well.

'Well, you two, how is the planning going for the Disfida?'

Erpicone was first to reply. 'Very well, Commissario. I was informing the ispettore here about the various Contrada Challenges that coincide with the Disfida. She is particularly interested in the bell tower climb.'

Moretti looked up at the church bell tower and whistled.

'Don't tell me they're including that in this year's programme. Some of the challenges are quaint and harmless, but this one is plain crazy. Who in their right mind would want to free climb to the top of the bell tower?'

'Well, the ispettore here, for one.'

Cristina's mouth gaped. 'I never said that, Signore Erpicone. I only remarked that it would take a great deal of skill to climb the tower with no ropes or climbing aids.'

Erpicone chuckled.

'Don't tell me you're not keen to try it. I heard how you brought up poor Domenico's body single-handed.'

'That was different. I was using ropes, and it wasn't a race.'

Moretti shook his head. 'Why are they even including the climb in this year's programme? It's not like it's always a part.'

Erpicone's eyebrows rose in time with his shoulders.

'Three of the contradas have climbers, and they decided to go ahead. So, there's a vacant side for you, if you want it, Ispettore.'

'I'm not in any of the contradas.'

'That's no impediment. There's nothing in the rules that say individuals can't enter. In fact, there was a precedent in the nineties – young American fellow – he persuaded the officials to let him enter. Told them how he used to climb some huge rock in California without ropes.'

'El Capitan? He climbed El Capitan?'

'I don't remember, Ispettore.'

'How did he get on? Did he manage it?'

'The poor young man fell and died. Shame, he was doing so well. In the lead for most of the climb.'

'How did it happen?'

'He drew the south side.'

Moretti and Cristina exchanged looks.

'The contrada captains draw lots to decide their allotted side of the tower. The south side heats up most, and there's no possibility of shade. Every brick, every hand hold, gets hot. The iron tie bars that stabilise the bell tower get so hot that they'll burn naked skin. He was climbing on a particularly hot day, without gloves, and kept taking his hands off the surface to cool them.'

'So, he was hanging from one hand.'

'Yes,' replied Erpicone. 'For most of the upper half of the climb.'

'He must have been fatigued and lost his grip.'

Moretti dusted off his hands. 'That settles it. It's out of the question.'

Cristina craned her neck to look at the top of the tower. 'Thank you, Commissario, but I'll decide for myself.'

'Hah,' chortled Erpicone. 'I'll leave you two to your discussion. If you do decide to go ahead, Ispettore, you must register with the Disfida committee and be present at the draw. Good luck.'

CHAPTER TWENTY-THREE

The Moka spluttered and hissed on the stove as Moretti collected Maria's mail and stuffed it into a large brown envelope. He wrote out her address and poured a cup of strong black coffee. As he raised it to his lips, a message made his phone buzz on the counter. Fabio. He put the cup down, grabbed the phone, and scrolled down the screen. Although Fabio had left all names out of his report, he confirmed that the sample belonged to a recently deceased drug-using petty criminal and sex offender who had a record of theft, burglary, dealing and supplying drugs, assault, extortion, and rape.

He left the phone and his coffee on the counter, stumbled to the dining table, and sat there propping up his head. For him, it had been an unsolved case. His only one. For Sergio's mother, it must have been torture to have to watch her husband being raped. Moretti did not want to imagine what she'd felt, nor to imagine what Sergio's father endured, but the thoughts, the images, the screams still came. He dug the heels of his hands into his eye sockets until a bright kaleidoscope of shapes appeared in the blackness behind his eyelids. How could he continue to blame Sergio for cleaning the scene when he knew that he might well have done the same? His action was that of a loving son preserving his parents' dignity, not of saving face.

Moretti stretched his arm across towards Maria's seat at the table, remembering how he used to share his feelings with her, and she would listen, hold his hand in hers, and stroke it. He rubbed the back of his hand, but it wasn't the same. He missed her. He depended on her. With a sigh, he stood and returned to the counter to collect his phone. The coffee was cold when he sipped it, so he threw it in the sink and left for town, where his ordeal at the post office was briefer than before but still left him in need of coffee.

'Good morning, ladies,' he said, striding past the three women seated at their usual table. 'I have a news bulletin for you.' He tapped the side of his nose and entered Bar Italia. 'A ristretto before my cappuccino, please, Carla.'

Carla beamed.

'Good morning, Commissario.' She started the two coffees side by side on the bar's vintage coffee machine and spoke over her shoulder. 'A rough night?'

While the coffees brewed, she turned and picked up a pastry in a paper napkin and handed it directly to Moretti before setting two saucers and teaspoons on the counter, turning their handles towards him. The ristretto finished first, and she placed the small cup on its saucer, turning its handle to him.

Moretti watched the fluid efficiency with which Carla moved in her space. She wiped clean the steam jet before frothing the milk, adjusting the rate of the steam and judging the depth of the jet by sound alone to produce the perfect creamy foam whose bubbles were almost invisible to the naked eye. Then, with three taps of the metal jug on the counter and a swirl, she poured the milk into the other cup as she brought it to him, leaving a perfectly smooth surface on the top. Simple precision, not a movement wasted, reaching without looking, in the knowledge that things would be where they ought to be. Such a contrast with his own life. He downed the ristretto in a gulp.

'Just a wretched start to the day,' he replied, biting into the pastry.

Carla glanced up from filling the circular dishwasher basket. He was grateful that she didn't pry. Halfway through both the pastry and the cappuccino, his phone buzzed.

'Moretti.'

'Commissario, I need to see you urgently. It's about Jupiter.'

'I'll be right there, Signor Nardelli.'

He gulped the remaining coffee, wrapped the rest of the pastry in a serviette, and brought out his wallet. 'Thanks, Carla,' he said, taking the change she had already counted.

He paused briefly at the table right outside the door. 'Ladies, an urgent call. I'll update you later.'

*

Nardelli, his son Beppe, and the loosely scattered pack of farm dogs were waiting for Moretti as he drove into the courtyard.

'Good morning, Signori,' called Moretti. 'You said it was urgent.'

'Come inside, Commissario. Beppe has something to show you.'

Moretti followed the others into the farmhouse and to a room where a computer was set up on a table in the corner. Beppe sat in front of the keyboard and clicked the mouse to bring up a full-screen image of a huge white bull.

'It looks like Jupiter,' said Moretti.

'It *is* Jupiter,' fumed Nardelli. 'But look where it was taken.'

Moretti studied the scenery behind the animal. 'I don't recognise it. Is it here on the farm?'

'I don't know where the hell it is, but I can tell you that it's not anywhere near here.'

'So, you think that the people who stole Jupiter took the photo?'

'I'm damn well certain they did. Show him, Beppe.'

Beppe clicked the mouse, and the image shrank to occupy the top of the screen. Writing filled the lower half.

Nardelli pointed at the screen. 'The bastard is selling Jupiter's semen.'

Moretti leaned forward and read the text.

BEGIN A NEW BLOODLINE.
MULTI AWARD WINNING PEDIGREE
CHIANINA BULL SEMEN FOR SALE.
OFFER MUST END SOON. STOCKS LIMITED.
YOUR CHANCE TO BREED A CHAMPION!!!

'He must've taken it before he made him a steer. What are you going to do about it?'

Moretti read the smaller print. There was an email address and the price per straw.

'Okay, here's what will happen. We'll order a sample and get it sent to one of the local farmers. That way we can test it against Jupiter's DNA, in case they are selling something that's not genuine.'

Nardelli stabbed his finger at the screen. 'But there's the bloody email address.'

'Dad, they'll have used a VPN. That email address will be untraceable.'

'I don't need a computer to tell me the address. It's that butcher Buina. He's rubbing salt into the wound. Go and search his computer.'

Moretti wrote down the email address.

'Let's not jump to conclusions, Signor Nardelli. It'll take time to buy the sample and have it tested, but I will visit Buina and find out what he knows.'

'Well, don't stand there, get on with it.'

'Good day to you both.'

Moretti punched a number into his phone as he strode to his car.

'Alfiero, have one of the tech guys meet me at the Buina farm. I'm on my way there now.'

*

Moretti waited just off the main road at the start of the dirt track that led to Buina's farm. When the technician's car arrived, both men got out.

'What do we have, Commissario?'

'Hi Renzo. Maybe something, maybe nothing. Someone is selling bull semen from this email address.' He handed over a slip of paper. 'I want you to check if it could have been sent from Buina's computer.'

'Commissario, if he's using a VPN—'

'I know, I know. I don't think that he's that clued up, but I want to rule him out.'

'Okay.'

A couple of minutes later, Moretti was knocking on Buina's door.

'Coming.' The farmer opened the heavy door. 'Commissario, what can I do for you?'

'Signor Buina, I'm sorry to disturb you, but we're chasing up a lead about someone selling bull semen on the internet.'

'Well, I sell it. You know I do. What's this all about?'

'We're checking everyone. I wondered if my colleague could check your computer.'

A guilty look appeared and vanished on Buina's face.

'And I wonder if you have the correct authority?'

'Signor Buina, I can go and get it, but that will mean confiscating your computer, taking it to the Questura, filling in the paperwork, and putting it into the workflow schedule. How long is that likely to take, Renzo?'

The technician scratched his cheek. 'We're short staffed at present, Commissario. Maybe four or five weeks?'

'Okay, Signor Buina, we'll be back in half an hour, and we'll take your computer away for the next month or so.'

Both police officers turned to go.

'Wait.' He opened the door wide. 'Come in and do it now.'

They followed Buina through to a room at the back of the house. A huge, beige-coloured monitor and keyboard filled most of the space on a table. Buina switched on the power. The monitor lit up, and the drive whirred for over a minute until the home page appeared.

'Please put in your password, Signor Buina,' Renzo said.

'There isn't a password. There's only me that uses it.'

Renzo sat at the keyboard and checked the directories. 'No sign of that email address, and there's no VPN.' He checked the internet search history.

'Hey, that's private!' Buina exclaimed.

'I've seen a lot worse, Signor Buina,' said Renzo. 'Nothing here, Commissario.'

'Okay. Thank you, Signor Buina. Let's go, Renzo.'

'A moment, Commissario. Signor Buina, since you were kind enough to let us examine your computer, would you like me to clean it up a bit? It'll make it faster.'

The farmer hesitated.

'You won't lose anything, I'll only tidy things up.'

'Alright, then.'

Renzo ran the disk cleaning programme. 'Your computer will switch itself off. When it restarts, you should notice a difference.'

'Thanks.'

Moretti led the way to the door. 'Thank you once again, Signor Buina.'

As they walked to their cars, Buina watched them from a window.

'What did you find on his computer, Renzo? Porn?'

The technician smiled. 'No porn, Commissario. The old guy has been searching on sites for Philippine brides.'

They shook hands and left for their separate cars. Renzo drove off while Moretti made a phone call.

'Signor Erpicone? Commissario Moretti. I wonder if I could ask for your help… No, nothing like that, I just need to use your address for a package… Entirely legal… In the next day or so… You can let me know when it arrives. Thank you.'

*

Cristina found the address of the Disfida committee in one of the narrow side streets that led up to the Castello. Like many of the former wine and oil cellars in the old part of Cassiatorre, it had been used to store old furniture and junk before being converted into a car garage. Then, as modern cars became too wide to squeeze through the narrow double-door entrance, it had been re-purposed as a meeting room and indoor entertainment area.

She used the side of her fist to bang on the multi-layered flaky paint.

'Come in.'

She turned the circular handle and pushed the door open.

'Ispettore,' roared a familiar voice. 'Come in and take a seat.'

Cristina smiled.

'Tell me, Corrado, are you involved in everything in Cassiatorre?'

Corrado stood and held out his large, hairy paw and they shook.

'Can I offer you anything, Ispettore? Water, coffee, wine?' He grinned, his mouth ringed by his permanent black stubble. 'Grappa?'

Cristina laughed as she sat at the opposite side of the refectory table from Corrado and the two men flanking him.

'Not this time, Corrado.'

Corrado resumed his seat. 'Mauro, Enzo, this is Ispettore Furlan. What can we do for you today?'

'I'd like to enrol in the bell tower climb.'

Corrado's smile vanished.

'I know you can climb, Ispettore. I was there when you brought up Domenico's body, but this is different. You won't have ropes or any climbing aids.'

'Thanks, Corrado, but I've done my fair share of free climbing. I think I should manage it.'

'Enzo.'

Enzo opened a ring binder full of plastic pockets, pulled out two sheets of paper, and slid them across to Cristina.

'Fill in both forms please, Ispettore,' he said.

'Two forms?'

'Yes, Ispettore, 'said Corrado. 'One is the enrolment form; the second one is a disclaimer in case you fall. Fill your blood type in the box at the top.'

CHAPTER TWENTY-FOUR

Moretti saw the people hurrying to the square from several hundred metres away. By the time he parked his car, there was a crowd encircling the enormous vehicle that was parked at the foot of the slope. All traffic was stopped, and the Municipal Police were already moving the onlookers off the road so that it could pass. But some drivers were equally curious, leaning out of their car windows or stepping outside, phones raised high, to snap photos.

The centre of the throng's attention was a huge, white, combined motorhome and horse transporter, painted like a circus truck with an archer, bow drawn to the limit, astride a coiling red fire-breathing dragon surrounded by Chinese characters. Every light on the truck was on, and an array of six powerful fog lamps on top of the cab flashed in time with all the indicators. Legs apart on the roof of the cab stood a slim figure, holding aloft a bow in one hand and a quiver of arrows in the other. Dressed in a yellow silk tracksuit with the same dragon design on the back, he waved and bowed to the people below him. In a sliver of space between the truck and the pressing crowd, his translator used a megaphone to address everyone.

'Thank you. Thank you for your welcome. Champion horseback archer Zou Leng is honoured to be here to represent the proud and ancient contrada of Girolamo in the Disfida.'

A gasp arose from the audience, and Moretti saw members of the other contradas exchanging astonished, shocked, or angry expressions, and gathering in twos and threes that dispersed out to the edges then escaped into the square only to join again in a noisy cluster whose mood settled on being irate. Since the Municipal Police were too busy with traffic to notice, and the huddle whose numbers had grown to almost twenty stood between him and the Questura, Moretti approached them himself.

When they saw him, they raised a thicket of fists and a chorus of voices in anger as they surrounded him like a team of protesting footballers around a referee.

'Commissario, you have to do something.'

'It's not fair.'

'It's illegal.'

Moretti waved both hands, palms down, to silence them.

'Gentlemen, let's move over there so that I don't have to compete with a megaphone.' He led them to the side of the square opposite the Questura. 'Now, one at a time, what's the problem?' He pointed. 'You start.'

'It's him,' replied the man. 'The champion archer. It's against the rules.'

Moretti pointed at another. 'Now you.'

'He's not even from here, never mind the contrada.'

'And you.'

'There's too much at stake. He must be disqualified.'

'Alright,' said Moretti. 'Now, I'm no authority on the Disfida and will have to check with someone like Ettore Erpicone, but what I can say is that Signor Leng representing the Girolamo contrada is not illegal.' He held up his hands to silence the protesting voices. 'It might not be fair, but no, I don't have to do anything. It's not a police matter. The four contradas must sort it out amongst yourselves. And as for the "too much at stake" comment, I hope that doesn't refer to bets being laid on the outcome of the competition.' He held the gaze of the one who had said it. 'Because that *would* be illegal, and I would have to do something about it.'

'We can boycott it then,' called someone from the back.

'That is always an option if you wish, but remember, the Disfida is a great tourist attraction. The whole reason for having it was to bring tourists into the town. Do you really want to risk losing all the income, all the jobs they provide?'

Heads went down and, amid grumbling and mumbled threats, the men broke up into disgruntled pairs and trios and shuffled off. At the same time, Zou Leng descended from the top of the truck, the announcement stopped, the large crowd dispersed, and the two occupants of the truck got on board, switched off the lights, and drove away.

Moretti felt the urgent need of caffeine and turned back down the slope to Bar Italia.

'Well, Commissario. What a disgraceful display that was.' Rosalia wore her indignation like a nun's habit.

Moretti managed a smile. 'Signora Seccavigne?'

Rosalia's hand waggled at the end of her extended arm, pointing to where the truck had parked.

'That man. Cavorting on top of his truck.'

'I think he was happy to be here, and he was advertising the fact that he is to be the horse archer for the Girolamo contrada.'

She sipped some water. 'He was advertising a lot more than that, Commissario. His silk trousers were very explicit.'

Moretti bit the inside of his cheek.

'I'm sorry, Signora Seccavigne, what exactly was the disgraceful display? The truck holding up the traffic? Leng's cavorting? Or the cut of his silk trousers?'

Donatella looked away, and Fausta covered the lower half of her face with her fan.

'Well, all of it.' Rosalia took another sip of water. 'The trousers especially.'

'All I can say, Signora Seccavigne, is you have remarkable eyesight – far better than mine. But I'll be sure to take your concerns up with Signor Leng. I'll make him realise that things are different here. He can't go about upsetting respectable women, waving his quiver around like that. You leave it to me. Now, if you'll excuse me…'

'You said you were going to update us on Signor Chen, Commissario.'

'Ah yes. Thank you, Signora Racano.' He leaned forward and lowered his voice. 'All I have to report is that Signor Chen's shop is one of the cleanest I've ever seen. Honestly. And his prices are very competitive. I'm afraid that once people get to know, the best bargains will be snapped up.' He looked up and down the street and whispered, 'If I were you, I'd get along there now. You know, before the rush.' He straightened up and tapped the side of his nose. 'Ladies.'

Their three heads came together as he left, and he heard the chorus of their whispering.

'A coffee, please, Carla.'

'Right away.' She turned to the machine and looked over her shoulder. 'Something to eat? Pastry? A slice of pizza?'

'Just the coffee, thanks.'

'The ladies were impressed by the truck then.'

Moretti grinned. 'More than the other contrada members were.' He picked up the small cup and sipped the strong hot coffee. 'No doubt Leng will be the subject of a formal complaint. Gennaro can deal with it.'

Carla tutted, shook her head, and smiled.

Moretti placed a coin on the counter and passed the empty table where the women had been. He stopped to light a small cigar and strolled up the slope of the square. An Na was crossing ahead of him. She saw him and waved, and an icy hand of guilt grabbed his insides. He waved back and she turned towards him.

'Hello, Moretti. Did you see Leng arrive?'

'I think most of the town saw him. He's quite the showman. Have you heard of him before?'

'No, but I'll get to meet him tonight. We're hosting a dinner in his honour. There's a special presentation, too. The mayor and the captains from the four contradas have been invited. Would you like me to reserve a table for you?'

'Have the other contradas accepted? I got the feeling that they weren't too pleased about Leng taking part.'

'They all accepted, but I'll contact them to confirm. I

hope that they can come, but if not, we have plenty of interest from the tourists.'

'In that case, I'd love to come. Save me the same table as before.'

'For one?'

'For one.'

'I'll see you tonight, then.'

She began to walk away, but Moretti stopped her.

'Signorina Cao, I haven't forgotten about your grandmother's trunk. I'm still looking for it. I haven't given up.'

'I know. You are a busy man and have other crimes to solve. But I know you will find it – I trust you, Moretti.'

He watched her walk off, leaving the burden of her trust upon his shoulders.

*

That evening Moretti walked past the small queue of hopefuls without reservations who waited outside the restaurant. Once inside he could see that it was full, with tables pushed together to seat a dozen or so, including Mayor Donati, CC Montanari, Cristina, the captains and representatives of the four contradas, Leng, his translator, and his driver.

He waited at the counter until An Na saw him and motioned him forward.

'Busy tonight.'

'Full to bursting.' She indicated his table. 'I hope you don't mind sharing, but we had to seat two singles together.'

Sitting at the corner table with his back towards him was Sergio Vanni. Moretti dismissed his first impulse.

'No, of course not. I quite understand.'

'Good. Thank you. Please take your seat.'

She busied away to the kitchen.

'Good evening, Sergio. It seems we're to be dinner companions tonight.'

Vanni beamed. 'Dino, good to see you. Please sit. Or would you prefer this side?'

Moretti sat with his back to the wall. 'Here's fine.'

Vanni passed him a menu.

'They've cut the menu, but I see that they have a

couple of specials. I think I'll try the straw mushrooms. What about you, Dino?'

'I had the Char Siu pork the last time I was here. I'll go for that again.'

Achille Donati, the Mayor, tapped a knife against a glass, and the noisy restaurant fell almost silent.

'Ladies and gentlemen, it gives me great pleasure to introduce Signor Leng, who will represent the Girolamo contrada in the forthcoming Disfida. Leng has newly arrived from Hungary, where he was runner-up in an international competition.' He turned to Leng. 'I'm certain that you will find our archers here equally tough competition.'

Leng and his translator leaned close to each other, and Leng smiled and nodded in reply. Conversation bubbled up again at the other tables, so Mayor Donati tapped his glass again.

'I know that you are all keen to enjoy this wonderful feast, but before we begin I have one other task to perform.' He nodded in the direction of the kitchen, and An Na brought over an ornately tooled and decorated saddle which she presented to Leng. 'This magnificent saddle arrived today with the instruction that it was to be used in the Disfida. So, Signor Leng, we wish you every success.'

Donati began the applause that filled the restaurant until Leng's translator stood.

'Champion Leng is thrilled at the reception he has had and looks forward to practising hard on the Disfida course and bringing victory to the Girolamo contrada. He wishes to thank you all for coming and wishes you a good appetite.'

He sat back to more applause and the sound of the first bowls arriving at the tables. A local teenager, dressed in black, helped An Na bring food and drink first to the top table then all the others. Vanni and Moretti were among the last to be served. They ate the clear chicken and vegetable soup without speaking until Moretti noticed the main courses being brought out behind Vanni.

'There's the mushroom dish.'

The doctor twisted in his chair. 'Looks delicious.' He turned back and finished his soup. A few minutes later their bowls were cleared away and the main courses arrived. Moretti began immediately, while Vanni examined his plate then leapt to his feet.

'Stop eating!' he shouted. 'Everyone, stop eating. Now.'

The room fell silent, and everyone stared at him.

'Raise your hand if you have eaten the mushrooms. Even a taste. DO IT.'

Several hands went up, including that of Vice Questore Montanari.

'Dino, call emergency services, tell them we need three ambulances, and then call the hospital and tell them to get ready to accept eight patients. I suspect Amanita poisoning.'

Vanni left the stunned detective to make the calls while he dashed into the kitchen. An Na followed him.

'Show me the mushrooms that were used for this dish.'

An Na translated and her father produced a carton of fresh mushrooms.

'Where are the others?'

His question needed no translation. Zhao fetched the food waste bin.

Vanni used chopsticks to rummage through it. 'Here we are. Give me a container please.'

CHAPTER TWENTY-FIVE

The townsfolk had already mown and fenced off the large field which served as the overflow carpark for the weekly market. Work parties were now assembling the second of the tiered metal bleachers – one for each contrada, each with its own stairway access – along one long side of the field. On the opposite side, which adjoined woodland, the perimeter fence of scaffolding poles was higher and lined with thin sheets of plywood, held in place by plastic ties. Three large cylindrical hay bales were positioned along this side – one in the middle, face-on to the bleachers opposite; the other two angled about forty-five degrees left and right of centre. Black and white roundels were fixed to the faces of the hay bales.

The grassy strip between the bleachers and the hay bales had received particular attention. This was the track along which the horseback archers would gallop and loose their arrows at the targets. Here, the grass had been inspected and combed of discarded plastic or metal and, as an additional precaution, covered in a thick layer of sandy soil that had been levelled smooth and compacted by the blade and bucket of a track excavator.

At one of the narrow ends of the field, a makeshift ticket box had been set up under a gazebo. At the far side, drawing a respectful but attentive crowd, Leng and his two companions swayed silently, slowly, and rhythmically to the sound of recorded flute music floating from the open door of their huge truck, following a familiar choreography in perfect synchrony. In front of the watching adults, a handful of small children copied the trio, adding their own pirouettes and variations of the men's Tai Chi moves, to the delight of their parents and grandparents.

In the remaining area of the field, between the bleachers and the main carpark, visiting traders set up a medieval village of tents and ferrying trestles, rectangular straw bales, and goods from their vehicles in the carpark.

In a normal year, the conversation would have been about which rider was favourite to win the Disfida, with secret bets being placed with impromptu bookmakers offering varying odds, or between friends or contrada rivals. But this was not a normal year. Leng's arrival had changed everything.

In a normal year, locals and tourists alike would be swarming like ants around the tented village, even as it was being erected, to discover what regional edible treats would be on offer.

This year, all conversation was about the poisoning in the Chinese restaurant.

So, too, in Moretti's office, where he sat facing Cristina and Gennaro.

'Are you both sure that you're alright?' Gennaro asked.

'I'm fine,' replied Moretti. 'And so is everyone else, I believe, thanks to Sergio's quick reactions. You went with CC to the hospital, Cristina. How is she?'

'Because we were at the top table, CC was one of the first to be served. So, unlike some of the others who put their hands up, she had eaten some of the mushrooms. I don't know how many of them were the poisonous ones, but she had her stomach pumped and a full plasma transfusion as a precaution. I think she'll be off the rest of the week.'

Moretti leaned forward with his elbows on the desk and tucked his thumbs under his chin.

'That gives us some time to try to find out who's behind it, how they did it, and why.'

'You don't think that someone made a mistake, Capo?'

'No, Gennaro. The mushrooms were supplied by Beppe Nardelli, but a mushroom producer wouldn't supply poisonous mushrooms, and he's hardly likely to make a mistake in identification. I think it was deliberate, but the culprit is elsewhere.'

'If it's a question of motive,' added Cristina, 'then any of the other contradas, or anyone who's staked a lot on their rider winning. Who knows, it might have been an attempt to poison Leng, and the other diners were merely collateral damage.'

'I'm not convinced, Cristina,' said Moretti, smoothing his moustache. 'How would anyone know what the menu was, and how could they be certain that Leng would choose the mushrooms? It's too haphazard, but I'll go and see Beppe – if only to rule him out.'

'Do you mind if I come, too?'

'Not at all. We'll go in your car.'

'That's right,' whined Gennaro. 'Leave the stroke victim on his own to run the show.'

On the way to her car, Cristina said, 'It's been odd not working together.'

Moretti shrugged. 'I'm all for accountability, but I've yet to see any evidence of increased efficiency. I also think that staff morale suffers.'

They set off.

'Here's a perfect example. We're going to interview someone, and there's an opportunity to catch up, to find out how the other person is feeling or coping with the job – time that would otherwise be wasted as merely travelling. You haven't had a chance yet to tell me about your Florence weekend with CC.'

'There's not that much to tell.'

'Well, before you do, I have a question for you.'

'What is it?'

'It might sound trivial, but it's been bothering me.'

'Sounds intriguing. What is it?'

'Did you know that Gennaro had a cat?'

She laughed. 'Poirot? Yes, of course. Don't tell me you didn't.'

Moretti slapped his knees. 'No, I didn't, although

everyone else seems to.' He exhaled loudly. 'Right, you'd better tell me about Florence, then.'

'I met lots of senior ranking officers and attended seminars.'

'Oh?'

'And I went with CC and some of them for a meal on the Saturday night.'

'Interesting.'

'Not really. The men went off to a club, leaving us alone. CC asked me if I wanted to go somewhere for a drink, but I reminded her that I was driving the next day, so we went back to the hotel and had an early night.'

'How did you feel about the Vice Questore of Police asking you to have a drink with her?'

'Awkward, embarrassed, angry, and like I was committing career suicide by refusing.'

'How was she the next morning?'

'Fine. Business-like. Like nothing had happened.'

Moretti opened his mouth to speak.

'Because nothing had happened,' Cristina added firmly. 'Now, do I turn left or right down here?'

She parked outside the barn, and Beppe came out to meet them and looked up at Cristina.

'Who's this? Reinforcements?'

'Beppe, this is Ispettore Furlan. We'd like to ask you about—'

Beppe interrupted him, 'You want to ask if I sold poisonous mushrooms to the Chinese. Well, the answer is no.'

'But you took a tray of mushrooms to the restaurant.'

'Yes.'

'And you picked them yourself and delivered them personally?'

Beppe shifted his weight enough for Moretti to notice. 'Yes, of course.'

'Who did you hand them to?'

'I carried them straight into the kitchen and left them on the counter.'

'Did you check them before you left?'

'I checked them here.'

'But not again at the restaurant?'

'No, why would I?'

'And you went directly from here to the restaurant?'

Beppe licked his lips. 'I had other deliveries to do first.'

'In Maghicchio?'

'Yes.'

'All to restaurants? Or did you manage to fit in a visit to Bea?'

Beppe looked at his feet. 'Fine, I dropped in to see my girlfriend. There's no law against it.'

'Where were the mushrooms while you were with Bea?'

'In the back of the van.'

'How long for?'

'Fifteen minutes – twenty at most.'

'Can we see the van, please?'

'It's in the shade round the side of the barn.'

The three walked around the corner, and a white van sat close to the wall.

'The window is open.'

'Everyone leaves their windows open in the summer.'

'True, but the fact that your van window is open means that anyone could gain access. Was the window open when you visited Bea?'

Beppe shrugged. 'I suppose so.'

Moretti turned to Cristina. 'That's the how. Now we need to figure out the who and the why.'

'Are you going to arrest me?'

'Not this time, Beppe, but if I see your van unattended with its window down again, I'll reconsider. Come on, Ispettore.'

By the time they reached Cassiatorre and parked the car, the four sets of bleachers were built, and the judges' table was laid out and lined on one side with tall, straight-backed chairs. Two men were testing the microphones hooked up to the large PA speakers at the ends of the table. Most of the tents of the medieval village were fully decorated with their scalloped trim. Their owners, wearing sandals and dressed in tabards or hessian shifts belted at the waist, had begun to sell their wares to curious tourists.

As if they had made a coordinated effort, a tent selling artisan beer and its immediate neighbour selling huge panini of porchetta, were already doing steady business.

Two fidgety lines of customers waited to be served, while others sat at trestle tables or more casually on hay bales to enjoy their food and drink. Some children whined, tormented, and dragged their parents to the tents selling brightly coloured foam spirals and batons, lollipops the size of saucers, candy floss and nut brittle, while others – in all probability fuelled by the sugar and colouring agents of the confectionery – ran amok brandishing plastic swords and spears. A bold few risked the castigation of the Disfida organisers by running in turn along the edge of the horse track, firing arrows tipped with rubber suckers at the roundels from their toy bows.

Above the crowds, stilt walkers carefully picked their way, stopping to be photographed or interacting with the jugglers and fire eaters who were tossing everything from hoops to Indian clubs, coloured balls or flaming brands between them.

The evening Angelus bell struck in the bell tower.

'The draw for the practice heats and the Disfida is about to take place,' said Cristina. 'Let's go and hear the order.'

They merged into the crowd that was slowly making its way to the bleachers.

The judges and contrada officials, dressed in medieval costumes, had already taken their seats along the table. Their leader tapped the microphone in his hand until the sound engineer was satisfied that the squelching feedback had stopped, and the volume was sufficient to convey the announcements to all those interred in the cemetery.

To a fanfare of trumpets, the beating of drums, and the waving of flags, a procession entered the field. The four archers sat on their horses, which were led by the contrada squires. Horses, archers, squires, the flag-wavers, and the musicians all wore the brightly coloured medieval costumes that represented their contradas.

The procession stopped in front of the judges' table, and the leading judge gave them a high decibel welcome. Three horses stood still, but Leng's horse – a sleek black creature not much bigger than a pony – stepped back and tossed its head, almost unseating its rider. Leng and his driver, in the role of contrada squire, only just managed between them to bring the animal under control, although its ears were pinned back, and its eyes were showing white. Leng leaned over the horse's neck and spoke to it. The leading judge signalled to the sound engineer to drop the volume.

After introducing those seated beside him at the table and expressing gratitude to all the sponsors, he announced the order.

'For the practice heats to be held on Saturday, the order will be as follows. First to run will be Bonaventura, then Lucia, followed by Girolamo, and finally Annunziata.'

The crowd applauded, cheered, and whistled.

'For the Disfida on Sunday, the order will be…' He paused while a small girl who was standing on the table put her hand deep into a black bag and pulled out a green and orange ball. 'Lucia.'

Cheering from the far-right bleachers.

The girl produced a blue and white ball. 'Annunziata.'

The crowd to the left of the judges table cheered.

A black and white ball was next. 'Bonaventura.'

Roars from the right of the table.

The girl finally produced a red and gold ball. 'And that means that Girolamo runs last.'

Now the far-left crowd joined the general applause and cheering.

The lead judge waited until the cheering had quietened down before announcing, 'Now we come to tomorrow's bell tower climb. I will ask the contrada captains, in the same order as the Disfida final, which side of the bell tower they wish to choose for their climbers. Lucia captain?'

'North.'

'Annunziata would have been next, but they do not have a climber this year, so I'll ask the Bonaventura captain.'

'East.'

'Girolamo?'

'West.'

'So that leaves the south wall for our independent climber, one of our local detectives, Ispettore Cristina Furlan.'

CHAPTER TWENTY-SIX

Moretti had left Bar Italia and was smoothing his moustache when his phone buzzed in his pocket.

'Moretti.'

'Dino, it's Dante. Where are you?'

'Just crossing to the square, why?'

'Can you come to the bank instead? There's a problem with your account.'

'I'll be right there.'

Moretti changed direction and arrived at the bank a couple of minutes later. He pressed the button and waited until a teller let him through the revolving glass door.

'Go straight through, Commissario.'

Moretti knocked on the door of the bank manager's office.

'Come in, Dino.'

The men shook and sat on opposite sides of the empty desk.

'You said there was a problem with my account. Has someone emptied it?'

Dante took a sheet of paper from the drawer and slid it across the table. 'Quite the opposite. There's been a deposit of twenty thousand euros.'

Moretti looked at the account total and rubbed the nape of his neck. 'I don't understand, Dante. How is that possible? Do you know where it came from?'

The bank manager half shrugged.

'How is simple. All anyone needs is your bank account details, and they are all too easy to discover. What do you do with your monthly statements?'

Moretti raised his brows. 'I don't usually pay any attention to them.'

'So, what do you do with them?'

'Put them out with the recycling, I suppose.'

Dante shook his head.

'Where the transfer came from is more difficult. The transaction was flagged as irregular by our security systems. I get a notification when it happens. Usually there's a simple explanation, but I always call in the customer to speak with them. This one is unusual because the sender has used an offshore electronic source that will be difficult if not impossible to trace. Which brings me to why. Why would someone send twenty thousand euros to your account, Dino?'

'I'm at a complete loss, Dante. I have no idea who or why. You said this sort of thing happens from time to time. What are the usual reasons?'

Dante puffed out his cheeks, exhaled, and counted on the fingers of his left hand.

'An inheritance, a gift, a windfall, a tax rebate, a refund.' He ran out of fingers. 'A bribe.'

'That's what I feared,' groaned Moretti. 'Can you send it back?'

'Possibly, but it might not be prudent to do so.'

'How can that be?'

'Let's say that you send the money back, then the original sender cancels the transfer, and the money is withdrawn from your account. You'd be out of pocket to the tune of twenty thousand euros.'

'So, what do you suggest?'

'Two things. First, that we set up another account and you put the money in there so that it is separate from your money. That way, you can say if asked that you had no intention of keeping it.'

'Then let's do that right way.'

'I'll do it from my office terminal. The tellers don't need to know.'

'What's the second thing?'

'That you switch to paperless banking so that you don't have your account details in the trash where anyone can find them.'

On the walk back to the Questura, Moretti called his wife. 'Maria, Dino. Can you speak?'

'Yes, briefly. I'm due in court shortly. What is it?'

'Did you send money to my account?'

'Your personal account? No. I still send money to our joint account for household expenses, but not to your personal account. Why? What's happened?'

'Twenty thousand has appeared from an offshore account. Dante called me this morning.'

'Oh, God. This is serious, Dino. You must get the money out of your account right away.'

'It's already taken care of. Dante personally transferred it into a suspense account.'

'Good. You need to report it, too.'

'I can't. Montanari is off sick until the beginning of the week.'

'Well, send her an email or, failing that, write down your version of events, get it witnessed, and put it in her office.'

'Okay, I will. Thanks.'

'Who could have done it?'

'Maria, I'm at a total loss. Someone who could afford twenty grand.'

'Dino, sorry to cut you short, but I really do need to get to court. Call me later if you need to. Bye.'

'Bye, Maria.'

Moretti entered the Questura and collected his mail and messages from the desk.

'She's back,' said Alfiero without looking up.

'CC? How come?'

The desk officer shrugged.

'Thanks, Alfiero.'

Moretti stopped at his office and rifled through his mail before dropping it on the desk, sighing, and rubbing his eyes and face. He smoothed his moustache and left for Vice Questore Montanari's office. He knocked and waited outside.

'Come.'

Moretti stood in front of the Vice Questore's desk and waited until she looked up from her screen. 'Well?'

'Welcome back, CC. I hope you're feeling better. We thought that you were coming back on Monday.'

'I'm feeling fine. I hardly ingested any mushroom, and I think I must have avoided the poisonous one, but I'm sure you aren't here to wish me well.'

'I want to alert you to something.'

'Alert me to what?'

'There's been a sum of money transferred to my bank account.'

Montanari pushed her chair back. 'How much of a sum?'

'Twenty thousand euros.'

'Joint or personal account?'

'Personal.'

'I take it you weren't expecting it?'

'No.'

'It'll have to be investigated, Commissario.'

'I know. It's been taken out of my account and put in a separate account while the bank tries to track down the source.'

'Anti-corruption will want to carry out their own investigation.'

'I understand.'

'Will they find anything else, Commissario Moretti?'

'No, Vice Questore.'

'Sure?'

'Certain.'

'That will be all then.'

'Vice Questore.'

He returned to his office, reached into his jacket pocket for a cigar, and found it empty. He rummaged in a desk drawer. Success. He stepped out onto his small balcony and lit up while scanning the square for inspiration. His mind cast for ideas like an angler in a river, until a knock at the office door called him back inside.

'What's up, Capo?' Gennaro asked.

'What do you mean?'

Gennaro tilted his head and smiled. 'Capo, I don't

have to be a detective to know that you only come out onto your balcony to smoke when something is bothering you.'

'Sit down, Gennaro. Someone put twenty thousand euros in my bank account from an offshore account.'

Santoro's eyes widened, but he remained silent.

'I don't know how or who. Dante called me, and he's taken it out and put it in a separate account. I told Montanari, and she said she'll have to get internal affairs to investigate.'

'What can I do, Capo?'

'Nothing, Gennaro, but thanks. I guess we must wait. Whoever put it there did it for a reason, and they'll follow it up with something – a blackmail threat, reporting me to CC… I don't know. But it didn't come from my fairy godmother.'

Gennaro was about to speak when the desk phone rang.

'Hi Alfiero, what is it?'

'A call from Buina.'

'Put him through… Signor Buina, it's Moretti.'

'Moretti, Hercules is dead. He's been murdered.'

'I'll come at once.'

*

The large doors of the cowshed were open, framing Buina who stood facing inside. Moretti parked close to him and got out.

Buina's head was slumped forward almost on his chest, his arms hung limply at his sides. The huge beast in its pen lay on the concrete floor, its left side horribly distended, its normal muscular contours seemingly enclosed in a dirigible.

'Look at him, Commissario,' Buina said without looking up. 'What a magnificent animal. The best I ever had.'

'What do you suspect happened?'

'Oh, I know exactly what's happened, Commissario. He died of bloat.'

'Bloat? Please excuse my ignorance, but what is that?'

'Look how distended his side is. That's caused by a build-up of gas that couldn't escape from his rumen. The pressure builds up so much that it prevents the lungs from expanding properly. The poor animal eventually suffocated.'

'Where does the gas come from?'

'All ruminants produce gas; it's normal. Millions of microbes in the rumen digest the food they eat, and the gas is released as part of that process. That's why ruminants belch all the time. It's a greenhouse gas and one of the reasons that environmentalists are trying to cut down on animal farming.'

'Well, if it's a natural process, how did Hercules die?'

'If the animal eats fresh, wet, high protein material, it doesn't need to produce as much saliva to swallow it. So, the soapy sugars and proteins released by microbes form a foam that prevents the gas bubbles joining together, and the animal swells up or bloats. With drier food, the animal produces more saliva, and there's a chemical called mucin in it that coats the food before it enters the rumen. Mucin prevents the build-up of foam, so the gas bubbles join together to form pockets of gas large enough to be belched out.'

'Couldn't anything be done?'

'Well, if I had found him sooner, I could've used a trocar.'

Moretti inhaled to speak, but Buina continued, 'It's a sharp knife with a tube in the middle. You cut through the skin and muscle as far as the rumen and let the gas out.'

'And there's no way this could have happened by accident?'

Buina turned to glare at Moretti.

'I know exactly what he eats. Look at his manger – there's stuff there that he didn't get from me.' He pointed at uneaten green material. 'That's clover and fresh alfalfa. I don't feed him that.'

'Signor Buina, have you checked your CCTV?'

'No. I've been here with Hercules.'

'Do you mind if we do that now?'

Buina forced himself to leave and went with Moretti to the farmhouse. They looked at the previous night's recording. A wandering fox and urinating farm dog had triggered the motion sensor, but there was also a recording of a man trying the door. He was carrying a sack and dressed in jeans, his face obscured by a scarf and hooded top.

'That's the culprit,' said Moretti, noting the time on the screen. 'How could he get in to feed the stuff to Hercules?'

'He must've climbed in at the side.'

'Let's look.'

The two men crossed the courtyard to the side of the cowshed. A pallet was propped against the wall, halfway along.

'That's how he got in.'

'Nardelli,' exclaimed Buina. 'Has to be.'

'Let's not jump to conclusions, Signor Buina,' said Moretti, taking out his phone. 'I'll get a forensics team down here, so don't touch anything. I'll also need a copy of that recording, and you need to call the vet to confirm your diagnosis.'

'Confirm my diagnosis? He's the size of a small bloody planet.'

'Call the vet anyway, please,' insisted Moretti. 'And stay away from the cowshed.'

*

Moretti drove directly to Nardelli's farm and parked in the shade of the barn. The dogs alerted the farmer to his arrival, and he emerged from the farmhouse.

'Any news?'

'Good morning, Signor Nardelli. The semen sample has arrived, and it's being tested against Jupiter's sample as we speak. I'll update you further when we get the results.'

'Any closer to finding out who's behind it?'

'Our investigations are ongoing.'

Nardelli folded his arms. 'So, if you've nothing new to tell me, why are you here?'

'I was wondering about what you fed Jupiter.'

Nardelli gawped at the detective. 'What?'

'Do you feed him fresh material?'

'I told you all this before. We feed him a mixture of fodder and grains.' He spat on the ground. 'Or at least, that's what we fed him when he was a stud bull. Now we've switched his diet to put on fat before we sell him for slaughter.'

'The fodder – I think you told me that you grow it all here on the farm?'

'Of course. Why would I trust anyone else?'

'Quite. And I think you said that it included alfalfa?'

'Yes, we add dried alfalfa as part of the mixture. Look, what's this all about?'

'Signor Buina's bull Hercules died of bloat last night. He found fresh clover and alfalfa in his manger.'

'And you think I did it?' Nardelli raged. 'I've seen what bloat can do to an animal It's a slow, horrible death. I could never do that.'

'Oh, I know it wasn't you, Signor Nardelli. We have the suspect on CCTV. Where was Beppe last night? Can I speak with him?'

'I haven't seen him this morning,' He turned and shouted into the barn. 'Beppe. Commissario Moretti wants a word.'

They waited, but there was no answer.

'You don't mind if I check for myself, do you?'

Nardelli stood aside. 'Be my guest.'

Moretti entered the gloomy barn, followed by the farmer. The air smelled of mushrooms.

'Beppe,' yelled Nardelli. 'Are you in here?'

Moretti's eyes adjusted to the light, and he surveyed the space. 'Where do you think he is?'

Nardelli shrugged. 'Try his secret girlfriend. He sneaks off to see her at all sorts of odd hours.'

Moretti nodded.

'Thanks, Signor Nardelli. Tell Beppe to get in touch with me when you see him.'

CHAPTER TWENTY-SEVEN

Easily the tallest of the four climbers, Cristina was dressed in a Lycra sports-back top, long stretchy pants, and climbing shoes with reinforced sticky rubber soles and heels. A crocheted chalk bag hung at the small of her back. Mindful of Erpicone's advice, she wore fingerless climbing gloves.

She craned her head back to study the bell tower of the church of Santa Lucia. Rising to a height of over 28 metres above the southern end of the church, its lower half was built from the same local light travertine marble as the rest of the building, while its three upper sections were of red brick, stabilised at intervals by large iron tie bars. She concentrated on the three tiers and began to break her climb into stages. Each section was defined by a continuous cornice that projected about eight centimetres from the vertical – enough to give a good hand hold. Another decorative course of bricks halfway up each section offered the possibility of a finger hold, or enough surface to catch an inside edge of her shoes. The corners of the tower were of large travertine blocks infilled with red brick, then the surface was indented as far as another vertical column of brickwork that framed the three tall Roman-arched windows. She mused that with her reach she might be able to grab the outside corner and the vertical edge of one of those columns.

The adjudicator's voice over the PA system broke her concentration.

'Ladies and gentlemen, boys and girls, welcome to the first of this year's contrada games – the bell tower climb.' The crowd applauded. 'The rules are very simple: each of the climbers has been assigned a face of the tower. Luca representing the Bonaventura contrada will climb the east side; Paolo from Girolamo will climb the west side; the home climber, Andrea, from Lucia was allocated the north face—'

'It's a fix,' shouted someone in the audience. 'Lucia never gets the south side.'

Some of the crowd mumbled in agreement while others shushed them. The tourists, unable to follow the local dialect, looked bemused or laughed.

'And the south side will be climbed by an independent climber, Ispettore Cristina Furlan.'

The three contrada climbers raised their arms aloft and waved to their supporters. Cristina merely raised one hand to shoulder height.

'On the signal to begin, all four climbers will start from the roof of the cloisters, and they will have to traverse the base of the tower to reach their own side. Once their climb has begun, they are not allowed to climb on any face other than their allocated one; they are not allowed to use any climbing aids except chalk; and they must not use the window spaces or edges in their ascent. Officials will watch that the rules are adhered to. The winner will be whoever reaches the roof of the tower and retrieves the pennant from the cross at the top. After reaching the roof, climbers can descend using the internal stairs.'

'Get on with it,' yelled a voice in the crowd to more laughter.

The adjudicator glared at no-one in particular.

'Points will be allocated depending on the order of finishing, and these will be added to the points gained in the other contrada games. Contestants, make your way to the cloisters roof.'

Cristina followed the others into the church and out into the cloisters, where a door led to the roof space and a hatch let them onto the pantiles.

Announcements were still being made to ensure that officials, timers, and ambulance crews were in position. The crowd wrapped itself around the church – the three sides with contrada climbers attracting most people.

'Climbers, are you ready? Climb.'

Andrea, the Lucia climber, pushed past Cristina and the others to get onto the wall. She went in the opposite direction and used the wide cornice that separated the travertine from the red bricks to nimbly get across the west face. When she placed her hand round the corner and touched the surface on the south side, she recoiled immediately. Even the bricks were hot to the touch, so she took advantage of the relative coolness of the west side to peer around the corner and confirm her route up.

'You're on my wall, Ispettore,' said Paolo behind her.

'Sorry, Paolo.'

Holding herself off the hot brickwork, she inched round the corner to her side, reached into her chalk bag, and began to climb. The heat reflected off the surface like a pizza oven, but she made good progress up the first third, finding edges for her feet and using the decorative middle course of bricks for her hands. Broken and pitted bricks let her reach the first of the cornices easily, and she stood on it to compose herself for the middle third. Her face was directly in front of one of the iron wall ties. She licked her middle finger and touched it to get an idea of how hot it was. Too hot to touch! So, she planned a route to the inside of it, to avoid it completely. She reapplied chalk to her hands and set off again. She pressed her toes into an indented brick, but its rough surface flaked away, and her leg dangled for an instant before she recovered. Planning ahead, she tapped potential footholds with either hands or feet before committing her weight to them, and despite her extra caution, she climbed efficiently to the second cornice and rested while contemplating how she would negotiate the projecting eaves onto the roof.

Some of the crowd on the west side, who could see her progress as well as that of the climbers on the west and north faces, drifted towards her side and shouted up encouragement.

'Keep going, Ispettore.'

'You're in the lead, Ispettore.'

Then a gasp and a scream from below.

'Andrea, help!'

Cristina looked down at the crowd. Some had their hands to their mouths, others were pointing.

She called down. 'What is it?'

'Paolo's slipped.'

Cristina moved gingerly to the corner and looked round it. Paolo was pressed against the wall, feet splayed, legs bent awkwardly, and gripping the middle course of bricks with white-knuckled claws.

'What happened, Paolo?'

'A brick flaked away, and I nearly fell.'

'Okay, how do you feel?'

'Scared.'

'Can you move?'

'No. I'm shaking.'

'Wait a moment.'

She carefully climbed down to his level and peered round the corner. He looked terrified.

'This has happened to me, Paolo,' she said softly. 'It happens to everyone. That shaking is a good thing. It means that your body is getting rid of adrenaline.'

His eyes were staring, and he pressed himself closer to the wall.

'Can you breathe for me? Breathe in while I count to five, then let it out sharply. One… two… three… four… five… exhale.'

She repeated the exercise four times.

'Good, Paolo, you're doing really well. Now, when I count to five, I want you to breathe in slowly and push up with your thigh muscles. I'll do it with you. One… two… three… four… five… Good.'

Cristina pushed herself up, and Paolo copied her so that his head and shoulders were much higher than his hands.

'Now relax your thighs without falling off.'

She lowered herself, and he eased himself back to the awkward position.

'Good. I know that you're scared, Paolo, but you can

do this. I want you to relax your grip with your left hand and shake it out.'

He gripped harder with his right but released his left. Cristina did, too.

'That's great. Now flex your fingers and shake out your arm.'

Paolo did as he was told.

'Now the other side.'

They both stretched out their arms.

'Reach behind and chalk your hands one at a time.'

Paolo seemed reluctant.

'Come on, Paolo, you can do this.'

He managed to chalk first one then the other hand.

'Now smile.'

'What? I can't.'

'Okay, then blow a raspberry.'

He looked at her crazily. 'What?'

'You heard me, blow a raspberry.'

He stuck out his tongue and blew but broke into a smile instead.

'Paolo, let's keep each other company for the rest of this climb. What do you say?'

'Okay, Ispettore.'

'Cristina.'

He managed a grin. 'Okay, Cristina.'

The pair climbed in tandem, with Cristina reassuring him until they reached the cornice between the middle and top tiers. They both stood and relaxed.

'What do you want to do?' Cristina asked.

'If I don't get to the roof, the contrada will lose points.'

'Paolo, I'll stay here and help you if you want, but this is only one game. Maybe the rest of the contrada can try harder to gain points. If you want to stop here, we can go in the windows. What do you think?'

Paolo nodded. 'You're right, Cristina, let's do that.'

They inched to the side and entered their respective windows.

Paolo hugged Cristina tightly. 'Thank you,' he said. 'If you hadn't talked to me, I'd have fallen. My muscles were already cramping.'

Outside, below them, the crowd cheered as Andrea held the pennant aloft. Cristina and Paolo descended the stairs of the bell tower, and when they stepped out into the bright afternoon sun they were met by an even louder cheer. Andrea, clapping loudest of all, handed the pennant to Cristina.

'You deserve this more than I do, Ispettore. You'd have beaten me easily.'

She shook her head and refused to take it. 'The rules are the rules, and I broke plenty of them. Anyway, there's always next year.'

Paolo's wife and Moretti arrived simultaneously and hugged Cristina from both sides at once, their arms crossing around the tall detective.

Cristina laughed, Paolo's wife cried, and Moretti gasped.

Along from the action, seated at their usual table, three women tutted in unison.

'Disgraceful behaviour,' said Fausta.

*

In the forested hillsides outside of Cassiatorre, archer Leng, followed by his driver and his translator, walked stealthily through the trees. Leng carried his bow, blunt arrow nocked, scanning the terrain from side to side. He stopped, drew his bow and loosed the arrow, hitting a stump. The small crowd of curious townsfolk who had followed the trio to the woods, and who kept a respectful distance behind them, applauded. His driver ran to collect the arrow, and the trio moved on.

Logs, tree stumps, fungi, and patches of moss on trees, all became targets for Leng's arrows. A few of the followers lost interest and began to drift away. Leng sensed this and, ever the showman, began to fire two arrows in quick succession – first at adjacent targets, then at objects on either side of him so that he had to nock, draw, loose, and turn in a whirl of movement that made the little crowd gasp and press closer. Now both his driver and his translator ran to retrieve the arrows as the excitement of the audience urged him to choose smaller, more awkwardly placed and further apart targets. Leng twisted, turned, and loosed arrows so quickly that he ran out of blunt arrows, and his men needed help from the onlookers to collect them.

Suddenly he froze and held up a hand.

Everyone stopped, and the woodland fell silent. He nocked a pointed arrow and stood motionless, gaze fixed on a spot ahead of him. He drew the bowstring, aimed, and held the position while everyone else held their breath, then loosed into the light undergrowth. This time it was he who ran forward, bent, and picked up his quarry – a large male pheasant, shot cleanly right through. He held it aloft to both cheers and wails from the crowd. Triumphant, he handed the bird to his translator to carry and headed back down the wooded hillside towards the town, accepting plaudits while his driver accepted the recovered arrows from those who'd picked them up.

CHAPTER TWENTY-EIGHT

Before the practice runs for the Disfida began, the judges called the four contestants, plus Leng's translator, to their gazebo to check the colours of their arrow fletching. Lucia's contrada colours were orange and green, Bonaventura's were black and white, Annunziata's blue and white, and Girolamo's red and gold. The first colour was on two of the feathers; the second was on the cock feather on the opposite side of the arrow from the bow. Leng's arrows for the Girolamo contrada were further distinguished by a thin, vinyl wrap decorated with Chinese characters under the feathers.

'For today's practice,' explained the Vice Questore adjudicator, 'each of you will have five passes, which must be performed at the gallop. We will use the runs to test our electronic timing equipment.' He paused to let the translator tell Leng. 'The targets today will be roundels, but for both the heats and the final, the target will comprise an image of the superimposed silhouettes of the heads of bear, boar, hare, and quail, with the smaller images earning more points.' Another pause. 'In the event of two or more archers gaining the same number of points, the average speed of the runs, as measured by the electronic timers, will decide the winner.' Pause. 'Are there any questions?'

He held out four straws and offered them first to

Leng. 'Please choose. The shortest straw goes first.' The riders picked straws, and Leng's was the shortest. 'Good luck to you all.'

The archers made their way to their mounts and readied themselves at the east side of the course. Marshals made sure that the area was safe, and one by one raised their hands as a signal. The chief adjudicator raised and lowered a flag.

Leng spurred his horse and leaned forward, standing out of his new saddle, and riding hands-free. He pulled an arrow from the quiver and loosed it at the first target, quickly taking another and turning side-on to the second target, and finally twisting round in the stirrups to loose his third arrow, before taking the reins in one hand and bringing his galloping horse to a canter then a walk. Three officials ran across the field to check the roundels. He'd hit two inners and a centre.

The other archers looked at each other but set off in turn to try and match him. They hit inners and even a centre on the first two targets, but the third, which demanded a backwards shot, scored only outers and inners.

Leng waited until the last of them had ridden then walked his horse back to the transporter, dismounted, and unsaddled his horse.

The three other contrada riders hesitated, unsure how to proceed, as their team captains surrounded the officials asking for a ruling.

'Practice rounds are not compulsory,' declared the Vice Questore adjudicator, waving them away. 'They are a means for competitors to familiarise themselves with the target field and nothing more.'

*

Moretti held up his hand to Santoro and picked up the desk phone. 'Moretti.'

'Commissario, we have the DNA results for the bull.'

'Ah, go on.'

'We cross-checked the two samples – the one that was taken from the animal Jupiter, and the semen sample that was sent to Signor Erpicone. They are identical. Someone is selling Jupiter's semen.'

'Thank you.'

'We also looked for DNA at the farm where the bull was poisoned. There was nothing on the pallet, the side walls, or the bull's pen. So, whoever did it was wearing gloves.'

Moretti cradled the phone and reached for a pad to map the sequence of events, repeating them out loud as he wrote.

'Chain cut at Buina's… Jupiter stolen from Nardelli's… Jupiter castrated by person unknown… Jupiter semen on sale by person unknown… Hercules poisoned at Buina's.'

He turned the pad around for Santoro to see. 'Well, Gennaro, what do you make of it?'

The agente scratched his head.

'On the face of it, it looks like Buina was jealous and stole Nardelli's bull, Jupiter, harvested semen from it, then castrated it. So Nardelli poisoned his bull Hercules in retaliation.'

'Except that Buina has a gold-plated alibi for the time of Jupiter's theft, and there's nothing to tie Nardelli to the poisoning apart from the fact that he grows clover and alfalfa – but then, so do all the other livestock farmers in the area. The CCTV image isn't that clear, but it's obvious that it's not Nardelli's build.'

'How about his son, Beppe?'

'He wasn't at home yesterday when I called, but I told Nardelli that I wanted to speak with him.'

The desk phone rang again.

'Moretti… Great, bring him straight in, Alfiero.' He hung up. 'Speak of the devil It's Beppe.'

Alfiero knocked, then opened the door. Beppe stood behind him.

'Beppe Nardelli to see you, Commissario.'

Both detectives stood, and Santoro moved his chair to the side. Moretti motioned to Beppe.

'Thank you for coming, Beppe. Please sit.'

Moretti and Santoro sat, and the young man dumped himself on the chair.

'You wanted to speak with me.'

'Yes. Can I offer you some water?'

Beppe nodded and scowled.

'Let's get this over with.'

Santoro left to fetch the water. Moretti pursed his lips.

'Certainly. Where were you last night?'

'I was with my girlfriend, Bea.'

'Specifically, where were you between eleven and midnight last night?'

'With Bea.'

'And she'll confirm that?'

'Of course.'

'Okay, now tell me when you got back to your farm?'

'Mid-morning.'

'Can you be a bit more precise?'

Santoro reappeared with a plastic cup of water, put it in front of Beppe, then sat quietly in his chair.

Beppe glanced at him then replied, 'About eleven o'clock.'

'So, to be clear, at no time did you visit the Buina farm?'

'And poison Buina's bull?' fumed Beppe. 'I've no interest in my father's business. Why would I be interested in someone else's?'

'You haven't said no, Beppe.' Moretti said calmly.

'You came looking for me when the restaurant served poison mushrooms. You came looking for me when someone poisoned a bull. Am I top of your list for every crime around here?'

'To be clear, Beppe, it was you who brought the tray of mushrooms to the restaurant. The poison mushroom in the tray was a particular type that has no antidote. That takes knowledge,' Moretti said, looking steadily at the young man. 'And Hercules wasn't poisoned. He was fed a specific mix of fresh feed that caused him to die of bloat. That takes the kind of knowledge that only someone from a stock breeding background would have. And you still haven't said no.'

Beppe leaned across the table.

'No!' he thumped the table spilling some water. 'I didn't go anywhere near the Buina farm. Not last night, not ever. Satisfied?'

Moretti slid open a drawer and produced a box of tissues.

'For now,' he said, mopping up the spillage. 'You can go.'

Beppe stormed out of the room

Santoro grabbed some tissues and helped mop up.

'Do you believe him, Capo?'

'I'm prepared to believe him – if his alibi stacks up. You can call Bea to find out. What about you?'

'I agree, but what I don't know is if we're dealing with a vendetta, a series of unrelated incidents, or something more organised.'

'I've been asking myself who stands to gain from it all,' said Moretti, preening his moustache with finger and thumb. 'If we think of it as a vendetta, then the advantage seems to flip from one party to the other.'

'In the way of vendettas.'

'Exactly, and we see the same thing all over Italy.'

'So, you think it's a planned series of actions?'

'I can't but think that there is a third party involved. Someone is trying to put the two farmers out of business and at the same time Zhao and his family. What I can't understand is why. If we can figure out their motive, then we'll have whoever is behind it all.'

Santoro screwed up his face. 'I'm reluctant to bring it up, Capo, knowing how you feel about the man, but could it be Ricci?'

Moretti ignored the pang in his heart that he always felt at the mention of the name of the agriturismo owner that he suspected of having an affair with his wife.

'Of course I considered him, Gennaro. If I'm honest, part of me would love it to be him, but I can't make the connections. I can't see how he stands to gain if two beef farmers in the valley go out of business – no matter how hard I try. So, I've ruled him out.'

The office door pushed open abruptly, and Vice Questore Montanari strode in.

'Ignoring my instruction about joint working, I see,' she snapped, glaring at the two detectives. 'Well, no matter. Moretti, I've spoken to Internal Affairs. You must leave the premises now and phone on Monday morning to find out when they will interview you.'

Moretti opened his mouth to speak but stood instead

and reached for the pad on his desk.

'Leave that,' said Montanari. 'I'll escort you out.'

*

Camilla Caprice Montanari stood at the entrance of the Questura and watched him go. She both despised and envied Moretti. He was tall and lean, despite his little paunch, where she was short and heavy set. How could he walk like that – almost a swagger – having been suspended? Did he know she was watching? She wouldn't give him the satisfaction and went back inside to her office and pulled out his file again.

She slipped the anonymous letters to one side and studied his career file. She even recognised some of the cases he'd worked on, important cases, where his expertise had been sought by other forces throughout the peninsula. In Rome or Milan, a record like his, peppered with award after award, would have shot him to the very top of the profession. Yet here he was, stuck in a backwater, a complete lack of ambition and waste of talent – a real talent that she wished she had.

Montanari leaned back and rubbed her eyes then closed the file folder. *He may be a hotshot, but I'm still his superior.*

She reflected on her own childhood in Bologna, her overbearing father who wanted no more for her than to be married and produce a litter of children like he'd given her mother. She did, though, thank her father for his disciplined and conscientious approach to work. It was that, paired with her own drive and determination to prove to him that women can do responsible and important jobs that brought her success. It hadn't been an easy path. Too many men who thought like her father, and when she spurned their offers of career progression in exchange for sex… She shuddered.

She brushed her fingers in a circle across Moretti's file. Her predecessors didn't appreciate who they had working for them and hadn't capitalised on Moretti's abilities. A few months of being assigned the most trivial cases, of working alone without his geriatric sidekick and Moretti would be banging at her door to get his teeth into a more demanding case. The sort of case that she was going to deliberately assign to Furlan.

Furlan. Now there was a prospect. Montanari smiled. Younger, taller, and fitter than Moretti, father a judge, Furlan would be her project, her legacy, Moretti's replacement when it finally occurred to him that he was more trouble than he was worth and moved on or retired. She'd mentor Furlan, remove obstacles, and give the young woman the kind of career help that she never had herself. She thought she sensed something in the tall ispettore, but she had to be patient, to be sure.

CHAPTER TWENTY-NINE

Moretti poured the strong black coffee into a small cup and carried it to the dining table where he had previously spread out the Vanni case files. He sat and picked out Sergio's testimony, sipping his coffee as he re-read it, and checked it against the notes he had made at the time.

Mancuso: What was the reason for you being at your parents' house?

Vanni: It was one of my regular visits to my parents' home. *How regular? Pattern?*

Mancuso: Describe the scene as you found it.

Does SV have a key?

Vanni: I entered their house and saw the mess. Drawers had been scattered onto the floor, cupboard doors thrown open, and shelves emptied.

Mancuso: What did you think the burglar was looking for?

Rossi: Objection. Calls for speculation on the part of witness.

Franchi: Sustained.

Mancuso: Dr Vanni, you are a family doctor. Do you ever store prescription medicines at your parents' house?

Vanni: No. Never. The only medicines there are for treating my parents.

Mancuso: Were your parents at the scene?

Vanni: No. I thought that they must still be upstairs. My father had dementia, and my mother was his carer. I called up to them, but there was no reply.

When did SV arrive?

Mancuso: What did you do?

Vanni: I ran upstairs and found them in their bedroom.

Mancuso: What was their condition?

Vanni: Both were dead. My father was covered in bruises.

Mancuso: Did you check for signs of life?

Vanni: Of course, but they were both cool to the touch. They had been dead for some time.

Mancuso: How long would you estimate they had been dead?

Vanni: I didn't take their temperatures, but I guess more than 18 hours. *PM time of death?*

Mancuso: What did you do then?

Vanni: I called for an ambulance and the police.

When was call made?

Then Moretti looked at the notes he had made after his recent conversation when Sergio had admitted scrubbing the crime scene.

SV with Maria. [check!!] Home help?! SV arrives – parents dead. SV scrubs crime scene.

He circled the note, *SV with Maria.* He knew what he had to do. He took the cup to the sink, rinsed it, then called his wife.

'Maria? Dino. How are you?'

'I'm fine, Dino. Is everything okay? Any progress on finding who put the money in your account?'

'That's ongoing. I've to speak to Internal Affairs next week.'

'Oh. Do you want me to shuffle things around here so that I can come up?'

There was a note in Maria's voice that Moretti had not heard for a while – concern? empathy? love? He was unsure, but there was something, and he changed his plans instantly.

'I was wondering about coming down to see you this weekend. How would that be?'

A pause.

'That would be lovely, Dino.'

The note had gone from her voice – replaced with a more guarded, bland timbre. Not the exuberant response he had been hoping for.

'I could drive down today.' He had to ask his questions face-to-face. 'I could be there around midday.' He had to see how she reacted. 'We could have lunch together, or maybe dinner?'

'Well…'

He faked a chuckle. 'Don't tell me you have to work on weekends, too.'

'No, it's not that…'

'Maybe you have other plans. That's it, you've a secret boyfriend down there.' The words tumbled out before he could stop them.

'No, Dino, it's nothing like that.' Her voice sounded taut. 'It's only that it's so unexpected, that's all.'

'So that's decided then,' he said before she changed her mind. 'I've a couple of things to do here. Let's say that I get to you mid-afternoon. Can you organise somewhere to eat this evening?'

'Of course, Dino. Leave it to me.'

'Good. I'll stop to stretch my legs on the way down. I'll call and update you on my progress.'

'Fine. See you later.'

'Thanks, Maria.'

She ended the call and Moretti stared at the screen of his phone until it went blank, conscious that neither of them had brought up the matter of where he would be sleeping. He dialled another number.

'Sergio? Dino. Can we meet?'

'Dino, good morning. Of course. When and where?'

'I was wondering if you were free now?'

'I can be in half an hour, if that's any use?'

'Do you remember where I live?'

'Yes. I'll see you in about half an hour.'

Moretti went to the bedroom, packed a few things into a holdall, and took it to his car. He tidied away the case files and his notes, and blocked thoughts of Maria by concentrating on how he was going to approach his conversation with Vanni.

Less than thirty minutes after their call, Vanni's car drew up outside. From the cool, unlit interior, Moretti watched the doctor step out and look around. He went to the door and opened it, letting the morning heat flow in.

'Thanks for coming, Sergio, won't you come inside where it's cooler?'

He stood aside to let Vanni pass then closed the door.

'Can I offer you something? Water, coffee, juice?'

'I'll take some water, thanks.'

Moretti took a jug of filtered water from the fridge and poured two glasses. 'Here you are. Let's sit at the table.'

They sat opposite, and Sergio looked around him.

'Just as I remember, Dino – maybe except for the light fitting.'

'Well, we're all saving the environment nowadays, aren't we?'

Vanni sipped his water. 'So, you wanted to meet. Social, business, personal, professional?'

Moretti smiled.

'A bit of everything, I suppose, Sergio.' He sipped his water, too. 'How are you settling in?'

'Very well. The practice is great – such a change of pace and workflow from Rome.'

'Thanks again for your quick work with Santoro, by the way. He's looking well.'

'Yes, I visited him at home a couple of days ago. I think he's managing to stick to the regime. And Poirot will help too. Such a lovely cat. Likes to be stroked.'

'Oh. You met Poirot? I never even knew Gennaro had a cat.' They both laughed. 'How are all of the restaurant casualties?'

'Luckily, we noticed quickly enough that no-one had eaten very much, so they are all fine.'

'Lucky that you were there, Sergio, or it could have been very much worse.'

'Okay, Dino, now that we've gotten the social bit out of the way, what do you really want to talk to me about?'

Moretti nodded. 'I've been going over the case files for your parents' deaths.'

'Uhuh?'

'Because some of the events didn't seem to match what you told me when we met in the forest.'

'Go on, I can feel a question coming on.'

'The court evidence—'

'You mean my evidence, Dino,' interrupted Vanni.

'Your testimony suggested that you arrived for a regular visit with your parents, found evidence of burglary and them both dead, and that you then phoned the police – that would be me – and the ambulance. But that was a lie, wasn't it, because you said you called your parents from the hotel, then you went to check on them?'

Vanni made no response.

'You also omitted to say that there was a home help; a valuable witness that we never knew about.'

Vanni stared at his feet.

'You then went on to say that you checked their pulse and so on, but they were dead. Both of them. You estimated for more than eighteen hours.'

'Did I? I can't remember.' Vanni drank his water.

'I got the lab boys to run the DNA sample you gave me, and you were right, the criminal died behind bars only a few weeks ago. But the odd thing is this, Sergio… before and after your parents' case, he was only ever convicted with theft, drugs offences, rape, and assault. Never murder. Why would a career criminal break his pattern of offences in only this one case? Why would the only people that he ever murdered be your parents?'

Vanni remained silent.

'Sergio, I'll be leaving shortly to drive down to visit Maria. We've lots to talk about. But one of the things I'm going to ask her is exactly when you two were away together – as you said you were – and when exactly you called your mother, and when exactly you got back to your parents' home. And there's one thing that I know about Maria is that she has an incredible memory. She'll be able to tell me precisely when it was.'

Moretti paused to sip his water.

'Comparing the two versions of events – what you told the court and what you told me – I think you're guilty of perjury and perverting the course of justice, Sergio.

You said you felt a question coming on, Sergio, well here it is. How did your parents really die, because the burglar didn't kill them?'

Vanni removed his spectacles and laid them on the table in front of him.

'Dino, I know that you've carried this case like a cross on your back all these years. I told you all that stuff in the woods because I wanted to give you closure. I was horrified to discover what had happened to Dad, and you're right, I did lie in court, and I did destroy evidence. But I told you why, and I've regretted it every day since.'

'You still haven't answered my question, Sergio. How did your parents die?'

Vanni sat, head down, shoulders forward, hands between his legs. 'I don't know. It looked like they were smothered by a pillow.'

Moretti had to swallow hard before he could speak. 'Sergio, after you had cleaned the place up, how long did you wait before calling me?'

'I stripped and changed the bed, changed both my parents' clothes, and took the lot with me. I told you how I washed my father. I don't know, maybe a couple of hours altogether. Then I went back to the hotel in the morning and told Maria that I'd been called out to an emergency. We checked out, I dropped her off at Cassiatorre, then drove to my parents' place again and called you.'

'How much of this does Maria know?'

'None of it, I swear. So now you know it all, Dino. The case you never solved.'

*

The four stands were full of excited tourists and noisy locals sporting the colours of their contradas for the heats of the Disfida. The roundels that had been fixed to the hay bales for the practice day were replaced with the competition targets – superimposed silhouettes of animal heads. The bear was black, the boar white, the hare black, and quail white. Unlike the roundels, however, the heads were not concentric, so that to hit the quail, the archers had to strike the target considerably off-centre.

Leng, who was used to the international convention

of aiming for the centre of the target, was caught unprepared, and after an agitated exchange with his translator, a protest was lodged on his behalf. The judges merely repeated the rules of the Disfida and dismissed the protest.

The four riders – from Bonaventura, Lucia, Girolamo, and Annunziata – galloped in turn along the course, cheered on by their supporters and booed by their opponents, with the spotters for each target calling out, 'Hare,' or 'Boar,' or 'Bear,' depending on the part of the target hit. After their five runs, only the rider from the Bonaventura contrada had managed to hit a quail.

'Thank you all for coming to today's heats,' announced the head adjudicator. 'All of today's scores will be totalled, added to the scores for the bell tower climb and the other contests, and publicised before tomorrow's final so that the archers will know what they need to do to win. Enjoy the rest of your evening, and we'll see you tomorrow.'

CHAPTER THIRTY

Cristina watched as the dignitaries and judges, all wearing richly decorated medieval costumes, processed behind the town band to the table of honour and took their places. The only exceptions were CC Montanari, who was wearing her dress uniform, and the emergency doctor who carried his medical bag.

The ispettore scanned the bleachers behind the long table. The final of the Disfida attracted a capacity crowd, and the four metal stands of seats were filled with tourists and locals who self-segregated. The tourists, armed with cameras, sat on the lower tiers near the front, while the predominantly young contrada fans encamped in the upper rows. It was from here that they waved their contrada flags. They had fixed their banners, proclaiming messages of support for their own rider and scathing comments about the opposition, on the scaffolding poles that supported the structure. Smoke flares were set off, sending thick clouds of coloured smoke across the field, and chants accompanied by air horns, tambourines, and referee whistles filled the air.

Cristina's role was to liaise with the Municipal Police and the Carabinieri, but since she was attending the Disfida for the first time, she stood close to, and followed the lead of, one of the white-hatted Municipal officers. She was about to speak when the first of the contradas appeared at the side of the field. The flag bearers were first – eight young people who swayed, swept, waved, and tossed the contrada flags in the air. They were accompanied by the musicians. Each contrada had its own fanfare – played on long trumpets from which hung the contrada flag – and marching rhythm, thumped out on side- and snare-drums.

Each contrada presented itself – in the order in which the riders would be running – before the table of honour, the flag bearers performing an ever more complex pattern of sweeps, tosses, and exchanges of their flags, to the applause and cheers of all. Each contrada's champion flag bearer competed to see who could throw their flags highest and still catch them, and to see who could juggle with the most. Most could manage five or even six, but Lucia's champion flag bearer managed eight.

The Lucia flag was a flaming orange chalice on a green background. Annunziata's had white lilies on a blue background. Bonaventura's black and white flag represented an open book with a quill resting across it, while Girolamo's blood red background bore a golden lion's paw pierced by a black thorn.

When the last contrada had completed its display, the chief judge stood and asked the audience for a final round of applause for all the participants. The Municipal cop beside Cristina informed her that points were awarded for the best flag waving performance and added to the overall total.

'Honoured guests, ladies and gentlemen, boys and girls, we will now begin the final event of the Disfida. The one which will decide the overall champion for this year.' Applause, cheering, whistles, and air horns from the crowd. 'I ask that during each ride, spectators must refrain from using whistles and air horns, to avoid accidents with the horses and riders.' Applause and one air horn tooted. The crowd looked to the source. Cristina followed their gaze and saw the culprit hold up their hand.

'Similarly, no smoke flares are to be set off when riders are galloping. There will be time for celebrating at the end.' The crowd applauded their approval.

The chief judge bent to take a slip of paper from an

adjudicator. 'I've been handed the points totals to date.' Shushing from the crowd. 'With the points for the flag waving displays added in, the scores are as follows: in fourth place, with three hundred and fifty points is Annunziata, who you will remember were not represented in the bell tower climb. In joint second place, with four hundred and twenty points each, are Girolamo and Bonaventura; and in first place with a slight lead, on four hundred and thirty points, is Lucia.'

Orange and green smoke drifted across the field in thick clouds, and a huge banner that stretched across the full width of the Lucia stand was unfurled and passed over the heads of their supporters, completely covering them. The youths on the other stands stamped their feet and booed noisily until the chief judge, with the help of the powerful PA system, brought everything back under control and the huge Lucia flag was furled again.

'The value for the targets for the final are: Bear – ten points; Boar – fifteen points; Hare – twenty-five points; and Quail – worth fifty points.' Oohs and gasps from the crowd. 'The points total will be announced after each round.'

'Chief judge – no points,' heckled someone in the crowd, to laughter.

The chief judge ignored the comment and continued. 'Marshalls, are you ready? Archers, are you ready? Let the final begin.'

The crowd settled, and the rider from Lucia rode first, his horse sprinting to the gallop as it passed the first of the electronic timers. The rider loosed his first arrow over the horse's shoulders, the second as he passed the middle target, and he twisted round in his saddle to hit the third. The crowd applauded as the marshals ran across to check his scores.

'Hare.' 'Hare.' 'Hare.'

'That's a good start,' said Cristina to the cop beside her.

'Yes, it is. They'll be difficult to catch.'

Annunziata galloped past next.

'Hare.' 'Hare.' 'Hare.'

'That's good, too.'

The Municipal cop frowned. 'They'll need to do better

than that. They've a lot to catch up.'

Bonaventura next.

'Hare.' 'Hare.' 'Boar.'

Gasps from the crowd.

'That third target is difficult.'

'He didn't nock his arrow fast enough.'

Leng for Girolamo pushed his horse to the gallop quickest.

'Hare.' 'Hare.' 'Hare.'

The cop whistled. 'That's fast. He's obviously thinking about having the best time if the scores are tied.'

The chief judge announced the results. 'The order after the first round is Lucia first, then Girolamo, Bonaventura, and in last place, Annunziata.'

Banners and flags were waved, and a chorus of air horns and whistles accompanied the four horses as their riders walked them back to the start. Leng's horse tossed its head, ears back, nostrils flared, and he had to fight to control it.

'Round two. Marshals, are you ready? Archers, are you ready?'

The second round saw Annunziata hitting a Quail to close the gap on the others. Girolamo hit a Bear, losing them points, but Lucia still led overall.

Round three saw all archers hit Quails, with Annunziata doing so twice to bring them within ten points of Bonaventura and Girolamo, with Lucia still in the lead. The Annunziata fans unfurled a huge blue and white flag in celebration.

In the fourth round, Annunziata's archer hit another two Quails to bring them into second place, with Lucia still ahead, and the other two tied.

'We go to the fifth and final round with Lucia on seven hundred and eighty points, Annunziata on seven hundred and seventy-five, and Bonaventura and Girolamo each on seven hundred and sixty. Good luck to all the archers.'

Quail, Quail, Hare for Lucia. The same for Annunziata. The Bonaventura rider spurred his horse to a reckless speed, kicking up great clouds of dust behind him, but scored three Quails to take the lead. The crowd went wild, with the Bonaventura fans ignoring the chief judge's instructions and setting off black and white flares and bouncing on the metal bleachers such that the Carabinieri and the Municipal Police closed in to prevent an accident.

'Please,' he shouted. 'Please calm down. We have one rider still to complete the course.'

The other three stands shushed, and as the smoke from the flares dispelled, Leng leaned over his horse's head and urged it to the gallop. He stood in the stirrups and took aim. Quail. It seemed like sparks were flying from his horse's hooves as his second arrow thudded home. Quail. He turned and followed the target, loosing at the last moment before urging his horse past the second electronic timer. Quail.

The Girolamo fans sent up an enormous cheer followed by a cacophony of whistles, air horns, and drumming.

'Bonaventura and Girolamo have tied,' the Municipal cop informed Cristina. 'It's all down to the times now.'

'Hmm,' said Cristina. Her attention was caught by something on the competition field. A sparkle. Glass, maybe? 'Excuse me,' she said, leaving the officer and walking towards it. She moved her head from side to side as she walked to keep it in sight as it reflected the strong sunlight. Behind her the announcement came over the PA system.

'The contrada with the fastest time, and the winner of this year's Disfida is… Girolamo.'

Cristina blocked out the noise of airhorns and whistles. She was oblivious to the fireworks and the smoke flares. Her focus was on finding the dangerous shard of glass on the dried grass ahead of her. She lost it and ducked and swayed until the angle of the sun caught it again. She paused, taking in its surroundings, noting hoof prints and minuscule changes in the colour and texture of the sandy soil in case she lost it again. She strode forward and dropped to her knees, arms outstretched, doing a fingertip search. There it was. She gasped, picked it up, and held it to the light. Not glass, but a perfect pink diamond.

*

'Moretti? Like the beer?'

'Like the beer,' he sighed. 'But the reservation will be in my wife's name – De Luca.'

The waiter checked his list.

'Of course, Signore. Signora De Luca is already seated. Please follow me.'

Moretti followed the waiter through the small trattoria, with its white painted walls covered in sepia-coloured and black and white family photographs, to a vine-covered pergola at the rear. Maria noticed him and gave him a shoulder-height wave.

'Here you are, Signore,' said the waiter.

'Thank you. Hello, Maria, how are you?' He leaned over and kissed her cheek.

'You've lost weight,' she replied. 'Your face is looking thinner. Are you eating properly?'

A woman at the next table overheard them and smiled.

'I'm fine. Work's been a bit busy.'

'Well, the food here is great, so have whatever you like. My treat.'

She picked up the menu and began reading. Moretti did the same, but he looked over the top of it at his wife. Maria was very tanned and looked as if she had gained a little weight. Her hair was cut a little shorter than she normally wore it.

'It suits you,' he said.

Maria looked up, eyebrows raised.

'Your hair. It suits you,' he explained.

She instinctively reached up to touch the nape of her neck. 'It's so hot down here, I had to get it cut.'

The waiter brought a bottle of water and a bottle of white wine sleeved in a frozen cooler.

'I hope you don't mind, Dino, but I ordered my favourite wine.'

'Of course not.'

The waiter showed them both the label and Maria nodded. He opened the bottle, sniffed the cork, and poured a little for her to try.

'Delicious.'

The waiter smiled, filled their glasses, slid the bottle back into its sleeve, and left.

'CinCin.'

'CinCin.'

'What would you recommend?'

'I would suggest the fish. It's always fresh and simply cooked.'

Moretti put down his menu and grinned.

'You know, since you're the host, I'd like you to choose for us both. You know the menu, and you know what I like.'

Maria returned his smile and nodded to the waiter. He approached, pad in hand.

'What's the fish of the day?'

'Line-caught sea bass.'

'Good, we'll both start with the *spaghetti ai ricci di mare*, then we'll share the *spigola al forno*.'

'And to accompany it?'

'How about some roasted potatoes, fennel, and tomatoes?'

'Good choice, Signora,' he said, picking up their menus.

Moretti became aware that his shoulders were hunched up, so he lowered them, sighed, and took a large sip of wine.

'Good choice, Maria. This really is a wonderful wine.' He slipped the bottle up out of its sleeve to examine the label.

'It's very local. I don't think you can find it outside of the area.'

The silence that quickly grew between them started to feel awkward. Maria broke it first.

'How was your drive down? It sounds like you've had bit of a rough time up there.'

Moretti shrugged. He noticed that Maria was fidgeting with her cutlery and felt that the woman near them was eavesdropping.

'The drive was a little tiring,' he said. 'So, let's enjoy our meal together. We can talk later.'

They clinked glasses again.

CHAPTER THIRTY-ONE

Cristina held the diamond tightly in her closed fist and looked around her. The PA system was still broadcasting the closing announcements, and the stands were beginning to empty of people who were diffusing in all directions. Crowds of fans were clustering around their contrada's horse and rider. Leng had already arrived at his trailer. The chances were that nobody was looking in her direction. She held the diamond up at eye level again between finger and thumb and turned it, watching the facets fracture the light, and wondering how much it was worth. *Not sparks from galloping hooves*, she gasped, and quickly hid it in her fist again, guiltily glancing at the dispersing crowds as she dismissed the temptation. She ran towards the Municipal officer she'd stood beside.

'Get two or three other officers and keep the crowds off the field.'

'We've been assigned to traffic duties, sorry.'

'I need you to keep the crowds off the field.'

The officer glowered at her. 'You don't have the authority to order me.'

'What's your name?'

'Carlotta.'

'Okay, Carlotta.' Cristina stood close enough that they were almost touching, and the officer had to stretch her neck back to look almost vertically upwards. 'I don't have time to discuss this with you right now, but if you don't get two of your pals to keep everyone off this field, right now, you'll be in front of Vice Questore Montanari first thing tomorrow morning to hand in your badge, gun, and say goodbye to your job and your pension. And I'll do what I can to personally see to it that you face a prison sentence for obstructing an officer in pursuance of their duties. Now, do I make myself clear? Close off this field now.'

The officer stepped back and saluted. 'Yes, Ispettore.'

Cristina sprinted away towards two Carabinieri who were casually chatting to a couple of American girls in very hesitant English. She held up her ID as she reached them.

'Excuse me, Officers, I need your help.'

Her request was met by looks of indifference and resentment, but Cristina was in no mood to be refused.

'Sorry to break up your public liaison,' she said sarcastically, 'but I need back-up at a potential crime scene.'

'Oh, it's the climber,' said one of the Carabinieri.

Cristina glared at him.

'Before you tell me I can't order you about, let me tell you in front of these witnesses that I'm reporting a crime, and I've asked for your help.' She turned to the Americans, smiled, and addressed them in English. 'You will be my witnesses that I've asked these officers to help at a crime scene, won't you?'

'Sure,' they chorused, holding up their phones.

The Carabinieri straightened up.

'Follow me,' barked Cristina. 'And try to keep up. You don't want your fan club to see that you can't match a woman, do you?'

'*Cazzo*,' spat one of the men, breaking into a jog.

'Go get 'em,' one of the American girls shouted after them as she filmed their progress.

Cristina was easily first to arrive at Leng's trailer. She held up her ID.

'Signor Leng,' she gasped in Italian. 'Please stop what you are doing.'

Leng had both hands on the saddle and was on the

point of removing it from the horse.

'Please stop what you are doing,' she repeated in English, as the two Carabinieri arrived.

Leng's translator emerged from the trailer and spoke in Chinese. Leng removed his hands from the saddle and stepped back. The translator stood between him and Cristina, and demanded in Italian, 'What is the meaning of this?'

'I have to impound this saddle,' Cristina replied.

The translator held up his left hand, revealing an unusual tattoo around the wrist. 'Do you have the authority? A warrant?'

'I have the authority, but not a warrant. I can get one, if you like. I'll get in touch with the judge first thing tomorrow morning, and in the meantime, I'll leave these officers here to make sure that no-one touches the saddle and that no-one leaves the trailer.'

'That's impossible. Champion Leng has another competition. We must be on our way.' He turned and called into the trailer in rapid Chinese. Leng's driver appeared – a stocky man, taller than Leng but much shorter than Cristina. He took up position between her and the horse, folded his arms, and stared at her unblinking. Cristina noticed the same unusual tattoo on his left wrist.

'What is your name?' Leng's translator asked.

'I am Ispettore Cristina Furlan.' She held up her ID again.

'Ispettore Furlan, you are making a very serious mistake. One which could result in international difficulties for your country and severe consequences for you personally.'

'It is not my wish to delay your onward journey. If you are detained, it will be as a consequence of a decision that you have made. You arrived here without the saddle that is currently on the horse. You are free to leave whenever you wish without that saddle, and to use the other saddle that Signor Leng practised in the other day.'

'Why the interest in this saddle? It was a gift to Champion Leng.'

'I suspect that it may be involved in an illegal

enterprise, and I must have it examined. If I am mistaken, it will be forwarded to you.'

'Are you accusing Champion Leng of being involved in illegal activity?'

'I suspect that the saddle may be. I am making no allegations about Signor Leng. You, however, seem to be very certain that there is nothing amiss. Perhaps you should stay with the saddle while it is being examined, and then you can take it personally if everything turns out okay.'

Leng fired what Cristina suspected was a string of questions at his translator. The two men withdrew and spoke quickly, while the driver stood implacably staring at Cristina. The translator nodded.

'Champion Leng has agreed that you may examine the saddle, but it must be done today. The tooling of the leather is of the highest artistic quality, and it would be an affront to the People's Republic of China if it were damaged.'

'Agreed.'

'And I will be present to ensure that you comply.'

'And what is your name, please?'

'Li.'

'Agreed, Signor Li. You will carry the saddle and come with me.' She turned to the Carabinieri behind her. 'You stay here until we return,' she said to the first, and to the other, 'You come with me.'

Her statement met with no demur from the first officer who took up position at the front of the trailer.

Cristina's eyes swept the field. Three Municipal officers had taken up position to turn onlookers away from the area where she had found the diamond. The other three riders and their supporters had left, and only stragglers remained at the public seating areas. A team of volunteers had already begun to dismantle the first of the seating stands. Standing still in the midst of all that movement, watching Cristina, stood the figure of Vice Questore Montanari, clearly visible in her dress uniform.

'Where's your vehicle?' she asked the other Carabinieri.

'Over there,' he pointed.

‘Lead the way,’ she said. ‘Signor Li, you walk ahead of me.’ The trio headed away from the Vice Questore and around the back of the farthest stand to the Carabinieri Jeep. The officer unlocked the car and Cristina held open the back door.

‘Please get in, Signor Li.’ She placed her hand on Li’s head and waited until he and the saddle were settled inside, then she climbed up beside him, saying to the driver, ‘The hospital in Maghicchio. We need a specialist. No lights.’

They drove off, picking their way through the crowds meandering along and across the road. Cristina noticed Vice Questore Montanari hurrying forward, so she turned away from her and they drove in silence down the hill to Maghicchio.

As they approached the hospital, Li asked, ‘Is there an X-ray department in the hospital?’

‘Yes,’ replied Cristina, then to the driver, ‘Drive past it and turn into the industrial estate on the right.’

Li fidgeted beside her. ‘You’re not taking the saddle to the hospital?’

‘No, Signor Li, the specialist we are going to is a saddle maker. Stop over there,’ she commanded. ‘Right to the door.’ Cristina and Li got out. ‘Park the car, then come inside and wait for us.’

‘Signor DiMarco,’ Cristina called into the shop as they entered. The smell of leather and the tapping of a hammer welcomed them inside. ‘Ispettore Cristina Furlan. I need your help.’

‘Coming.’

DiMarco emerged from a back room lined with shelves of tools and boxes. He wiped his hands on a rag that he produced from a pocket in his leather apron, changed spectacles, and whistled.

‘Oh, my goodness,’ he said, ignoring Cristina and Li. ‘What a magnificent saddle.’ He motioned to the counter. ‘May I?’

Li lifted the saddle onto the counter, and DiMarco tilted his head to examine it from every angle.

‘This is quite the most beautiful piece of work I’ve ever seen.’ He wiped his hands again and ran his fingers over it with the lightest of touches, tracing the tooling and stitching. 'There's damage here,' he said, peering at the place his fingers had found. 'Some of the stitching has come undone. See? Do you want me to repair it?'

'On the contrary, Signor DiMarco,' replied Cristina. 'I want you to open it up. All of it.'

*

Moretti used a *scarpetta* of bread to mop up the last of the sea urchin sauce from his plate, then dabbed his napkin on his moustache, finally preening it left then right with his index finger.

Maria smiled. 'Good?'

'Stunning,' he replied.

'I'm glad.'

The waiter cleared away the empty plates.

The awkward silence between them returned. Even the woman at the next table seemed aware of it.

Moretti felt the need to change the atmosphere.

'Did you know that Gennaro has a cat?'

Maria looked up brightly. 'Black, with a white patch between its eyes? Yes. What's he called again?

'Poirot.'

'Poirot. That's it. Haven't you seen it?'

'I only found out when I had to go and feed it.'

Maria grinned. 'Some detective you are.'

They both laughed.

Two waiters arrived. One laid the roast vegetables on their table while the other deftly filleted the fish, using two spoons at a side table before placing a fillet each on their warm plates.

'Enjoy,' he said as he left.

Moretti enjoyed the sea bass but not the prospect of going back to Maria's rental. They skipped dessert and had a coffee.

'How far to your place?'

'Not far. Where did you park your car?'

'Behind the trattoria.'

'It'll be safe there. Let's fetch your bag and we can walk.'

Ten minutes later, Moretti followed his wife inside her apartment – an open-plan kitchen and living room, with a couch, an armchair, a table spread with folders, and no television.

'It's lovely.'

'It came like this. I've had nothing to do with it. I only use it as a place to sleep.'

'Talking of which,' he said, 'I might be restless after the drive and keep you awake, so if it's alright with you I'll sleep on the couch, unless there's a spare bed.'

Maria's shoulders relaxed enough for him to notice, and she smiled. 'Of course. I'll bring some sheets and help you make it up.'

They held the corners of the crisp sheets and billowed them open before draping them on the couch.

'I'm sorry, Maria, I haven't asked how your case is going.'

'Cases,' she sighed. 'It turns out that the case that originally brought me down was only the start of it, and my success in that has led to a whole string of other interest.'

'Can't they be dealt with as a class action?'

'If they were against the same defendant, yes of course, but the abuse of corporate power down here is so widespread that I'm representing clients – and yes, sometimes in groups of five or six – against a whole range of employers, including local and regional government departments who really ought to know better than to exploit people simply because they're a different colour, or poor, or immigrants, or don't know their rights.'

'That's happening in Cassiatorre now, too.'

Maria smiled as she tucked in the edge of the sheet. 'Now?'

'What?'

'You know what.'

'Do I?'

She paused from stuffing a pillow into a pillowcase. 'Yes. You were dreadful when I first met you.'

'I suppose I was a bit parochial.'

She threw the pillow at him. 'Parochial? You were racist.'

'Not really.'

'Yes, really.'

He handed back the pillow. 'I didn't know better.'

'That's no excuse. You hated outsiders. You saw foreign tourists as a means to an end because they brought money into Cassiatorre. You used to think that it was alright to employ people from the south to work in the hot sun for peasant wages. Then when the first refugees and immigrants began to arrive, you thought it was okay to pay them even less. Dino, that's exactly what I'm still up against down here.'

Moretti nodded and held her hand.

'It's true, Maria. I'm ashamed to admit it. But you made me better.' He pressed his lips to her knuckles. 'It doesn't sound like you'll be able to come home anytime soon, then.'

Maria's head dropped and she raised her eyebrows, her gaze focussed on some point deep underground.

'No, Dino. Not anytime soon.'

CHAPTER THIRTY-TWO

The two men looked aghast.

'All of it?' DiMarco repeated.

'Start with the pommel and the cantle,' said Cristina. 'Then we'll see.'

Li stepped between DiMarco and the saddle and gripped it just as the Carabinieri officer returned.

'Ah, perfect timing. Please assist Signor Li to that chair over there and stay beside him while we examine this saddle.'

The officer held Li firmly by the wrists and pulled him away from the counter. Li shrugged him off and sat down.

'Please proceed.'

DiMarco looked from Cristina to Li then back to the saddle. He briefly went into the back room and returned with a few tools.

'You're sure, Ispettore?'

Cristina nodded. 'Certain.'

DiMarco began at the high cantle at the rear of the saddle, cutting open the stitching from the point where it was damaged until the smooth laminated wood of the saddle tree was revealed.

He sighed. 'Beautiful.'

He carefully peeled back the leather then gasped.

The wood was drilled like a honeycomb, with cut pink

diamonds in each hole.

'Careful, Signor DiMarco. Remove them one at a time and put them on the counter.'

She turned to Li, who watched grimly, arms folded. 'Of course, you know nothing of this.'

'How could I, Ispettore? The saddle was a gift.'

DiMarco worked steadily away until all the leather was stripped from the saddle tree. There were even more gems packed into the tall, wide pommel. He placed the last of them on the counter that now twinkled like a small pink ice floe.

'There,' he said, straightening up and surveying the mess of the destroyed saddle. 'The saddle is so full of holes that I'm surprised it didn't fall apart when it was being ridden.'

'You're not quite finished,' said Cristina. 'Check the stirrups.'

The metal had been drilled there, too, and another dozen or so gems were added to the haul. Almost a hundred perfect pink diamonds had been found.

Cristina spread them in a single layer and took a photograph. 'Please bring a box that I can take them away in.'

DiMarco disappeared into the back room and returned with a plastic box with a snap lid. Cristina filled it and snapped it tightly shut.

'Thank you. Send a bill for your time to me at the Questura in Cassiatorre.' She turned to Li. 'Signor Li, I now need you to come with me to the Questura. I have a few questions for you.' Finally, she addressed the Carabiniere. 'Please bring the saddle with you and drive us back.'

No-one spoke on the return journey. The Jeep stopped immediately outside the Questura and the three entered – Li first, then Cristina, and finally the officer with the saddle.

'Put it there,' Cristina said, pointing to a table beside Alfiero's counter. 'Alfiero, please escort Signor Li to my office and wait with him until I arrive.' She waited until they had gone and spoke to the officer. 'Thanks for your help today.'

'No problem, Ispettore. What do you want us to do about the other two and their trailer?'

'I don't think we'll be too long. Signor Li will no doubt insist on speaking to someone at the Chinese Embassy and I'll be told to release him. Please wait at the trailer until I bring him back.'

The officer saluted and left. Cristina made for her office but was intercepted by Vice Questore Montanari.

'I'll sit in on this, if I may, Cristina.'

Li and Alfiero sat, both with folded arms, side by side in front of Cristina's desk. Cristina sat behind her desk and placed the plastic box in front of her while CC took a seat at the side.

'Thank you, Alfiero,' said Cristina. 'You can get back to your desk now, but please enter the saddle into evidence for me.'

Alfiero rose. 'Vice Questore Montanari, Ispettore.'

'Signor Li, what can you tell me about the saddle?'

He unfolded his arms and sat forward, jabbing a finger at Cristina. 'I can tell you that I watched while it was systematically destroyed. It was a unique piece. A masterpiece – your own saddle maker said so – and now it resembles a spatchcock chicken.'

'From which about one hundred pink diamonds were recovered,' said Cristina, opening the box and spilling the diamonds out like a pink waterfall.

Li folded his arms again and stuck out his chin.

'I know nothing about them. How could I? They were sewn into the saddle. And nor could Champion Leng,' he added quickly.

CC cleared her throat. 'Why did you not take the saddle to be x-rayed, Ispettore?'

Li looked smug. 'We drove past the hospital. I'm sure they could have done it.'

'Some years ago, I was on assignment to Venice Marco Polo Airport.' Cristina began putting the diamonds back into the plastic box. 'We received information about a shipment of diamonds arriving on a flight from the Far East. We knew from the passenger manifest who was supposed to be carrying them, and the person was detained, searched, and x-rayed.' She closed the lid. 'The diamonds didn't show up on the scanner because they are what's called radiolucent. There are techniques and equipment found in diamond mines which use much higher doses of radiation, but a hospital set-up would not have detected the diamonds in the saddle.'

'But it would have detected the holes bored inside.'

'Yes, but then we would have had to go to the saddle maker afterwards anyway. And Signor Li made it clear that he and Champion Leng are on a tight schedule.'

CC nodded. 'I see.' She turned to Li. 'Signor Li, I have had a phone call that instructs me to release you, so you are free to go.'

Cristina's jaw dropped.

Li slapped his hands on his thighs. 'And the saddle? The diamonds?'

'They remain with us,' replied Montanari. 'They are now part of an ongoing investigation and may or may not be released to the original owner, if they come forward in person to claim them. In the meantime, I'll enter them into evidence.'

Li muttered something in Chinese and strode out of the office, leaving the door swinging.

Montanari moved to the seat Alfiero had been in.

'I had two phone calls,' she said. 'One from a Chinese Embassy official – though, how they knew, I don't know – and the other anonymous. That's the one I want to talk to you about. It concerns Commissario Moretti.'

*

Along the corridor in his own office, Agente Gennaro Santoro flicked through the notepad that he had pocketed from Moretti's desk. He copied details into a page in his own notebook of all the little nuisances that had befallen Moretti – the anonymous letters, the photographs, and now the mysterious appearance of the money in his account. On the facing page he wrote a list of potential suspects – ex-Vice Questore Innocenti; the three gossips; Vanni; new Vice Questore Montanari. He drew pencil lines between the possible suspects and each event.

The gossips could certainly be behind the anonymous

letters and the photographs. He knew for certain that they had done it before, but twenty thousand euros from an offshore account was beyond them. Innocenti could have sent the letters. Certainly, there was enough detail to suggest inside knowledge, but twenty thousand? He ruled out Montanari for the same reason. So, that left Vanni. Was it a coincidence that this all began when Vanni returned? He was sure that the doctor could afford the cash, but did he know people in Rome who could have put it into Moretti's account? Gennaro knew that his own contacts there would be able to find out. Then a thought struck him, and he wrote another name on the suspects' page.

What if Vanni's return was linked to Moretti's wife Maria? He looked at her name, circled it, then shook his head and scribbled it out as his phone rang.

'Hello, Santoro here.'

'It's Pino Mancini. I heard you'd been unwell. How are you?'

'This is unexpected. I'm fine. I've to follow doctor's orders, and I'm confined to the Questura while I recover fully, but I'm good. How about you?'

'The truth is, I'm bored. Can you escape long enough to have coffee with me?'

Santoro chuckled. 'For all anyone here pays attention to me, I could drop down dead and not be noticed. When and where?'

'I'm at Bar Italia. Why not join me?'

'Ah, Pino, there are three very good reasons why I won't join you there, and they're probably sitting at the outside table nearest the door. Tell you what I'll do, I'll sign out for lunch and walk home. Why don't we meet there?'

'I'm on my way.'

Shortly later, the two men sat with freshly made coffee in front of them. Poirot curled his tail around Mancini's sharply pressed trouser leg and pressed his head into the hand that was stroking it.

'So, you're not finding retirement easy, then?'

'That's it, Gennaro, it's too easy. It's hard to fill the days.'

Santoro shook his head and smiled. 'You've run out of young women to seduce, you mean?'

Mancini laughed.

'Not yet, but I need something else.' He drained his cup and placed it on the table. 'Imagine you leave a car in the garage for a year, two maybe. What happens to it?'

'Well, I guess the battery will go flat, and eventually parts will seize up.'

'Now imagine that the car is a Ferrari.'

'Ah, well, that would be a catastrophe. Are you comparing yourself to a Ferrari?'

Mancini looked Santoro steadily in the eyes.

'Gennaro, I quickly became more than a cop. I trained with special agents from the Italian Secret Service and with a Special Forces group drawn from five NATO countries. Although my original assignments were anti-Mafia, I was deployed here and abroad in a number of roles – witness protection, extraction, all manner of covert activity that I can't go into.'

Santoro rubbed his chin then pulled his notebook out and laid it open on the table between them.

'What's all this?'

'Pino, ever since the new Vice Questore arrived, Moretti seems to have had one bit of bad luck after another. Look.' He explained the events and his thoughts about who was behind them

Mancini's eyes darted across the pages, and he nodded. 'This is more than coincidence, Gennaro. Someone is out to destroy Moretti.'

'I agree, but unfortunately I'm banned from driving for the moment, so I can't get about to do anything about it.'

'Mind if I take a copy?'

'Go ahead. For what it's worth, Moretti thinks that ex-Vice Questore Innocenti is behind it all.'

Mancini clicked his phone camera over the page. 'Okay, I'll have a think about it and see what I can come up with. Anything else?'

'Well, Cristina has discovered a diamond smuggling scheme.'

Mancini sat up brightly. 'Oh? That sounds interesting.'

‘There was a fortune in pink diamonds stashed in the saddle of that Chinese rider. She discovered it by luck.’

‘And I guess the authorities have shut down the investigation?’

‘You guess correctly. Phone call from the embassy.’

‘Now that sounds like something that I could get my teeth into. I used to have connections with Chinese law enforcement. Let’s see if they are still around, and maybe I can come up with a lead or two.’

Mancini stood to leave.

Gennaro shook his hand. ‘Thanks, Pino.’

‘I haven’t done anything yet.’ Mancini laughed. ‘I might find out that the Ferrari has become a Fiat Panda.’

‘Well, pandas are Chinese, so maybe a Fiat Panda is good enough.’

CHAPTER THIRTY-THREE

'Concerns Commissario Moretti, how exactly?' Cristina gasped.

'The informant said that there is an Etruscan artefact hidden in his house.'

'Who is this informant? Where did they call from? Do you have their number?'

Montanari crossed her legs.

'The call came from an internet app, so the number wasn't displayed, and I don't know where they were calling from. The informant's accent was local, however, and they gave very precise details of the inside of Commissario Moretti's house. Have you been inside?'

'No.'

'Me neither, but the caller clearly knows the house well.'

Cristina slid her hand up her forehead and grabbed her hair until it hurt.

'Ispettore.' Montanari uncrossed her legs and leaned forward. 'Cristina, I know this must be difficult for you, but we must investigate. Rather, *you* must investigate.'

'I can't believe it.'

'I know, but I need you to go there and do your job. I've already called to get a warrant, and I've arranged for a forensics team to meet you there. The State Police will give you back-up.'

'I don't think that will be necessary, Vice Questore.'

'It's procedure, Cristina. Just in case.'

'It must be a mistake.'

'Cristina, your loyalty does you credit. It's one of your qualities that I most admire. But I trust you to do a thorough job, and if it is a mistake, then all and well. No harm done, and we'll all move on.' Montanari lowered her voice. 'But if it is true, then I want you to be ready to step immediately into Moretti's shoes, first as an interim replacement, then full-time. I know from Vice Questore Innocenti's files that's what he wanted.' Montanari stood. 'Get yourself ready, and I'll check that the warrant has arrived.' She picked up the plastic box from the desk. 'I'll get these entered into evidence. Report back to me with what you find.'

The Vice Questore left, closing the office door behind her. Cristina rubbed her eyes then reached for her phone to call Moretti but hesitated, stopped, and put it back in her pocket. She inhaled deeply and shrugged her shoulders.

Thirty minutes later, she was outside Moretti's house. The team of four forensics officers was already there and dressed in their white suits. Two State Police officers, with pistols drawn, stood behind her. She put on her gloves and knocked on the door.

'Commissario Moretti, it's Cristina. Open up, please.'

No reply.

She knocked and called inside again.

Still nothing. She tried the door handle. It turned, and the door opened. The officers levelled their weapons.

Cristina turned to one and pushed his arm down. 'No need for that.'

She slipped on shoe covers and stepped into the dimly lit, cool kitchen, letting her eyes adjust to the light.

'Commissario Moretti, it's Cristina. I have a warrant to search your house. I'm inside, and there are other officers outside. If you are here, I need you to come out and make yourself known.'

No reply. Not a sound.

She switched on the light, walked to the counter, and surveyed the room. Everything was in order in the kitchen, though the dining table was covered with neatly stacked bundles of papers. The two armed officers came in as she crossed to the table. She nodded, and the two men checked the rest of the house while she examined the papers.

'All clear, Ispettore.'

'Thank you. Please take your car back to the road and let me know if Commissario Moretti appears.'

They holstered their pistols, saluted, and left as the forensics team came in.

'We are looking for an Etruscan artefact. I don't know what type or what size but let me know when you find it.'

One of the white-suited men returned to the front door while the other three began a search. Cristina picked up a small stack of papers and flicked through it. Witness statements from the Vanni case, with Moretti's handwritten notes in the margins. She put it back.

'Ispettore, come here.'

Cristina followed the voice to a bedroom. An officer was crouching in front of an open wardrobe. He pointed to a neat tower of shoe boxes on the floor of the wardrobe.

'Look here.'

He slid the boxes aside to reveal a perfect Etruscan vase.

Cristina bent to look.

'Photograph everything,' she said. 'Then carefully bring it out to the kitchen and place it on the counter.'

The other two officers stopped their search and joined their colleague. Cristina watched them make a meticulous record of the scene but wondered why there were so many empty hangers in the space above.

Her phone rang, breaking her musings. 'Furlan.'

'Ispettore, Commissario Moretti's here.'

'On my way. Thanks.'

*

Moretti drove home with the radio on the whole time to block out the thoughts that haunted his nights and now the quiet parts of his days. He had not been able to bring himself to ask Maria about the timeline around the death of Vanni's parents. Nor had he pursued his suspicions that she had a secret boyfriend down there. At least she looked well and happy.

From some way off he noticed the police car parked on the verge at the entrance to the dirt road that led to his house, and he gave the officers a wave as he turned onto the track. Around the curve below him the scene caused him to slow down so that he could take it all in. His house was surrounded by incident tape. And several vehicles, including the forensics team and Cristina's car, were parked in front of it. He stopped a little way back and got out. The police car that had been at the main road had followed him down and now sat sideways across the track, blocking any chance of escape.

Cristina emerged from his house wearing shoe covers and gloves.

He closed the car door and called to her. 'What's all this?'

She pulled off her gloves and shoe covers and walked over to him, producing a piece of paper from her pocket.

'Commissario Moretti, this is a search warrant.' She handed him the paper.

He hardly glanced at it. 'This is a joke, right?'

Cristina looked uncomfortable but grim.

'Unfortunately, sir, it's no joke.'

The officers from the car blocking his drive had made their way down the track and now stood a little way behind him. One of them had undone the flap over his revolver.

'How did you get inside?'

'I tried the handle, and the door was open.'

'Well, I'm aways careful to lock up. Did you examine the lock?'

'I didn't have to.'

Moretti addressed the forensics officer near the door. 'Check the lock for damage.'

'I'm sorry, sir, but according to Vice Questore Montanari, as of now you are suspended from duty. You don't have the authority to ask the officer to do anything.'

Moretti rubbed the back of his neck. 'Well, could you ask him then, Cristina?'

She turned. 'Please examine the lock and take prints from the area.'

'So what, am I under arrest now?'

'Not at the moment, Commissario, but I'd like you to come inside and answer some questions.'

Moretti shook his head. 'Of course.'

They both went inside. The vase was on the kitchen counter being photographed by a forensics officer.

Moretti pointed at it. 'What's that doing here?'

'I was hoping that you'd be able to tell me.'

'What I can tell you is that I've never seen it before. Where was it?'

'We found it at the bottom of a wardrobe, behind some shoe boxes.'

'My wife's wardrobe?'

Moretti immediately recalled the conversation he'd had with Maria when she had acted as unpaid counsel to the immigrants.

'You sold some artefacts for the immigrants, didn't you? Where did you hide them? We searched both cars after you and Cristina came back from collecting the men from the tomb.'

'Ask Alfiero. He searched me and all the men.'

'Where was your bag? Did he search that, too?'

'I put it on the counter. You'll need to ask him if he searched it.'

She must have kept this one for some reason. *But why?* He had to protect her until he had a chance to speak with her. He sighed deeply and began thinking clearly.

'So, Cristina. Sorry, Ispettore Furlan. You found an artefact in my house. I guess you had an anonymous tip-off.' He paused, but Cristina remained silent. 'As I thought. Okay, when your colleague checks the front door, I'm sure that he'll find that the lock has been tampered with.' He reached into his pocket. 'These are my house keys. This one is for the main lock. Try it for yourself and tell me if it feels normal.' He held out the bunch of keys.

Cristina didn't take them. 'I wouldn't know what it should feel like.'

Moretti jabbed his thumb over his shoulder.

'Well, let him try then, or better still, get Moscardini here. He's a locksmith. He'll know.'

'All in due course, Commissario. Are you saying that

you think someone broke in and planted the vase?'

Moretti didn't want to think where the vase came from.

'Well, it sounds the most likely explanation, don't you agree?'

'It's one possibility, but there are others.' She counted on her fingers. 'You could have brought the vase here. Your wife could have brought it here. A visitor might have brought it.' She broke off. 'Oh, I'll need the details of any visitors who have been here since the tomb was discovered, if you can remember them.'

'That's easy, only Sergio Vanni.'

'Not Gennaro?'

'No.'

Cristina hesitated. 'Carla?'

'No, Cristina, only Vanni.'

'Alright.'

'Look, someone broke in here. If you won't call Moscardini, then I will, because I'll need to change the locks.'

Cristina looked past him to the police officer at the door.

'Call Signor Moscardini and ask him to come here, please. Don't tell him what it's about.'

The policeman nodded and stepped away from the house. His colleague took up position at the door.

The three forensics officers came back into the kitchen area. 'We've finished here, Ispettore, unless there's anything else you want us to look at?'

Moretti spoke. 'Have you checked the outside area for tyre prints or shoe prints?'

The forensics team looked at Cristina.

'Have you?' she asked.

'No.'

'Then please do that before you go. Oh, I need one of you to stay until Moscardini arrives.'

'Yes, Ispettore.'

'May I offer you something to drink, Cristina?'

'Nothing, thank you, sir.'

'May I pour myself some water?'

'Of course.'

Moretti filled a glass from the tap and drank deeply, then smoothed his moustache.

'Look, I know this is difficult for you, Cristina, but I really don't have a clue about the vase.' He took another sip. 'Maybe you should get the museum guys to identify it to see if it came from the tomb that was discovered last year. If not, then the problem isn't only local.'

'Commissario—'

'Sorry, I'm telling you how to do your job. I'll shut up.' He drained the glass and wiped his hand across his moustache. 'May I sit down?'

'Yes.'

Moretti sat at the table.

Cristina joined him. 'Do you keep copies of all your old case files?'

'No. This one was special.' His eyes flicked across the neat piles of papers. 'It was personal, and it was the only one I didn't solve.'

'That's some record, sir.'

Moretti motioned to the papers. 'May I?'

Cristina nodded, and as he began to stack them together into one pile, Vanni's admission of guilt rose to his lips desperate to be shared. But Moretti swallowed it down. When everything was back in the banker's box, Moretti leaned back in his seat, crossed his hands on his stomach and closed his eyes, while Cristina made notes into her phone until the locksmith came.

The sound of car tyres outside broke Moretti's chain of thought and he sat up.

'I'll take those keys now, if I may,' said Cristina.

Moretti handed them over and remained seated while she went to greet the locksmith.

'Signor Moscardini, thank you for coming. I wonder if you could look at this door.' She handed him the keys.

Moscardini took them, found the correct one, placed the tip of it in the lock and turned it. 'Hm.'

He removed the key, knelt, and looked closely at the lock. Then he produced a strong LED light and a magnifying glass and looked again.

'This has been picked,' he said, craning up at Cristina.

'Picked? How do you know?'

Moscardini smiled.

'A lifetime's experience, Ispettore, and it would take me a lifetime to explain, but it's enough for you to know that the moving parts inside the lock are out of alignment, and the front surface has two tiny scratch marks where two picks have been pushed in.'

'Scratch marks?'

'Every lock has scratches. Every time a key touches the metal, a microscopic layer is worn away. But over time these form a microscopic groove that is smooth, because it more or less happens in the same place. The marks that I'm referring to have been made more recently, so their edges are more ragged and not in the position that a key would follow.' Moscardini stood up and dusted his knees. 'No, Ispettore, this lock has been picked. Where is Commissario Moretti? Does he know about this?'

'In here,' called Moretti. 'Thanks, Gianni. You've confirmed what I said a while ago.'

Moscardini poked his head in the door. 'Hi Dino. You really should change that lock, you know.'

Moretti chuckled and sat up. 'Why don't you come back today and fix me up with one of your top-of-the-range locks?'

Moscardini looked at Cristina. She nodded.

'Will do. I'll be back in an hour.'

Moretti waited until the locksmith had left, then said to Cristina, 'So, Ispettore, am I under arrest?'

'No, sir, but I will need your badge.'

CHAPTER THIRTY-FOUR

Cristina held the cardboard box under her arm and knocked the Vice Questore's door.

'Enter.'

Cristina pushed open the door.

Montanari didn't look up from the papers on her desk. 'Please sit, Cristina.'

Cristina brought a chair from the side, placed the box on her lap, and sat quietly.

Montanari closed the folder and looked up. 'Well, what do you have for me?'

Cristina set the box on the desk, opened it, brought out the vase, and removed the bubble plastic that it was wrapped in.

'We found this in the bottom of a wardrobe.'

Montanari gasped and reached out to touch it but withdrew her hand. 'It's beautiful.' She stood and walked around the table to see it from every side.

'To think that someone made this two thousand years ago,' she whispered. 'Look, you can still see the thumb marks of the potter on the lip.' She sat down again. 'Put it back in the box. I don't want it to be damaged.'

Cristina wrapped it carefully and returned it to the box.

'What did Commissario Moretti have to say about it?'

'He claimed that someone had broken into his house

and planted it there.'

Montanari smirked. 'Well, he would, wouldn't he?'

'We brought Moscardini the locksmith to examine the door, and it had been picked.'

'So, you think that proves Moretti's innocence? You've a lot to learn, Ispettore. All it proves is that Moretti is clever enough to be able to fake a break-in to cover himself.' She stabbed her finger into the desk for emphasis. 'Did Moscardini say when the lock was picked? Could he say that it was someone other than Moretti? Were you able to say that the vase wasn't there before the lock was picked? Of course not.' CC shook her head. 'No, Cristina, you have been deceived by a corrupt officer who has used his knowledge of evidence to lead you to draw a false conclusion. Moretti is using your loyalty and the fact that you don't want to believe he's corrupt.'

'He seemed genuinely surprised.'

'Of course he did. That's part of the act, but he doesn't fool me. Did you tell him he was suspended?'

Cristina nodded. 'Yes.' She placed Moretti's badge on the desk.

Montanari put it in her drawer.

'Good work, Cristina. Now take the vase to evidence and write up a full report. That will be all.'

Cristina put the chair back against the wall and left.

Santoro beckoned her into his office. 'Close the door,' he said.

They sat on opposite sides of his desk, the box with the vase on Cristina's lap

'What was all that about?'

Cristina told him all about the warrant, the search, and Moretti's suspension.

When she finished, Santoro spoke quietly but firmly.

'I've known Dino for a long time, Cristina. He's not corrupt. If he says he knows nothing about the vase, it's the truth.'

'CC's alternative version of events is plausible, though. The break-in and the presence of the vase might be unrelated.'

Santoro opened his notebook.

'These are notes that I copied from the Commissario's

notebook – the one that Montanari told him to leave on his desk. I've written some names of people who could be behind all this.' He turned the notebook for Cristina to see. 'The name that I wrote and scribbled out, the one at the bottom of the list. That was his wife's name.'

'Maria? The lawyer?'

Santoro shrugged. 'Look, I don't know the whole story, but I know they're going through a difficult patch at the moment. I think it has something to do with Vanni being back in town. But Maria acted for the immigrants, remember? She met with them and could have accepted that vase as payment. Who knows?'

Cristina fidgeted with the lid of the box.

'It's all so confusing.'

Santoro smiled. 'It's our job to untangle it, Cristina, and when I say us, I mean you, seeing as how I'm confined to the office.'

Cristina took a deep breath and exhaled loudly. 'Okay, Gennaro, what do we need to do?'

'I don't know how long the boss will be suspended, so it would be good if we… you… could follow up on a couple of his investigations.'

'What was he working on?'

'Well, right before he was marched out by CC, we were talking about the two cattle farmers. I called Beppe's girlfriend Bea, and she confirms that he was with her all night. The Capo thinks that a third party might be involved, someone who'd gain from them and Zhao going out of business.'

'Did he put that to Beppe?'

'No. We didn't know at the time and anyway Beppe was in no mood to listen to anything. So it might help if you told him that as far as the death of Buina's bull, he's in the clear.'

'Fine, I'll speak with the Buinas myself.' Cristina frowned. 'But first I'll go and ask An Na and her family what they know about the saddle.'

Santoro made a shooing movement with his hands. 'Right then, you'd better get going.'

'I'll check this vase into evidence first.' She rose and paused at the door. 'You're sure about the commissario,

Gennaro?'

'Absolutely. I'd stake my life on it. Now go.'

Cristina left the vase with Alfiero and walked the short distance to Chībăo and knocked on the door. An Na opened it.

Cristina held up her ID. 'I'm Ispettore Cristina Furlan. May I come in? I have a few questions for you about the saddle.'

'Where is Moretti?'

Cristina swallowed. 'I've been asked to speak with you.'

An Na pushed the door, but Cristina held it open.

'Please. I need two minutes of your time.'

A Chinese voice from behind asked a question. An Na called back an answer. She opened the door.

'Two minutes.'

'Thank you.'

Cristina stepped in and was immediately embraced by the fragrant aromas from the kitchen.

An Na stood, arms folded.

'What can you tell me about the saddle that Champion Leng had on his horse?'

An Na shrugged. 'It came by messenger. A gift for Leng from China.'

'Do you know from where in China? From whom?'

An Na's expression was unreadable. 'China is a big place. There are many people. Why do you want to know?'

'The saddle is part of an enquiry.'

'One minute.'

'I won't keep you. Can you tell me the significance of a tattoo?'

'Tattoos mean many things.'

'This one was unusual. It went round almost all the wrist and was shaped like a rat but with a scorpion's tail?'

An Na's face fleetingly betrayed fear and panic before she controlled it.

'It means something, doesn't it? You've seen it before.'

An Na stabbed her finger at Cristina. 'I have a question for *you*. Where is my grandmother's luggage? Moretti promised he would find it. Where is Moretti? Where is the trunk?'

'I must be honest, Signorina, I don't know. This was an investigation that Commissario Moretti was handling personally. What I will say is that if he promised he would find it, he will do everything in his power to do so, and I will get in touch with him to find out how it is going.'

'Next time, send Moretti I trust Moretti. Now go, we must prepare for customers.'

Cristina was glad to leave. She strode to her car and drove down into the valley thinking about An Na's reaction to the mention of the tattoo – and that she'd tried to hide it.

When she reached Nardelli's farm, the dogs approached her car until she stepped out and they retreated to the shade. Nardelli appeared from the cowshed at the same time as Beppe emerged from the barn.

'Good day, Signori. I wonder if I could have a word with you, Beppe? It's about Signor Buina's bull.'

'It's okay, Dad can hear what you have to say as well.'

'We checked with your girlfriend, and she confirms that you were with her all night.'

'Told you so,' said Beppe hotly.

'So what now?' asked Ignazio. 'Is that it? Case closed?'

'Well, obviously if any new evidence comes up, we'll follow it but Commissario Moretti has a notion that some third party could be behind all of it.'

'Third party?'

'Yes, someone with a grudge, maybe?'

Ignazio shrugged.

'I don't believe that any of the other cattle breeders would be involved.'

'What about Cosimo?' offered Beppe. 'Does anyone know where he is? I heard he's back?'

Cristina frowned. 'Cosimo? Who's he?'

'Buina's son,' replied Beppe.

'Buina's estranged son,' said Ignazio.

Cristina brought out her phone and began to make notes. 'I don't think we knew that Signor Buina had a son.'

'Huh. I'm not surprised.'

'He never speaks about him, Ispettore. He brought

shame to the family. Some people think that his behaviour caused his mother's death.'

'What behaviour exactly?'

'It started as petty crime, stealing, shoplifting, but he spent some time in prison, and when he came out, he was involved in drugs, violent crime, and housebreaking. You must have him on record.'

'I'll look him up. Thanks.'

'And check if anyone has seen him around Maghicchio.'

'Have you seen him, Beppe?'

'I don't know. Maybe. I was driving to visit Bea, and I thought I caught a glimpse of him as I passed the station, but I couldn't be sure. It's worth checking anyway. He was always a shit.'

'Look, I'm sorry about everything that's happened here, but I'll follow up on Cosimo. Thank you.'

'You do that, Ispettore,' spat Beppe. 'You do that.'

Cristina called Santoro from her car.

'Gennaro, what do we have on a Cosimo Buina?'

'I remember the name. I think he was involved in some petty stuff locally. Did some prison time, but I've not heard anything recent. I'll check and get back to you. How did you get on with Beppe?'

'He's still raging. It was he who gave me Cosimo's name.'

'Okay, leave it with me.'

'Thanks.'

Buina was in the courtyard when Cristina drove in. She stopped beside him, got out, and held up her ID.

'Signor Buina, Commissario Cristina Furlan. I wonder if you can help with a case that I'm working on?'

'Is it the case of who poisoned my prize bull?'

'That, and who mutilated the Nardelli bull.'

'Don't know anything. Goodbye.' The grizzled farmer turned and walked away.

Cristina called after him. 'Then maybe you can tell me where I can find your son Cosimo?'

Buina's progress faltered. He called back over his shoulder, 'I have no son.'

Cristina caught up with him in three strides and

blocked his path.

'Whether you want to admit to it or not, Signor Buina, you do have a son, a son who has served time in prison, and who I need to speak with.'

'I haven't seen him for four years, and if I don't see him this side of infinity, it'll be too soon.'

'You haven't heard of him returning to the area? You haven't seen him around the farm?'

'If I saw him here, I'd shoot him like the vermin he is, Ispettore. Now, unless you've any news about who's ruined my business, I need to get on.'

By the time Cristina returned to the Questura, Santoro had pulled Cosimo Buina's file from the records.

'In here, Ispettore,' he called, as she passed his open door.

She slumped into a chair. 'What do you have for me, Gennaro?'

'Good news or bad news?'

'Either.'

'Okay, Cosimo got into trouble from a very young age. Fights at school, bullying, stealing things. That led on to theft, scamming tourists and shoplifting, for which he was handed a six-month prison sentence not long after his eighteenth birthday. He came out but instead of going straight, he branched into burglary, assault, and possession of drugs.'

'What class of drugs?'

'He moved up the scale there, too. Started with magic mushrooms and cannabis then onto ecstasy, and cocaine. He got two years in prison.'

'Then what?'

'Then nothing. When he came out of prison, it's as if he vanished. There's no record of him committing any crime, not even a parking ticket.'

'Do you think he's dead?'

'Either that or he's left the country, or he has a new identity.'

'So, we've no way of tracing him, Gennaro. Is that what you're saying?'

'Not exactly, Ispettore. I've made some enquiries using unofficial channels. Let's see what comes of those.'

CHAPTER THIRTY-FIVE

Moretti sat at the table looking at the questions he had written in a notepad in preparation for his meeting with Internal Affairs.

Where did tourist get the magic mushrooms that led to the fatal car accident?

Not from Beppe, the obvious source – of that he was certain – but who? Hallucinogenic mushrooms were not part of the usual drugs on offer locally. He preened his moustache, first left then right, and sent a message to Santoro.

Gennaro, I don't want to call you at the Questura, but could you find out if forensics opened the phone of the tourist in the car crash? He must have bought the mushrooms locally.

Thanks.

He looked back at the pad.

Why was Buina's cowshed broken into?

Nothing was taken, yet someone went to a lot of bother to cut through a hefty chain. But why? He walked to the sink and poured a glass of water, sipping it as he paced up and down.

Of course.

He picked up his phone and messaged Cristina.

Cristina, go to Buina's farm and get him to check the security system in the cowshed.

Make sure that it hasn't been tampered with. Thanks.

He finished the water and returned to the notepad, writing down the idea that had only then occurred to him. His phone rang.

'Moretti.'

'Capo, it's Gennaro.'

'Gennaro. Is it safe to talk?'

'Yes. I've stepped out on the balcony in your office. Nice view.'

Moretti grinned. 'Don't get used to it, I'm planning to be back at work very soon. What have you got for me?'

'Forensics opened the dead man's phone. There are no messages, unfortunately, but there's a phone number that he called and that called him back the day before and on the day of the accident.'

'Good work, Gennaro. Try and trace the number and get back to me with a name and address if possible.'

'Will do.'

'Oh, Gennaro, have you noticed that Chen has a tattoo?'

'A tattoo? Capo, are you okay? I thought that you'd be preparing for your grilling by Internal Affairs.'

Moretti chuckled.

'I'm fine, thanks, Gennaro. It's only that I have all this swirling inside my head. Chen has a tattoo around his wrist – a solid black band – it's as though he's covered up another tattoo.'

'Capo, it's probably the name of a former girlfriend.'

'Look, you know him well, and his shop is on your way home. Pop in after work and find out what's under that tattoo. What else is new?'

'Of course, you won't have heard. Cristina found about a hundred diamonds hidden in Leng's saddle.'

'What? The one that was presented to him at the contrada meal?'

'Yes. About a million euros' worth.'

'*Mannaggia*. Montanari will love her for that.'

'I thought so, too, but she's kept very quiet about it. Probably planning a press conference or something. Cristina spoke with An Na about it, but she knew nothing.'

'Damn. That reminds me. I haven't been in touch about the trunk that her grandmother lost.'

Moretti looked down at his notepad.

Where is stolen trunk? Who took it? How? Further check of CCTV?

'Gennaro, I'm afraid until I clear things with Internal Affairs, I have to depend on you and Cristina.'

'Capo, it's fine. Really. I'm using some of my contacts to dig about. I'll report back before your interview.'

'Oh, there's another call coming in. Must go. Thanks, Gennaro.'

'Take care, Capo.'

'Moretti.'

'Cristina, sir. I got your message and I'm on my way. I'll report back to you if I find anything.'

'Thanks, Cristina – and congratulations. I hear you foiled a major diamond smuggling attempt.'

'It was luck more than police work, Commissario. I'll send you a copy of my report.'

*

This time, when Cristina parked in Buina's yard, the farm dogs stayed where they were. The farmer was not outside so she knocked on the door of the farmhouse.

'I can see who you are,' called a gruff voice. 'I saw enough of you yesterday. Clear off.'

'Signor Buina, I need to check your cowshed.'

No response.

'It may help answer some of your questions.'

She heard a chair being pushed back from a table and the clumping of feet. 'What exactly do you need to see?'

'Your security system.'

Buina sighed loudly. 'Fine. Come with me.'

They walked across the yard to the cowshed, and Buina pointed up to the eaves. 'There. Look all you want.'

Cristina craned her neck to see.

'Signor Buina, can you explain the set-up to me?'

The farmer tutted and pointed up.

'These are two lights activated by motion sensors. There, between them, is a camera that is linked to the same motion sensors. It sends signals direct to my computer in the house when any movement is recorded.'

'I understand. And over here,' she said, pointing further along, 'what's this?'

Buina looked to where she was pointing. 'I don't know. Is it a camera?'

'I think it is. Can we see inside the cowshed?'

Buina opened the padlock and dropped the chain.

'Help yourself.'

Cristina stepped inside and looked up.

'There, see, that camera has a lead going along to the electricity supply that feeds your security system.'

'Well, I never installed it.'

Cristina pulled out her phone. 'Can I call one of our tech guys to get it checked out?'

'Of course.'

Half an hour later, the technician had arrived, taken down the camera, and was able to give Cristina and Buina his report.

'What we have here is a remote surveillance camera. It was connected into the modem on your computer system, Signor Buina, and whoever installed it could monitor your movements.'

Buina picked up the camera and turned it in his hands. 'How is that possible?'

'Well, the person would need to be able to access your computer – and, as I found, it isn't password protected. They would also have to get into your house to access your electrical supply to switch off your security system. Do you know of anyone who has a key?'

'No. No-one. And I always take care to lock up securely.'

'Signor Buina,' said Cristina, 'does Cosimo have a key?'

*

Santoro looked at the message on his phone and left his office for the balcony of Moretti's office. He noticed Mancini sitting on a bench in the square below and called him.

'Hello, Pino, what do you have for me?'

'Is that you on the balcony?'

'Yes, it's safer to phone this way.'

'Well, you can rule out ex-Vice Questore Innocenti. He's living a simple life in Rome and unsuccessfully trying to get work as a security consultant.'

'Hmm. Moretti was sure he was involved. What else have you found out?'

'There's a connection to Ricci.'

Santoro gasped. 'How come?'

'I got in touch with some of my grey contacts.'

'Grey?'

'Yes, the ones who work both inside and outside the legal boundaries.'

'Okay, and what did they tell you?'

'The number you sent me – the one that the car death guy called – it's from a mobile phone bought in Rome, but my contact hacked the triangulated data from it, which placed it in this area.'

'Go on.'

'The bulk of the time is spent in two locations, Ricci's agriturismo and the train station in Maghicchio.'

'That's amazing.'

'But not all. It has also been traced to Erpicone's farm, and both the Buina and Nardelli farms.'

'This could be the breakthrough that we need. Do you fancy doing some real police work again and interviewing the owner?'

'No. I need to protect my identity, but I can give you a name. The phone is registered to a Damiano Buono.'

'Damiano Buono, got it. Wait. That's Cosimo Buina! Don't you see? He's changed Cosimo to Damiano and Buina to Buono.'

Mancini laughed. 'Careful or you'll fall off that balcony. Yes, I did make the connection but that's all. It's up to you now.'

'Oh, before you go, any update on the diamonds?'

'Still working on that. I'll be in touch. Bye.'

Santoro hung up and lifted his hand in a little wave, then he called Moretti and Cristina simultaneously.

'Capo, Ispettore, listen carefully. I might have to cut this short.'

'Gennaro, I hear traffic. Are you on my balcony again?'

'Yes, Capo, but please listen. The reason that Cosimo Buina disappeared is because he's taken a new identity. He's now called Damiano Buono.'

'Ah.'

'Aha.'

'He's in the area and spends most time at the train station in Maghicchio and at Ricci's place.'

'Go on, Gennaro.'

'He's also been to both bull farms and to Erpicone's place. What do you want to do?'

'I'm on my way back to Cassiatorre from Buina's place,' said Cristina. 'Someone installed a surveillance camera there. Almost certainly Cosimo. I'll visit Erpicone, then Ricci, and find out what they know.'

'I'm suspended, but I guess I can take a drive down to the railway station to check train times,' said Moretti.

'Commissario, you can't interview Cosimo while you're suspended. Your evidence would be thrown out of court.'

'It's a while since I had a train trip, Capo. Why don't you give me a lift to the station, and *I'll* check the train times?'

'Sign out, Gennaro, and I'll meet you at your place. And send us both a copy of Cosimo's photograph.'

*

Cristina drove into the tidy farmyard and saw Erpicone talking to the immigrants who were now shareholders in the farm.

'Can I have a word, Signor Erpicone?'

'Of course.' He left the workers and met her at her car. 'What can I do for you today?'

Cristina showed him a photograph on her phone. 'Have you seen this man?'

'Yes, a couple of months ago. He came here looking for work, but I told him I had all the help I needed.'

'How was he?'

'Pleasant enough and seemed to know about farming. I think he'd maybe worked before raising cattle. If I didn't have Yusuf and the others, I would have given him a chance. What has he done?'

'We're not sure. That's why I want to talk to him. Did he come back at all?'

'No, Ispettore. I suggested that he try Ricci's place. He sometimes uses seasonal workers.'

'Thank you. I'll ask there. How are things with you?'

The old farmer's eyes twinkled. 'Never better. I have a new girlfriend, and my daughter is coming to visit.'

Cristina smiled. 'A girlfriend, eh? Anyone I know?'

'Signora Luchia, Donatella.'

'Ah, one of the three…' Cristina stopped herself in time. 'One of the three friends who sit outside Bar Italia?'

Erpicone laughed.

'It's alright, Ispettore. You mean one of the three gossips. Yes, that's her. She's due here in a little while to help me get the place spruced up for my daughter's visit. You know, a woman's touch.'

'That's wonderful, Signor Erpicone. Let me know when I have to buy a wedding outfit.'

'It's early days, Ispettore. We're both widowed and we like each other's company.'

'Well, I wish you both happiness, but if you excuse me, I'll visit your neighbour, Signor Ricci.'

She got back into her car, drove the short distance to the agriturismo, and stopped at the entrance barrier. She pressed the button.

'Yes?'

'Ispettore Cristina Furlan for Signor Ricci.'

'One moment.'

The barrier rose and she drove down the drive, parked, and entered reception.

'Hello Alicia, can I speak with Signor Ricci?'

'Hello, Ispettore. I'm sorry, he's away on business. I expect him back tomorrow. Is there anything I can do?'

Cristina showed her the photograph on her phone. 'Have you seen this man?'

Alicia peered closely.

'It looks like Damiano, but he has a shaved head and a beard now. What's this about?'

'Oh, some ongoing enquiries. Where did you see him?'

'Why, here of course. He lives here, in one of the farmhand cabins behind the olive grove. Is he in trouble?'

'I can't say at the moment, but I need to speak with him urgently. Is he on the estate today?'

'No, he only helps out now and then. He works full-time at the railway station in Maghicchio.'

Cristina called Moretti immediately.

CHAPTER THIRTY-SIX

'Jump in, Gennaro.'

'It's good to see you, Capo. How have you been?'

'Oh, fine. Better now that you're here. It's been so frustrating not being able to get anything done because of this stupid vase.' They set off. 'Thanks, Gennaro, it's taking my mind off the interrogation tomorrow.'

'Are you prepared?'

'As much as I can be. There's so many loose ends.'

'Well, if it is Cosimo and we can speak with him, some of those loose ends might get tied up.'

'How are you doing? Is your health improving?'

'It might not look it, but I've lost some weight. The only thing that's getting me down is this stupid individual working regime that CC imposed.'

Moretti laughed. 'Well, that's working well for her.'

Santoro joined in.

'Goodness knows what she'll do when she finds out.'

Moretti's phone rang. He fished it out of his pocket.

'Answer that for me, Gennaro, I haven't figured out the hands-free stuff yet.'

'I don't think your car is modern enough.' He took the phone and put it on loudspeaker. 'Moretti's phone, Santoro here.'

'It's Cristina. I checked with Erpicone. Cosimo went there for work. He stays at Ricci's place but works full-time at the rail station. His appearance is different from his photograph. He's shaven-headed and bearded now.'

Moretti turned his face towards the phone.

'Thanks, Cristina,' he shouted. 'We're there. Speak with you soon.'

The two detectives entered the busy station moments after a train from Florence had disgorged its passengers. They waited until the confusion died down then looked on the platforms and at the ticket office for Cosimo. He was nowhere to be found.

'He could be anywhere,' said Santoro. 'In one of the outbuildings, having a coffee in a bar, anywhere.'

'Well, we know he's at work. Let's ask someone.'

Santoro took out his ID and went to the front of the queue at the ticket office, excused himself to the American trying to buy a ticket, and spoke to the woman behind the counter.

'I'm looking for Damiano Buono. Can you tell me where he's likely to be, please?'

'If he's not on one of the platforms, he'll most likely be downstairs organising the stores. Which one, I don't know. There was a delivery of boxes on another train this morning.'

'Thank you.'

He returned to Moretti. 'Downstairs in a store. She didn't know which one.'

'Let's go and find out how many there are.'

Downstairs they found three doors marked *Staff Only*.

Moretti took out his phone. 'You take the farthest away, and I'll take this one and listen.'

He dialled a number, and a phone rang from the store beside Santoro. Moretti hurried to join him. They entered the store, and at the end of a corridor of cardboard boxes, was a bearded young man with a shaven head. Santoro held up his ID.

'Cosimo Buina, we need to talk.'

'What's this about?'

'Signor Buina, I'm Agente Santoro I have a number of questions for you. Is there somewhere we can go?'

Buina looked from one to the other.

'I recognise you. You're Moretti.'

Moretti nodded.

'Here's fine,' said Buina, sitting on a box.

The detectives sat, Moretti behind Santoro.

'You changed your name to Damiano Buono,' said Santoro. 'Why was that?'

'Do you know how hard it is to find work if you're an ex-con?'

'I know that it's expensive,' replied Santoro, producing his notebook. 'Where did you get the money?'

'Borrowed it. It's not against the law.'

Santoro looked at his notebook.

'And you're staying at the Ricci agriturismo.'

'Correct.'

'An expensive place to stay.'

'I'm in staff accommodation.'

'But you work here.'

'I also do work there.'

'Oh?'

'IT work.'

'Does Ricci pay well?'

'Bed and board.'

'That's a pity. With Trenitalia wages it'll be years before you can pay off your loan.'

Buina shrugged.

'Is that why you stole the trunk? To sell off the contents?'

'That's not what happened.'

'Tell me then.'

'I found the trunk on the platform, and I looked for the owner but there was no-one, and I needed to clear the platform for the next train, so I brought it here.'

'And hid it at the back of the store.'

'I put it where it wouldn't get in the way.'

Santoro referred to his notebook again.

'You did prison time for supplying drugs.'

No answer.

'Including magic mushrooms. They're unusual for this area.'

Buina stared at the floor.

'You supplied an English tourist with mushrooms, didn't you?'

'You've no proof.'

'We've CCTV footage from when he arrived off the train until he drove away in the hired car. Including the time he spent in the bar at the station.'

Buina shook his head.

'You know he died in a car crash, Cosimo? You could be going back to prison.'

Silence.

Santoro softened his tone.

'You said you use your IT skills for Signor Ricci. How did that come about?'

'When I got out of prison a few months ago I was looking for farm work. I got a start at the agriturismo. I was talking to the estate manager, and he found out I could use computers, so I switched from field work to office work.'

'What's Ricci like to work for?'

'He's okay.'

'Sounds as though he's a bit stingy if you only get bed and board. I'd resent him if it were me.'

'You can't be fussy when you're desperate, and anyway I'd heard about this job, so I started here and did Ricci's work in the evenings.'

'What sort of IT work are you doing for him?'

'He wanted to catalogue all his wines, so I set up a spreadsheet.'

'I'd have thought he already had a system.'

'He did but only for the wines in the new cellar. The old one was a disaster.'

'What do you mean?'

'It's an ancient cellar carved out of the tufa. The bottles are valuable but they're in a helluva mess – different wine varieties mixed up, reds and whites bundled together in crates.'

'Must have been difficult to sort that lot out.'

'Wasn't my problem, I only had to catalogue them, but that's why the job is taking so long.'

'So, did you turn up anything unusual?'

Both detectives noticed Buina's eye movements and the expressions that flitted across his face.

'You did, Cosimo,' said Santoro. 'What was it?'

Buina rubbed his thumb into the palm of his other hand.

'Let's come back to that. Was it you that installed a surveillance camera on your father's farm?'

Buina shook his head.

'A security camera. I just wanted to make sure the old fool was safe.'

'Even though he disowned you?'

'I'm a loving son.'

'We also have footage of someone with your build on the Nardelli farm.'

Buina shrugged.

'Nothing to do with me.'

'You see, we're looking for someone with the knowledge of how to harvest bull semen and castrate the animal. Someone with the skill to set up a website and sell the semen online.'

'Not me.' He twisted his thumb deeper into his palm.

'Someone who grew up on a cattle farm.'

'Not me.'

'Someone with maybe a grudge against the Nardellis.'

'Not me.'

'Our experts in gait analysis might tell us different and with your record, you'll be going down for a long time and your debt will never get paid. Do you know what will happen to you? The loan shark will need to set an example.'

Buina dropped his head into his hands.

Moretti spoke for the first time.

'Did you plant an Etruscan vase in my house?'

Buina looked up and met Moretti's gaze.

'I want to speak to a lawyer.'

'Let's go to the Questura, Cosimo,' said Santoro. 'And we'll provide a lawyer. There's a whole lot more to discuss.'

CHAPTER THIRTY-SEVEN

Moretti finished the last of his cappuccino and used the paper serviette to clean the froth and pastry crumbs from his moustache. He placed a ten on the counter and swept his index finger first across the left then right side.

'How do I look?'

Instead of reaching over with his change as usual, Carla came round to his side of the counter and gave it to him.

'Very smart,' she said. 'Let me fix this.'

She brushed some errant pastry flakes from his jacket, straightened the knot in his tie, and made sure it was centred. She stood back, hands on hips, and looked him up and down.

'You look very handsome in a suit.'

He blushed and she smiled. Tutting came from the table immediately outside the door of the bar.

'Wish me luck.'

'You won't need it.'

He felt the need to hug Carla, but instead picked up his folder and left.

'Good morning, ladies,' he said as he passed their table.

'Very handsome today, Commissario,' said Rosalia.

'I'm almost swooning,' added Fausta, fanning herself furiously.

'Important meeting, Commissario?' Donatella asked.

'You could say that.'

He checked in with Alfiero at the desk.

'Good morning, Commissario. They're ready for you.'

'How many?'

'Three. Two from Internal Affairs, and an officer of equivalent rank from Siena.'

'Who's observing?'

'Not sure. The Vice Questore, for certain; I think the ispettore; and I don't know about Gennaro.'

'Okay.

'Good luck, Commissario, you look the part.'

'Thanks, Alfiero.'

Moretti stopped outside the interview room, glanced at the door of the observation room next to it, then took several deep breaths and cleared his throat. He knocked and entered the room where he had conducted so many interviews over the years. The set-up was familiar. The three investigating officers sat on one side of the table, each with a folder in front of them. A recording machine was ready at the end of the table. On his side of the table sat three small bottles of water, a glass, and an empty chair.

'Good morning, Commissario Moretti,' said the female officer in the middle, as Moretti placed his folder on the table and sat down. 'I am Adelina Giordano. On my right is my colleague Davide Conti, and on my left is Commissario Gori.'

'Good morning.'

'Please help yourself to water throughout this meeting.'

'Thank you.' Moretti opened a bottle and poured a glassful.

Conti started the recording.

'We have a number of issues to resolve today so that a decision can be taken about your suspension. We plan to work though until twelve thirty, then take a one-hour break for lunch. We'll resume at one thirty precisely and hope to be finished by five o'clock. Do you have any questions?'

'No.'

'Very well.'

The Chair opened the folder in front of her.

'There are several items in the report that has been given to us, and I intend to begin with the last and potentially most serious. Is that agreeable to you?'

'Yes.'

'It concerns the finding of an Etruscan vase in your home. Are you aware of the item in question?'

'Yes.'

'The vase was discovered after a warranted search was conducted. It was hidden in a wardrobe.'

'If you say so.'

'What do you mean?'

'At no time did I see the vase in the wardrobe, nor anywhere else in my home, for that matter. The vase was allegedly found in the wardrobe before I arrived home. The first time that I saw the vase, it was on the counter in my kitchen.'

Conti produced three photographs from his file and laid them in front of Moretti. 'Do you recognise the shoe boxes in these photographs?'

'They look like boxes at the bottom of my wife's wardrobe.'

'And do you see the Etruscan vase hidden behind them?'

'I see that a vase has been placed there, yes.'

'Commissario Moretti, are you suggesting that the officers conducting the search put the vase there?'

Before Moretti could answer, he heard raised voices outside the door of the interview room, then a knock on the door and Alfiero came in.

'Excuse me,' he said breathlessly. 'Signora Maria De Luca insists on coming in. She says that she is representing the commissario.'

Giordano looked at Moretti. 'Is that correct?'

'Yes.'

'Then permit her to join us.'

Alfiero opened the door and Maria swept into the room, dressed in a white blouse, white bib, black skirt, and her black toga billowing out behind her.

'Please bring me a chair, Alfiero,' she said over her shoulder, before addressing the three sitting across from her husband. 'I'm sorry I was delayed. Ah, thank you, Alfiero.' She sat and arranged the folds of her robes. 'How far along are the proceedings?'

'We have only just begun. Commissario Moretti was calling into doubt the integrity of his colleagues.'

Maria looked at him. 'Is this true?'

'No.'

'Please replay the recording.'

Conti looked at Giordano. She nodded.

'Do you recognise the shoe boxes in these photographs?'

'They look like boxes at the bottom of my wife's wardrobe.'

'And do you see the Etruscan vase hidden behind them?'

'I see that a vase has been placed there, yes.'

'Commissario Moretti, are you suggesting that the officers conducting the search put the vase there?'

'Ah,' said Maria. 'On the contrary, it seems that it is you… excuse me, who are you, exactly?'

Moretti bit the inside of his cheek to prevent a smile.

'I'm Adelina Giordano, this is Davide Conti, and this is Commissario Gori.'

'Thank you. As I was saying, it appears to be you, Signora Giordano, that is calling into doubt the integrity of the investigating officers – or in any case, trying to put words into my client's mouth.'

'I was doing no such thing.'

'Then in that case you will retract your last statement and order that it should not form part of the transcript of this meeting. Do you agree?'

'Yes.'

'Then retract it.'

'Pardon?'

'Say the words so that they are recorded.'

'I retract my last statement and order that it shall not form part of the transcript.'

Maria crossed her legs and arranged the toga over her knees. 'Thank you. You may proceed.'

'Commissario Moretti, I ask you bluntly, did you place the vase in the wardrobe?'

'No.'

'Could your wife have placed it there?'

'Yes.'

Giordano narrowed her eyes towards Maria. 'Ah, now we're getting somewhere.'

Maria sighed.

'Did your wife in fact place the vase in her wardrobe?'

'No.'

Giordano frowned. 'I don't understand, Commissario. First you say she could, then you say she couldn't. Which is it?'

'I said she could have, then I said she didn't, not that she couldn't.'

'I'll try again. Do you know where the vase came from, Commissario?'

'Yes.'

'Where did it come from?'

'An Etruscan tomb.'

'Can you be more specific?'

'No, I'm not an expert, and I haven't been able to examine the vase personally.'

'Could it have come from the tomb discovered in Cassiatorre last year?'

'Yes.'

'A tomb discovered by Somali immigrants?'

'Somali and Ethiopian.'

'Somali and Ethiopian immigrants whom your wife represented?'

'I must caution you,' interrupted Maria, 'that you are embarking upon a line of enquiry that is not only hypothetical, but also outside the competence and jurisdiction of this hearing. If you have issues to raise about my involvement with previous clients, it would be dangerous, career damaging, and hugely expensive to you personally if you were to forgo the proper channels of presenting evidence before the proper authorities so that I could be called to answer for my actions.'

Giordano swallowed hard.

'Commissario Moretti, do you know how the vase got into your wife's wardrobe?'

'Yes.'

'Then please tell us how?'

Moretti looked at Maria, who nodded.

'It was placed there by Cosimo Buina who, for the

sake of clarity, also goes by the name of Damiano Buono.'

'Just how do you know this, Commissario?'

'I asked him yesterday.'

'While you were suspended?'

'Yes.'

'Did you tell him that you are a police officer?'

'No.'

'Commissario Moretti, you barely managed to escape disciplinary action a few months ago because of the way you acted while suspended from duty. It seems to be a habit with you. Look, this hearing would proceed much more smoothly if you simply told us everything that you know without me having to drag the answers out.'

Moretti glanced again at Maria. She half nodded and blinked.

'I gave Agente Gennaro Santoro a lift to the station in Maghicchio – he's had a health scare and can't drive. I was with him while he identified himself as a police officer. I stayed while Agente Santoro interviewed the suspect about a number of different matters then Agente Santoro cautioned Signor Buina or Buono, and I drove them both back to the Questura here. And, yes, I did ask him if he had planted the vase in my house.'

'Did he think you were a serving police officer?'

'You'll have to ask him that. I certainly did nothing to indicate that I was, and I am certain that Agente Santoro will testify to that. Shall I go on?'

'Please. What other matters did you and Agente Santoro discuss with Buina or Buono?'

'He admitted to selling magic mushrooms to a tourist whom he met in a bar in Maghicchio. That tourist was then involved in a fatal car crash. He also admits stealing and hiding a trunk, also to castrating a bull having first harvested it of semen which he has been subsequently selling online. He also installed a surveillance camera in his father's farm.'

'He sounds like a one-man crimewave, Commissario.'

'Quite.'

'And you say that he is here?'

'I guess safely locked in one of the cells along the

corridor.'

'And Agente Santoro has his statement?'

'I'm certain of it.'

'Did he say whether he was acting on his own behalf or for others?'

'You'll have to check with Agente Santoro for the details.'

Conti shuffled papers and scored out items from a list which he slid to Giordano.

'You've cleared up a major part of today's investigation, Commissario, and given us a whole lot besides. There remains one other item, however. There was a sum of money transferred into your account. Where did it come from, and what was the sender hoping to gain by sending it?'

Maria placed her hand on Moretti's knee.

'My client reported the arrival of funds into his account as soon as he was made aware of it,' said Maria. 'Furthermore, the money was the same day removed from his account and placed into a separate account, with instruction that if the person who sent it did not make themselves known to the authorities, the money in its entirety should be donated to charity.'

Giordano turned to the two men flanking her. They nodded.

'I think in the light of all that we have been told we will halt proceedings and call an early lunch to give us time to speak with Agente Santoro and Signor Buina or Buono. We will still reconvene at one thirty.'

Conti switched off the recording and everyone stood. Moretti and Maria left and hurried out of the building. He put his arm around her waist, turned her towards him, and hugged her tightly before kissing her on the lips. She kissed him back.

'You were formidable in there. Thank you, Maria.'

She leaned back in his embrace and smiled up at him. 'You weren't half bad yourself.'

'Let's grab some lunch. I want to visit the Chinese restaurant with some good news.'

They hurried along to Chībǎo.

'Oh, this used to be Bar Roma,' said Maria.

'It's been transformed. Wait until you see inside.' Moretti knocked the door.

An Na opened it a little, then wider.

'Moretti. Where have you been? Do you have news of my grandmother's luggage?'

'An Na, this is my wife Maria, and yes, I have good news. The trunk has been found, and it is at the police station.'

'I'll go and collect it.'

'I'm afraid you can't do that today. It's part of an open investigation, but you can certainly go and identify it.'

An Na frowned.

'Has it been opened? Is anything missing?'

'I can't say. That's why you need to check, maybe with your grandmother.'

'When?'

'I guess it would be okay to go after four o'clock.'

'Four o'clock. Good.'

'We were wondering if we could have lunch?'

An Na smiled, stood back and waved them in. 'Of course. Not everything is prepared but we can arrange something.'

CHAPTER THIRTY-EIGHT

The investigating officers Giordano and Conti, and Santoro, sat across from Cosimo who had taken off his blue jerkin and sat in the Trenitalia regulation short-sleeved shirt and dark trousers.

Giordano read from the statement provided by Santoro.

'…I saw the trunk on the platform and thought that someone had abandoned it there. The platform was very busy because many passengers had disembarked from the Rome train. So I decided to take the trunk into safe keeping until the owner came back for it.'

'So, that was your initial thought, Signor Buina. To move the trunk to a safe place.'

Buina scratched the back of his hand. 'Yes. I know it looks bad, but I didn't mean to steal it.'

'Were you aware that the police had come to the station looking for the trunk?'

'Not at first, but when I found out, I was scared and panicked.'

'So, what did you do?'

'I hid the trunk at the back of one of the underground storage areas. I know that was wrong, but I needed time to think.'

'What did you need time to think about? The trunk wasn't yours, and people were looking for it.'

Buina looked down his hands.

'I know, but you don't understand. I was newly out of prison, and I thought that if I said I took it then everyone would assume that I stole it, and I'd lose my job and end up back inside.'

'So, after you had time to think, why did you not return it?'

Buina shook his head.

'I don't know. I couldn't think of a way of doing it without throwing suspicion on myself. I thought I could put it back on the platform, or that maybe another worker could find it, but no-one did.'

'It says in Agente Santoro's report that he explained what the law means by "theft by finding" and that you admitted to that. Is that true?'

Buina nodded. 'Yes.'

'Let's leave that for the moment and turn to the magic mushrooms. You supplied these to an English tourist, correct?'

'Yes. He went into the bar near the station. It's one that younger people go to. He was there and asking around if anyone could sell him some hash. Someone gave him my phone number and when we spoke, I said I'd no hash but that I had some mushrooms.'

'Where were these mushrooms?'

'I had them at my place at the agriturismo.'

'So what happened next?'

'I arranged to meet him in the bar, I collected the mushrooms from my accommodation, brought them back and sold them to him.'

'And that was it? You didn't check that he was driving?'

'I asked him if he'd taken them before, and he said yes. I thought he'd be okay with them. I didn't know he was going to take them straight away.'

Giordano rubbed her chin.

'So far, Signor Buina, it seems you've been very unlucky. What you thought was doing a good deed – that is, moving a trunk to a safe place and selling a few mushrooms to an adult who was used to taking drugs – have both had unintended bad outcomes for you. Is that how it appears to you?'

Cosimo raised his head and nodded vigorously.

'Yes, that's it exactly,' he said. 'Unintended outcomes.'

Santoro cleared his throat and shifted in his seat.

Giordano shuffled through the papers in front of her. 'Tell me about your relationship with your father.'

'What do you mean?'

'How do you both get on?'

'I'd like to get on better with him, but he's ashamed of me. Ashamed of the things I've done in the past and that I've been in prison.'

'That must have been difficult for you.'

Cosimo looked at her. 'Yes, it was. Particularly in prison. Other guys would have visits. He never came to see me. He never sent a letter. He even refused to take phone calls from me.'

'So, he really cut you out of his life?'

'Exactly. His own son. His only son.'

'I imagine that you were curious about how life was going for him. After all, he's not a young man.'

'Exactly. When I was inside, I had time to reflect, and I realised how selfish I had been. He was right to disown me, but you're right, I was worried about him.'

'Is that why you installed the camera?'

'Yes, it is.'

Giordano turned to Santoro. 'This aspect is not picked up in your report, Agente Santoro.'

'No.'

Giordano faced Cosimo again.

'Installing a camera like that looks like a tricky job, Signor Buina. Where did you learn those skills?'

'I took some courses in prison, and of course there were other guys with experience. When I told them that I was worried about Dad, they were happy to help me. They told me all that I had to do.'

'Let me see if the agente has the details correct. You went to the farm when you knew that your father was away.'

'Yes. He wouldn't have understood.'

'Quite. Then you entered the house. Oh, did you break in, or did you have a key?'

'I used my key.'

'Good. Then you switched off the electricity which disabled his security cameras?'

Buina nodded.

'You then used bolt-cutters to cut the chain and gain access to the cowshed, where you installed your camera.'

'Yes.'

'Then I imagine you went back into the house and tapped into his computer system.'

'It's called port forwarding. It allows me to access the camera remotely.'

'Ah, interesting. It all sounds so sophisticated.'

Cosimo smiled. 'Well, you know, I wanted to be reassured that Dad was alright.'

'Very thoughtful. Don't you agree, Agente Santoro?'

Santoro sighed. 'Very thoughtful.'

'Thank you,' said Buina.

'Which makes me wonder,' said Giordano, 'why you didn't install the camera *inside* the farmhouse? You know, if you wanted to ensure that your father was okay.'

Cosimo swallowed and scratched the back of his hand again. 'I thought about that first, but then I thought he'd see it, so I changed my mind.'

'Ah, so you thought that even though you'd prefer to check on him inside, given your strained relationship with him, at least if you had an outside camera, you could have some idea of how he was.'

'Yes. That's it exactly.'

'Very commendable, eh, Agente Santoro?'

'Very commendable.'

'Can we turn now to the matter of the castration of the bull Jupiter? What was your thinking behind that?'

Cosimo's head went down again.

'It says here in your statement, *"I was so angry that all my father's work and expense, his very livelihood, was being threatened by Nardelli."* Can you say more about that?'

'Nardelli and my father have always been rivals for the Fiorentina market. The Nardellis always seemed to have more money behind them, and Dad was always trying to catch up. He has a great stud bull called Hercules, but Nardelli's bull, Jupiter, was bigger. And in the beef cattle world, bigger is better. So yes, I did it, I castrated Nardelli's bull.'

Santoro and Conti shifted in their seats.

'I'm not from a farming background, but I imagine that to castrate an animal of that size must be dangerous for you and painful for the animal.'

'I waited until I knew that Dad and Nardelli were going to be off their farms at the stock auction. I put Jupiter into what's called a squeeze crush. It's a sort of cage that holds him still. Then I cleaned and anaesthetised the scrotum and cut the balls out. I set him free in a field.'

'And harvesting semen? How is that even possible?'

'I thought that it would be a waste if Jupiter couldn't sire any more offspring, so I used electrostimulation to—'

Giordano held up her hand to stop him.

'Thank you, Signor Buina, but to save my colleagues further discomfort, you don't have to continue. And you sold this semen?'

'Yes. I admit that I also needed the money.'

'But you have a well-paid job with the railway.'

'I needed the extra money to pay for my change of identity.'

'That's very honest of you.' Giordano turned to Santoro. 'Do you have any further questions?'

'I have nothing to add to my report. Thank you. I'd like to ask Cosimo why?'

Buina inhaled and sighed deeply.

'My father comes from a long line of beef farmers. It's been his life. He wanted me to follow in the family tradition, but I told him that I didn't want to. I hate the prospect. It's too hard a life, you never have any time off, there's so much that can go wrong. I told him how I felt, and that's when the trouble started between us.'

'It looks like you are a rather naive young man who has made some stupid decisions, rather than a career criminal.'

Buina nodded.

Giordano turned to Conti. 'Do you have anything you'd like to ask?'

'Yes. Signor Buina, where did you get the Etruscan vase, and why did you plant it in Commissario Moretti's house?'

Cosimo blanched.

'I… I… can't tell you where I got it,' he stammered. 'I was paid to put it there. I told you that I needed money to pay off a debt. But I can't say who gave it to me. They'd have me killed.'

'You understand you're facing prison time?'

Cosimo put his head in his hands. 'I can't say any more.'

'Maybe you can answer this, then,' said Giordano. 'When the lock on Commissario Moretti's house was examined, it had marks and scratches consistent with being picked. Did you pick the lock to gain access?'

'Yes.'

'I guess this is something you also learned in prison.'

'Yes.'

'You said previously that you took the trunk to keep it safely until the owner came to reclaim it. So, can you explain why the same type of marks as were found on Commissario Moretti's lock were found on the locks of the trunk that you hid in the store?'

'I don't know what you mean.'

'Forensic examination suggests the same set of pick tools was used on both locks.'

'I don't know anything about the locks on the trunk.'

'Well, that I believe is because the trunk is very old and uses a type of lock that is not found in the West. It is a Chinese design that doesn't require a key, only that you know the trick to open it. These trunks have a false lock which I suggest you tried to open but couldn't.'

'Not true.'

'And that you hid it at the back of the store until you could get in touch with some of your criminal friends who have greater experience in lock-picking than you, so that you could open it and profit from the contents.'

'That's not true.'

Giordano stacked the papers and closed the folder.

'Well luckily, Signor Buina, it isn't me that you'll have to convince. It will be the judge and jury that hears your case.' She turned to Santoro. 'Call the officer to take Signor Buina back to his cell.'

'But I didn't do it.'

‘I suggest that your father is right. You are not the simple farm boy who has found himself in a bit of bother through naivety and stupidity, but a fully-fledged career criminal who, having served an apprenticeship in prison, was ready to do anything and everything to further his own selfish aims.’

Santoro returned with Alfiero.

‘Take him away.’

The two officers each grabbed one of Cosimo’s arms and led him to the door.

Cosimo twisted in their grip and called over his shoulder, ‘Bea’s lying. She was with me the night Hercules was poisoned.’

CHAPTER THIRTY-NINE

The meeting reconvened at one thirty, in Vice Questore Montanari's office instead of the interview room.

Giordano, flanked by Conti and Montanari, sat at CC's desk opposite Moretti and Maria. Santoro and Cristina sat at the side of the room.

'Thank you all for arriving so promptly,' said Giordano. 'Earlier we heard testimony from Commissario Moretti, then from Cosimo Buina. We have deliberated on what we discovered, and our findings are as follows. First, Commissario Moretti is cleared of all charges against him, and his suspension is revoked with immediate effect.' She went into the desk drawer, took out Moretti's badge, and handed it to him.

Moretti relaxed his shoulders. Maria patted his knee. Montanari's mouth tightened.

'Although we cannot prove it, there seems to have been an orchestrated campaign against him, involving the spreading of half-truths and rumour, to the planting of artefacts in his home and sending money to his personal account. Second, the details of this suspension will be expunged from his record. Third, we wish on behalf of the Police Force to commend you for your outstanding work and to apologise for having to put you through this process.'

Moretti held Maria's hand. Montanari clenched her

teeth. Cristina and Gennaro smiled.

'May I say a few words?' Moretti asked.

'Please do.'

'I want to thank you and Signor Conti for the way in which you have conducted this hearing, and I would like it to be noted that I owe this result to the team working that we have in this Questura. It has always been a strength of the department, but since her arrival, Vice Questore Montanari has encouraged each of us to work more closely together than ever, and as a result each member of the team played a part in bringing the disparate investigations to a successful conclusion.'

'Thank you, Commissario,' said Giordano turning to face Montanari. 'We would also like to acknowledge how difficult it must have been for Vice Questore Montanari to instigate the process and to praise her, too, for fostering such a strong spirit of joint working and cooperation within the department. At a time when some departments are chasing targets and quotas, it is refreshing to see that there are still others who believe that the best way of solving crime is to utilise the collective experience and expertise of the officers in the field.'

Montanari glared at Moretti and her mouth remained tightly shut, but she lifted the edges of her lips into something resembling a smile.

'I am certain that after we have filed our report, other Questure will be in touch to find out how you have established and maintained such a healthy working environment.'

'I am always at the disposal of colleagues to assist in any way that I can,' said Montanari tersely.

'If you will all excuse us, we have a few details to conclude with Vice Questore Montanari before we leave.' Giordano stood, followed by the others. She held out her hand and shook with Moretti then Maria.

'Good luck, Commissario, and keep up the excellent work.'

Moretti followed by Maria, Cristina, and Gennaro, filed out of CC's office. He removed his tie, stuffed it into his pocket and kissed Maria, then shook hands with Cristina and Gennaro, who almost choked laughing.

'She's encouraged us to work more closely than ever? You sly fox, Capo. Now she can't go back to her way.'

Moretti shrugged.

'Well, her way did make us work harder together.' He laid a hand on the arms of Cristina and Gennaro. 'Thanks, you two. You really came through for me.' He turned to Maria and took both her hands in his. 'And you were terrific, Maria, thank you. Let's all go back to my office.'

'You go on,' said Maria. 'I want a word with Dino.'

The two detectives left them.

'Dino, I can't stay. I really ought to be in court today but asked off for a family issue. I must get back. People are depending on me.'

Moretti held her arms. There was still so much he needed to say to her, to ask her, to tell her. He smiled and stroked her cheek with the back of his fingers. 'Of course, Maria.' He swallowed. 'Message me to let me know that you've arrived safely.'

She leaned into his caress. 'I will.'

They kissed lightly on the lips and parted. Moretti watched her walk away until she disappeared around the corner. He cleared his throat, preened his moustache, walked to his office, and closed the door.

'Welcome back, Capo.'

'Yes, welcome back, Commissario.'

'Sit down, guys, and fill me in on how you did it. You first, Gennaro.'

'It was Mancini, actually.'

Moretti and Cristina stared at him.

'He got in touch, asking if he could help, so I told him about the car crash guy, and he managed – don't ask how – to check on a local number and its location. That was Cosimo's phone, and linked him to Nardelli, Buina, Ricci, and the rail station.'

'That was the breakthrough,' said Moretti. 'Cristina, tell me about the diamonds.'

'Leng's saddle was drilled full of holes, each of which held diamonds but weakened the saddle so that it flexed. A seam came undone, and a diamond popped out during the Disfida. I saw it and followed up on it from there. I don't know where the diamonds came from other than

China.'

'I can help with that,' said Santoro. 'Or rather Mancini can. He got in touch with some contacts in the Chinese police force. There's a regular traffic in high quality, cut diamonds into Europe. Chinese triad gangs are infiltrating the lucrative drugs market, and this is how they bring in their start-up money.'

'So Leng—'

'No. Leng was a convenient excuse for the gang. He's innocent. I'm not so sure about his sidekicks, but nothing shows that they were directly involved.'

'Mancini has really come up trumps.'

'Yes, Capo, and it seems that we have contacts in common in the south.' The agente rubbed his chin. 'You asked me about Chen's tattoo, Capo. He wouldn't talk about it. Said that it was part of a past that he'd left behind and would rather forget.'

'Fair enough.'

'Leng's translator and driver had odd tattoos, sir. I don't know if it's relevant.'

'What was odd about them, Cristina?'

'It was the image. It was like a rat but with the tail of a scorpion. I asked An Na about it, and she recognised the description. It upset her so I didn't press her for more.'

'And where are the diamonds now?'

'Vice Questore Montanari checked them into evidence herself.'

'Typical. Trying to get some credit for your work, Cristina. Okay, well the Chinese have left, so we can leave that for now. What about the farmers? There's the matter of who poisoned Buina's bull.'

'That and the old woman's trunk,' said Cristina.

'I've an update about the bull,' said Santoro.

'Hold on, we'll come back to the bull.' Moretti called forensics. 'Moretti here. Have you guys finished with the trunk belonging to the old woman? …Good … Now? …Thanks.' He hung up. 'Okay, we can collect it from evidence and return it.'

'Now, Gennaro, what's the update?'

'Cosimo blew a hole in Beppe's alibi. He claims that he was with Bea on the night of the poisoning.'

'Did you check back with Bea?'

'She's gone. Packed her things and gone.'

'Beppe?'

'Haven't been in touch yet,' said Santoro. 'We could get him in here and spring it on him.'

'We could call the farmers here for a meeting and return the case before they arrive,' offered Cristina.

'Great plan, Cristina. You call the farmers. We need Buina and Nardelli – both father and son. Ask them to come in half an hour. Gennaro, call Mancini and tell him how my hearing went and that I'll thank him personally later. I'm going to take the trunk back to the restaurant.'

The three detectives left together.

Moretti had the trunk brought up from evidence and wheeled it to Chībǎo. He knocked on the door. An Na opened it and gasped when she saw the trunk. She called behind in Chinese, and both her father and grandmother appeared. She opened the door fully and Moretti hauled in the case. The old woman wept and clasped her hands together. She said something to An Na.

'My grandmother wants to apologise for all the trouble that she put you and your colleagues to by losing the trunk. She wants to know if you would like to drink some water and have a seat?'

'Apologise? It's me who should be apologising that someone took it.'

An Na smiled and nodded. 'It is how we say that we are grateful, Moretti.'

'Please tell her that no thanks are required. We were only doing our jobs.'

An Na translated and the old woman replied.

'My grandmother said that I was right to trust Moretti.'

Moretti grinned. 'I'm sorry but I must go. I have a meeting.'

He left and returned to his office. A short time later, Alfiero rang though to say that three visitors had arrived.

'Bring them through, Alfiero, and let Cristina and Gennaro know.'

The office was crowded with six people, so Cristina and Gennaro stood at the sides.

'I've asked you here to tell you about Cosimo Buina's actions, and to look at a way forward.'

As Moretti summarised events, Cosimo's father's head lowered closer to his chest.

'The situation that we face now is that one son will be going back to prison, and we could be looking at sending another son there with him if you press charges against Beppe, Signor Buina.'

Buina raised his head and spoke in a shaky voice.

'Press charges against Beppe? What for?'

'It was Beppe that fed the fresh feed to Hercules.'

All eyes turned to the young man.

'Beppe said that he was with his girlfriend Bea all that night,' continued Moretti. 'But that's not true, is it, Beppe?'

Beppe's mouth opened and he inhaled to speak. His father, Ignazio, grabbed his wrist.

'Tell the truth, son,' Ignazio said, his eyes filling up. 'I'll stand by you no matter what.'

Beppe swallowed hard and looked at the circle of faces.

'It's true,' he said. 'But I didn't mean to kill Hercules. I thought that Signor Buina would find him in time to release the gas.'

Ignazio shook his head and released his son's wrist.

All eyes now focussed on Buina.

'I saw what prison did to my son and I wouldn't wish that on anyone else.' He turned to Ignazio. 'I'm sorry for what Cosimo did to Jupiter, but sending Beppe to prison won't bring Hercules back. I have other bulls. I simply must wait until they are ready to sire.'

Beppe hung his head.

Ignazio spoke. 'I'm grateful for this generosity and kindness. For too long we have been vying with each other. I propose that we have a new beginning and work together, pooling the genetic stock of our herds and going into business as partners, not rivals. What do you say?'

He held out his hand. Buina took it, and the old farmers shook vigorously.

Moretti smiled and sat back in his chair.

'Well, it seems that there is nothing further for the police to do here.' He stood. 'I'm sure that you've made the correct decision, and I wish you both success.' They all shook.

Moretti held Beppe's hand for longer while he spoke. 'Acting out of revenge only does harm, Beppe. There is always a better way to live your life, as your father and Signor Buina are demonstrating. Learn from this.'

'I will, Commissario. Thank you. And thank you, Signor Buina.'

Much later at home, changed out of his suit, Moretti stood outside watching the light fade across the valley where the farmers raised their beef cattle. He puffed on a small cigar and thought of his time with Maria – from the early days to the present. She had come, unbidden, to help him today. Their lunch together at Chībāo had gone well – talking about the hearing, laughing together about memories – so why was the rest of their life so difficult? If Nardelli and Buina could settle their differences and move forward together, why couldn't he and Maria?

His phone rang so he stubbed out the cigar and went indoors.

'Dino? Maria. I'm home safely.'

Home? Did she now really think of her apartment in the south as home?

'Thanks for letting me know and thanks again for today.'

'Glad to help. You'd have done the same for me.'

He smiled. 'Take care.'

'I will. You, too. Goodnight.'

'Goodnight.'

John MacDonald writes atmospheric, socially-charged crime fiction set deep in the Tuscan hills. A lifelong lover of Italian culture, language and literature, he spends part of each year immersed in small-town life, learning how modern Italy balances tradition and change.

Inspired by authors like Andrea Camilleri and Donna Leon, John tells stories where small-town secrets, social tensions and personal grief collide – wrapped in gripping mysteries with emotionally complex characters.

The Cassiatorre Quartet, set over four seasons in a fictional Tuscan town, is his debut series.

When not writing, John is drawn to the quiet rhythms of Tuscan life – long walks, slow meals, and the occasional espresso-fuelled plot twist.

John MacDonald

https://www.instagram.com/johnmacdonaldwriter/

@johmacdonaldwriter.bsky.social

Printed in Dunstable, United Kingdom

80945369R00163